The Shadowed Trail

Center Point
Large Print

Also by Arthur Henry Gooden and available from Center Point Large Print:

Painted Buttes Roaring River Range
The Trail of Vengeance

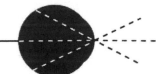

This Large Print Book carries the Seal of Approval of N.A.V.H.

The Shadowed Trail

Arthur Henry Gooden

CENTER POINT LARGE PRINT
THORNDIKE, MAINE

This Center Point Large Print edition
is published in the year 2017 by arrangement with
Golden West Literary Agency.

First US edition: Houghton Mifflin
First UK edition: Harrup

The text of this Large Print edition is unabridged.
In other aspects, this book may vary
from the original edition.
Printed in the United States of America
on permanent paper.
Set in 16-point Times New Roman type.

ISBN: 978-1-68324-419-6 (hardcover)
ISBN: 978-1-68324-423-3 (paperback)

Library of Congress Cataloging-in-Publication Data

Names: Gooden, Arthur Henry, 1879–1971, author.
Title: The shadowed trail / Arthur Henry Gooden.
Description: Center Point Large Print edition. | Thorndike, Maine :
    Center Point Large Print, 2017.
Identifiers: LCCN 2017010242| ISBN 9781683244196
    (hardcover : alk. paper) | ISBN 9781683244233 (pbk. : alk. paper)
Subjects: LCSH: Large type books. | GSAFD: Western stories.
Classification: LCC PS3513.O4767 S53 2017 | DDC 813/.52—dc23
LC record available at https://lccn.loc.gov/2017010242

Affectionately inscribed to

My Nieces
Esther and Hilda

Contents

The Shadowed Trail

Chapter I
ENCOUNTER

The horse moved with an easy rocking gait up the dry wash that twisted between low-lying hills covered with a sparse growth of piñon trees. Silence lay heavy in that remote spot. The only sound was the grind of shod hoofs in the harsh sand, the creak of saddle leather.

The rider swayed easily to the motion of his horse. The brim of his hat was pulled low over watchful eyes against the sunlight, and smoke curled lazily from the cigarette that drooped from his mouth. A firm-lipped mouth, with a hint of humor in the corners that belied the somewhat grim set of his shadowed, bold-featured face.

A coyote drifted across the wash, paused for a brief look at the lone rider, and then streaked like a gray wraith into a tangle of brush that crawled up the slope. Almost instantly the desert prowler reappeared, doubling back at top speed for cover on the opposite bank.

The rider's reaction to the little incident was immediate. He swung the red horse behind a sprawling mesquite tree and drew to a standstill. He sat erect in his saddle, hand closed over the butt of the gun in his holster, the indolence gone

11

from his hard body, his head bent in a searching look through the branches of the mesquite.

Long moments passed. Finally the man relaxed, and something like amusement crinkled the corners of his eyes, showed in a glint of white teeth that broke the stern set of his lips.

He shook his head impatiently. It was obvious that something had startled the coyote, and a coyote was too smart to be fooled by anything except a very real danger—a man, perhaps, lying in ambush somewhere in the piñon scrub just beyond the tangle of brush.

He continued to watch, eyes again hard, alert, his ears keyed for any telltale sound in that blanketing stillness.

Some two hundred yards above the big mesquite the low hills that confined the sandy, boulder-strewn wash drew in close and became high ridges that broke down from sheer red cliffs. The narrow portal of Cañon Los Diablos. Sunlight drew silver gleams from water that fell thinly over the boulders in the canyon's mouth and disappeared magically beneath thirsty sand to subterranean gravel beds.

The watching rider's gaze roved up the wash to the waterfall where the trail looped up around the boulders and was lost in the dark gorge. His straining ears caught the sharp whip of wings and a pair of mourning doves took off in swift flight from the pool.

The man's eyes narrowed. He seemed hardly to breathe. Something had startled the doves. Not himself. He was too far from the pool to have caused the alarm. Like the prowling coyote, they had fled from some danger his own senses had failed to identify. He only knew from the signs that he was not alone.

A new sound touched his ears, the crackle of brush, the unmistakable rattle of loose stones underfoot. A shape lurched into view from the desert willows below the pool.

Surprise widened the lone rider's eyes. In an instant his horse was in motion and pushing into the willow brakes that fringed the pool.

The man stumbling over the boulders toward the water turned a pain-distorted face in a look at the approaching horseman. There was stark despair in his eyes, and defiance. He stopped his forward movement toward the pool, lay sprawled on a boulder, watched in silence while the other man slid from his saddle.

The newcomer stood looking down at him with frowning intentness.

"Who shot you?" he asked abruptly.

The wounded man shook his head. "Don't know." His voice was hardly more than a whisper. It was plain that he was in the last stages of exhaustion. He spoke again, more loudly, "You— one of them?"

"What do you mean?"

"One of the gang that's chasing me?"

The owner of the bay horse shook his head. "No," he answered curtly. He bent over the wounded man, touched the blood-soaked shoulder with light, expert fingers. "You've bled a lot," he went. "How long ago did it happen?"

"An hour—maybe less . . . It seems an eternity . . ."

The man bending over him lifted his head in a brief, curious look at the haggard face. There was culture—and breeding—in the painfully articulated words. He resumed his examination of the wound—not the only hurt, as he quickly discovered.

"Your leg, too," he diagnosed briefly.

The wounded man's hand lifted in a weak gesture of confirmation. "I'd like some water . . ." The fear had left his eyes. It was apparent that he was drawing comfort and new hope from the bronze-faced young man bending over him.

"I'll bring my canteen . . . easier than getting you down to the pool," the rider said.

He took the canteen from the saddle and held it to the other man's lips. "That's enough for now," he said presently, and went back to the horse and hastily retied the canteen to the saddle, his face turning in quick looks at a faint haze of dust drawing along the crest of the opposite ridge. He made haste to return to the wounded man.

"Somebody coming," he said laconically.

He read a wordless appeal in the eyes staring up at him. "They won't find you." There was confidence, reassurance in his quiet voice. "Hang on with your good hand," he added, and with a quick movement lifted the helpless man bodily into his arms.

It took all of five minutes to circle the pool and make the ascent up the slippery granite rocks that led into the gorge. Fortunately, the man was of lean, wiry build and not too heavy.

Tall cliffs shut out the sunlight. They could hear the quiet murmur of the gently cascading falls outside the portal. The creek was narrow at this point, a deep and boiling torrent during the rains, but now a placid, shallow stream.

The young man found what seemed to satisfy him, a great split boulder screened by a clump of piñons. He worked his way around and into the crevice and made the hurt man as comfortable as possible. The wound and leg needed proper attention. The enforced delay might prove fatal.

"I hate leaving you like this," he said. "There's no alternative." He smiled, added reassuringly, "I'll be back—"

He returned to his horse and led the animal down to the pool. The big bay snuffled the water, took a few swallows and moved leisurely toward an inviting bunch of drying grass a few feet away. He halted, swung up his head in an interested look at the slope.

His master, sitting indolently on a boulder, also heard the sounds. He plucked tobacco and papers from a pocket and began fashioning a cigarette. As if suddenly aware of the approaching riders, he turned his head and watched with poker-faced indifference until three men halted their horses before him. They returned his lazy stare with frowning intentness. One of them finally broke the silence.

"Hello, Severn. We wasn't expecting to run into *you* down here. Sure is funny." The wide grin that creased his dusty face failed to disguise the hostility in his hard eyes.

Kirk Severn put a match to his cigarette. "What's funny about it, Clint? Why not here as well as any other place?" There was a hint of irony in his lazy smile.

"Huh?" A scowl replaced the grin on the other man's face. "Don't savvy what you mean."

"You've been foreman of the Bar T years enough to know you're off your own range," drawled Kirk. "I can hand back your own words. It's sure funny what business Bar T riders can have on K7 range. Answer *that* one, Clint."

The Bar T foreman reddened. He was perhaps in his late thirties, a long-framed, tough-looking man with carroty hair and angry, protruding blue eyes. He said blusteringly: "Nothing funny about it. We're trailin' a damn cow thief we jumped other side of the ridge, and it ain't your K7 over that way."

Kirk finished a brief scrutiny of the two silent riders who flanked their foreman. One of them he had never seen before, a short, stocky man whose swarthy stupid face was belied by a pair of vicious and cunning eyes. His companion, a slim black-haired youth with an engaging grin, was Clint Sleed's right bower. Severn was under no illusions about him. Dunn Harden was dangerous for all his soft-spoken voice and gay smile. He could shoot from the hip with either hand, and always a split second faster than his unfortunate opponent.

Severn gave him a recognizing nod. "Hello, Dunn."

The black-haired cowboy seemed oddly embarrassed. He said unsmilingly, "Hello, Kirk."

Clint Sleed's eyes took on a calculating look as he continued to stare at Kirk. "How long have you been settin' here?" he asked.

Kirk gave him a mirthless smile. "Is that *your* business?"

"I told you we're chasin' a cow thief," fumed the Bar T foreman. "Sign says he headed down this way from the ridge." He added menacingly, "I aim to get him, Severn."

"Not on K7 range," Kirk said frostily. "You do your rustler hunting on your own range, Sleed. When K7 needs your help, I'll let you know."

Anger and suspicion bristled from the man like quills from a ruffled porcupine. "That talk don't set good in my craw, Severn."

"Don't be a damn fool," Kirk drawled.

"You've got that hombre hid out some place," insisted Sleed furiously.

"I've no more use for rustlers than you have," countered Kirk. "You know me, Sleed."

"You're too damn soft with 'em," sneered the Bar T foreman. "Sure I know you."

"I believe in leaving rustlers or any other criminal to the law," Kirk said coldly.

Sleed's thin lips curled. "There ain't no law in Soledad," he derided.

"That's our fault," Kirk retorted.

"You're loco," grumbled Sleed. "Only one way to fix a cow thief . . . dangle him from the nearest tree or hand him a dose of hot lead." His scowl deepened. "Where's that hombre hid out?"

Kirk's eyes narrowed thoughtfully. He shook his head. "There's no cow thief hid out here, Sleed." His voice hardened. "I don't want any more talk from you about it."

There was a long silence. Sleed slanted a look at Dunn Harden. Something he read in the cowboy's eyes seemed to hold him in check. Both men knew Kirk Severn too well to be deceived by his apparent indifference to the crisis provoked by his words. He was one against

18

three, but there was a warning in his smile that restrained them from reaching for their guns.

The Bar T foreman broke the silence. "I reckon we're wasting time with this fool palaver," he said gruffly. "Come on, boys." He started his horse toward the mouth of the canyon.

"No, you don't, Sleed," Kirk called sharply. "Head back the way you came. Hunt your rustler some other place—not on K7 range."

Sleed said sulkily, "To hell with you," swung his horse and headed down trail. The two Bar T men followed. Dunn Harden's head turned in a look at the tall man still lounging carelessly on the flat boulder. There was a hint of sly amusement in the brief grin he sent back at Kirk.

Kirk watched until sure they were well up the hillside and lost to view in the piñons. Dunn Harden's odd look puzzled him. Frowning over the incident, he hastily stepped up to his saddle and headed for the portal.

He was anxious to get back to the wounded stranger. One good reason why he had so abruptly terminated the argument with Bar T's bellicose foreman. He believed he had spoken the truth when he told Sleed he had seen nothing of the rustler the foreman claimed they were hunting. A juggling of the truth, perhaps, but entirely justifiable. The fugitive he had hidden was no doubt the man Sleed was chasing, but Kirk was reasonably positive he was *not* a rustler. The signs were too obvious for argument. The man was an Easterner, a tenderfoot. Sleed had deliberately lied, which perhaps explained Dunn Harden's secret amusement.

The wounded man's eyes questioned him eagerly.

"They've gone," reassured Kirk. "Bar T men." He added grimly, "Seem to think you're a rustler."

The man shook his head feebly. "No," he gasped, "not a rustler."

"My idea of it," Kirk said dryly. "You don't look it to me."

He refrained from further questioning for the moment, went swiftly to work. Using his bandanna and strips torn from the sufferer's shirt, he improvised a bandage for the shoulder wound. Fortunately the bullet had passed through without touching bone. The broken leg proved more difficult.

"Fell from a cliff," the man explained. "One of their bullets killed my horse . . . I tried to climb down . . . couldn't quite make it with only one good arm . . . took a bad tumble." A shudder ran through him. "It's a miracle I got away."

Kirk nodded. "We'll have to put that leg in splints," he said. He was gone for some minutes, returned with several short pieces of willow from the thicket below the pool.

"It's going to hurt," he warned.

The man nodded, closed his eyes. Kirk set the broken bone and skillfully adjusted the splints. Beads of sweat stood out on the man's face.

"You're as good as a doctor," he said between gritted teeth.

"We pick up lots of tricks in the cow business," chuckled Kirk. "I'm a cowman myself," he added casually. "I own the K7 outfit."

"You're Kirk Severn?"

"Yes," Kirk replied. He was watching the man closely, aware of an odd panic in his eyes. "I don't know who you are," he went on, "but I've an idea I know where you live." He smiled reassuringly. "Don't get excited."

"A K7 man found us there . . . told us to clear out." The injured man spoke in a troubled voice. "He was rather unpleasant, said that Kirk Severn wouldn't stand for nesters."

"Don't get excited," repeated Kirk.

"I'm not a nester," the man went on feverishly. "I'm an archaeologist. The place seemed suitable for my purpose and we moved in. We didn't know we were trespassing." He sensed the question in Kirk's look. "My wife," he explained. "She came west with me." He sat up with a painful effort, added despairingly, "She'll be worried . . . I was to have been back long ago."

"I'll get you back to her," Kirk assured him. "How are you feeling? Strong enough to sit in a saddle?"

"It doesn't matter how I feel," answered the man doggedly. "I've got to get back to my wife. She'll be frantic."

"Hang on—" Kirk took him up in his arms and carried him to the horse. "Easy does it," he said, and slid his burden into the saddle. "Hurt you?"

"Damn the hurt!" The man gave Kirk a pain-twisted grin. "I haven't told you my name . . . Chase."

Kirk swung up behind him and turned the horse into the trail, unaware of the man crouched under the rocks below the falls.

A satisfied grin creased the watcher's swarthy face. He slid down the ledge and made his way swiftly around the pool and vanished into the fringing willows.

Chapter II
CABIN IN THE CANYON

The bluff overlooked the wide floor of the canyon some two hundred feet below and was well covered with a growth of stubby junipers. A weather-beaten log cabin and a fair-sized corral stood in a small clearing. Attempts had been made to bolster the sagging split rails with stumps trimmed from the junipers. A brown mare and two burros drowsed near the gate, cocking expectant ears occasionally at sounds of movement in the cabin.

A woman appeared in the doorway. The mare nickered softly. The woman—she was young and slender—turned and looked, and after a moment's hesitation, picked up a tin bucket contrived from a five-gallon kerosene can and went with swift, graceful steps to a small spring that bubbled up at the base of the low red cliffs near the cabin. She dipped the bucket into the water and carried it to the small trough in the corral. The mare nuzzled her bare brown arm as she emptied the bucket, began to drink thirstily. The burros crowded in, big flop ears cocked eagerly.

The young woman stood watching them for a few moments. "I just plain forgot you," she said,

23

aloud, self-reproachfully. She reached out, patted the mare's neck. "I've been so worried—"

She walked slowly back to the cabin, replaced the tin bucket on a flat stone near the door and went inside. Presently she reappeared, a pair of binoculars in her hand, and, swiftly now, made her way through the junipers to the edge of the bluffs.

For a long moment she stood motionless, gaze fixed across the canyon, on the green-forested hills, unspoiled, majestically remote. She knew that somewhere over there lay the Mexican border, less than a half-day's ride away.

The wind caught at her dark chestnut hair, fluttered her full skirt. She put up a hand against the sun reaching down to the peaks, moved closer to the edge of the bluff and, adjusting the binoculars, gazed for a long time into the deeps of the canyon.

She could see the trail, where it broke away from the bluffs and followed the windings of the creek down the boulder-strewn floor. She studied it carefully with the glasses.

Of a sudden she went rigid, a slim, trim shape in the wind that pressed revealingly against her. Something was moving out of the narrow gorge a mile or so away.

The young woman seemed hardly to breathe. She kept the glasses focused on that moving dot drawing so slowly into the wider sunlit reaches of the upper canyon. Something like incredulity spread over her face. With a startled exclamation she lowered the glasses, drew the back of her hand across her eyes, and again leveled the binoculars. She had not been mistaken—the horse was carrying a double burden—two men.

She continued to watch, a growing fear in her eyes, and presently the horse was lost to view in the ravine up which the trail twisted to the rimrock.

The girl lowered the glasses, stood there, her face pale, frightened, her eyes fixed in a blank look down the canyon. Something flashed there, like sunlight on metal. She lifted the binoculars quickly, stared at the moving black dot outlined against the white cliffs. A lone horseman.

She lowered the glasses, her expression bewildered. When she looked again, the lone rider had vanished.

She shook her head dubiously. Perhaps she had been mistaken. Her nerves were too taut. She had been watching down the canyon for so many hours her eyes were playing her tricks.

Excitement seized her, a wave of eager hope, stabbed with cold prickles of apprehension. She began to run, the binoculars clutched in small brown hand.

She came to a standstill midway between the corral and the cabin. It was no time to be swayed by blind panic. She must keep her wits.

She stood there, struggling for self-control, wide-open eyes fixed on the juniper scrub beyond the corral. The brown mare's head lifted in a sharp look in the same direction. She snorted, trotted toward the far end of the corral. The burros followed, huge ears cocked.

The girl looked down at the binoculars in her hand. She ran back to the cabin and placed the glasses on a wooden bench that stood outside the door. Sounds drifted up from the juniper scrub, the thud of shod hoofs.

Kirk saw her standing by the cabin door as he rode out of the junipers, heard her anguished voice, and then she was running toward him.

"Dick!" she cried, *"Dick!"*

Kirk halted the horse, met her terrified look. He had an arm around the limp body of the man in the saddle.

"Hold on to him," he said.

"Dick!" The girl's low voice was husky with alarm. "What—what have they done to you?"

"Hold on to him," Kirk repeated, almost harshly. "He's unconscious."

The sharpness in his voice steadied her. She put up her hands, supported the unconscious man while Kirk slid from the horse. "Now," he said, "let me have him." He spoke gently, reassuringly. "Where do you want him, Mrs. Chase?"

She went with quick steps into the cabin. Kirk followed with his burden. It was a good-sized room, lighted by two square openings in the log walls. Pieces of canvas hung over the openings in lieu of windows. An iron pot simmered on the cookstove and there was a warm, pleasant smell of stewing meat. Odds and ends of a camping outfit were heaped in one corner, and there was a homemade table with wooden benches on either side.

The girl motioned him into the adjoining room. Kirk obeyed, carefully lowered the injured man to the bed and turned his head in a look at the girl. He saw with relief that her nerves were under control. Her face was pale, but the panic had left her eyes.

She met his look composedly. "We have a medicine kit," she said, and went swiftly to a duffel bag that lay in a corner of the room.

Kirk's gaze followed her, an oddly startled expression in his eyes. He was still staring at her when she hurried back with a small wooden box in her hand. She half-paused, gave him a frowning, puzzled look, as if resentful of his intent scrutiny.

He reached for the medicine kit. "Fine," he said. "Have you any whiskey?"

Mrs. Chase nodded, ran into the other room and returned with a half-filled flask.

"It's been a tough ride for him," Kirk said. He's lost a lot of blood—but we'll soon have him out of it."

He removed the improvised bandage and laid the wound bare. The girl's eyes dilated.

"He's been shot!" Her eyes went to Kirk in a fierce look. "Your work?"

Kirk shook his head. "No." His tone was grim, but not resentful. "Get some water—in a basin," he added.

She obeyed, helped with quick, sure hands while he dressed and bandaged the bullet wound, now and again glancing anxiously at her husband's face.

"We'll leave the leg alone," Kirk decided. "It's a job for a doctor."

A little cry escaped her. "He's coming to!" She sank on her knees by the bedside. "Dick!" Relief choked her voice.

"I'm all right," Chase mumbled. "I'm all right." His eyes took on a curious look of terror as he stared up into her face. "Are *you* all right, Esther?"

"Yes, yes," she reassured quickly. "I'm all right, Dick." She put the whiskey flask to his lips. "Drink some of this—and—and don't worry."

Chase obediently drank. Esther recorked the flask, continued to kneel there, watching him anxiously, one of his hands in hers. She seemed to have forgotten Kirk.

He stood there, gravely silent, gazing down at her, and, suddenly glancing up at him, she again saw that odd mixture of surprise and bewilderment in his eyes. She got to her feet and faced him, resentment and fear in her answering look.

"Why do you keep staring at me?" She flung the question in a low, tight voice.

Kirk suddenly smiled. It was a warm, reassuring smile and seemed to mollify her. "I didn't mean to be rude," he said.

The girl looked at him doubtfully. "You see— this is all very frightening—" She spoke in a troubled voice. "You bring Dick home—wounded, unconscious—his leg broken. I don't know what to think, except one thing."

Chase's voice interrupted her. "Kirk Severn didn't shoot me, Esther," he said weakly from the bed. "I'd never have got here but for his kindness."

Esther's eyes widened. "Kirk Severn?" Her voice was panicky. "*You* are Kirk Severn?"

"Yes," Kirk admitted laconically.

She continued to look at him, growing distrust in her eyes. "I think I understand—*now*—" There was contempt in her voice—and bitterness.

"*I* don't," Kirk said.

She clenched her hands. "Don't pretend. One of your cowboys was here the other day. He told us to get out—or there'd be trouble."

"Esther—you wrong Mr. Severn," reproached her husband.

"He sent his men to kill you," insisted the girl. Her eyes sparkled angrily.

"My dear, you are so dreadfully wrong. He hid me from those men. What he told them, I don't know. I *do* know that he sent them away—saved me from being shot to death—or hung for a cow thief."

Esther's face went the color of chalk. She gave Chase a compassionate look. "Don't try to talk, dear," she said gently. Her look went back to Kirk. "The fact that you could send those men away, as Dick says, is proof they were your own cowboys."

"This talk is not doing him—or yourself— any good," Kirk said quietly. "What your husband told you is true, Mrs. Chase. I was heading into Cañon Los Diablos when I ran into your husband."

"You *must* believe him, dear," Dick Chase broke in feebly.

Some of the tension went from the girl's face. She was extraordinarily lovely with her burnished gold-brown hair and tawny eyes. Kirk was again aware of stark amazement as he looked at her.

"I—I'm sorry," she faltered. Kirk shook his head at her.

"Forget it," he said brusquely. "What else could you think?" His smile went to Chase. "Feeling more comfortable, feller?"

"It's better than sitting in that saddle," Chase assured him with a wry smile.

30

"I'll send a doctor out from town," Kirk promised. "Nothing more *I* can do here."

"You are very kind," rejoined Chase in his cultured and precise voice. "I can never thank you enough, Mr. Severn."

"Forget it." Kirk gave him an embarrassed grin and turned to the door.

Esther Chase followed him outside, stood silent as he felt in a pocket for tobacco and cigarette papers. Slanting sunlight brought out warm glints in her soft brown hair. It was Kirk who broke the silence.

"Have you any idea who would want to kill your husband?" he asked abruptly.

Esther shook her head. "We're strangers in this country," she answered. "Why *anybody* would want to kill Dick is more than I can imagine." She smiled faintly. "Unless it was your own men."

"That's out," Kirk dissented curtly. "K7 men aren't murderers."

"I suppose we *are* trespassers," Esther went on ruthlessly. "We didn't know we were trespassing. We packed in from Deming and stumbled on the place quite by chance. Awfully tumbledown, but it seemed ideal—right in the heart of things for Dick's archaeological work."

"You are welcome to stay as long as you wish," Kirk assured her. "An old cow camp . . . we haven't used the place for years."

31

"Your cowboy didn't think we were welcome to stay," the girl reminded him.

"Chuck's bark is worse than his bite," smiled Kirk. "It's in his blood to hate nesters."

"Dick tried to explain—told him he was an archaeologist."

"That got Chuck all the more worried," smiled Kirk. "He thought the word meant some new kind of nester." His face sobered. "It was Chuck's story that started me over this way."

She nodded, her expression thoughtful. "It was lucky for us you *did* start," she said, a bit unsteadily.

"Come to think of it, the thanks are due to Chuck," argued Kirk. "If he hadn't had that run-in with your husband and told me about it, I wouldn't be here now."

"Thank God you *did* come," Esther said, with a little shudder. She went back to his question. "No—the whole affair is a complete mystery." She hesitated, "Do you know the men who were chasing Dick?"

"Yes." His tone was bleak. "Claimed your husband was a rustler. They lied."

"It frightens me," the girl said miserably.

"How did you happen to come to this Soledad country?" questioned Kirk.

"Dick's always been wild to do some exploring in New Mexico. He's a professor of archaeology, and really quite famous. Well—this is his sabbatical

32

year, and so we came." Esther Chase hesitated. "It was partly on my account, though, that he chose this Soledad country."

"*Your* account?" Kirk's brows lifted.

She looked at him irresolutely, seemed to be debating with herself. "You have lived here a long time, haven't you, Mr. Severn?" she finally asked.

"All my twenty-nine years," Kirk told her solemnly. His eyes twinkled. "Is that long enough for your purpose, Mrs. Chase?"

"Oh, yes—by at least nineteen years." The girl hesitated again, fingered her dress nervously. "Do you know, or did you ever hear of a man by the name of Worden Taylor?"

Kirk hid the surprise he felt. "I know a Warde Taylor," he replied cautiously.

She looked doubtful. "My Worden is spelled with an *o*."

"This man I know might be your Worden Taylor for all the spelling," speculated Kirk. "He owns the Bar T outfit—one of the biggest ranches in this part of New Mexico."

"What does he look like?" She asked the question breathlessly.

"A grizzly bear of a man—over six feet—wears a beard."

Disappointment chased over the girl's expressive face. Kirk studied her curiously. "Nineteen years can change a man's looks," he reminded.

33

She shook her head doubtfully. "It doesn't sound like him." She turned to the cabin door. "I have a picture of the man *I* mean. I'll get it."

She was back in a few moments, a faded daguerreotype in her hand. Kirk studied the likeness attentively, a man in the early thirties and wearing the uniform of a Confederate cavalry captain. He shook his head. "Not the same man," he said positively. "No, Mrs. Chase—the Worden Taylor you're asking about is certainly not Warde Taylor of the Bar T."

Esther mutely held out her hand for the picture. Her face was without expression, but Kirk sensed a poignant suffering that profoundly moved him.

"Your father?" he asked gently.

She stood looking at him with frowning intentness. "Yes, my father." She spoke sadly, in a low voice hardly above a whisper, and then more clearly, "Have you ever heard of a man known as Pecos Jack?"

The question startled Kirk. "Why—yes," he admitted. "A long time ago—when I was a kid—" He hesitated, troubled by the bitter look in her eyes. "I don't remember much about the fellow—"

"He was a stage-robber," interrupted Esther. "A mob lynched him for murder. An old man in Deming told me all about it." She gave Kirk a twisted little smile. "Isn't that right, Mr. Severn?"

34

"I was only a kid," Kirk repeated. "I think it was something like that." He shook his head. "I only vaguely remember the name. Such stories are common enough." He glanced appraisingly at the sun. "It's time I head for Soledad and get hold of Doc Williams."

Esther Chase nodded assent. "You're very kind." She picked up the glasses from the wooden bench, gave Kirk a startled look.

"What is it?" he asked sharply.

"I—I've just remembered something," replied the girl. "I was watching down the canyon—for Dick. I saw you coming out of the gap—and then I thought I saw another rider." She paused, her face troubled. "I was excited . . . I might have been mistaken."

Kirk made no attempt to conceal his dismay. His frowning gaze swept the fringing juniper scrub. "I don't like it," he said.

"I'm not afraid—and we *must* get the doctor—"

Kirk was not deceived. He knew she was afraid. He regarded her with worried eyes. "Have you a gun?"

"Dick's rifle—and a revolver—and I know how to use them."

"Fine." Kirk stared thoughtfully at the cabin. The log walls were stout, and the door a heavy affair of two-inch planks strapped with iron. "We mustn't take chances," he said. "Stay inside until I get back with the doctor. Keep the door barred and slide the shutters over the windows. This cabin was built years ago by my father when he had to fight off Apaches."

"Yes." The girl's voice was cool. "I understand—"

Kirk gave her an approving smile. "Fine," he repeated. "Stay inside and you won't catch a bullet from some prowler in the brush. Nobody can get at you if you keep the door barred and the shutters in place."

"I understand," she said again.

"It's a long ride to Soledad," Kirk reminded. "The doctor won't get here until morning. If I don't come with him, I'll send two of my men to stay with you and help." The incredulous expression came back to his eyes as he looked at her. "You remind me a lot of a girl I know," he added in a puzzled voice.

"I've wondered why you seem so—so surprised when you look at me," Esther Chase commented with a faint smile. "The resemblance must be startling."

"It is," Kirk agreed. "Have you a sister out here, Mrs. Chase?"

She shook her head. "No sister." She paused, added in a low voice: "I was only about three when father came west to look into the cattle business. My mother accompanied him and they left me with an aunt in Virginia." She faltered. "I—I've never seen them since—" A hint of tears clouded her eyes.

"Poor kid—" Kirk broke off. He sensed that the fine metal in this girl would resent pity. He said briskly, "All right, Mrs. Chase—get inside and fix the door and the shutters. Don't open up for anybody until Doc Williams comes."

She nodded, threw him a quick, grateful smile and went swiftly into the cabin. Kirk stood waiting until she closed the door and dropped the wooden bar. He walked slowly around the cabin while she slid the heavy shutters. Satisfied, he went to his horse and swung up to the saddle.

Chapter III
THE SWARTHY MAN

It was still a good hour from sundown. Evening shadows made a blue mist in the deep canyon below the bluffs, spread up the lower slopes. The complete stillness oddly affected Kirk as he rode past the corral. It was an ominous quiet that sent a tingle down his spine, the awesome silence of the jungle when a tiger lies in wait for the kill. He knew he was taking a chance, but it was necessary to draw into the open a killer more ruthless than a tiger.

Esther's story of a second rider had disturbed him far more than he had cared to let her know. The answer was plain enough. Clint Sleed was determined to get the man he claimed was a cow thief and had sent one of his riders to follow the trail. Not Dunn Harden. The temperamental cowboy was not *that* kind of assassin, which left the swarthy, stupid-looking man with the vicious killer eyes.

The juniper trees closed in, hid cabin and corral from sight. Kirk kept the red horse moving briskly along the trail and swung into the left fork for the short cut over the ridge, a harder ride than down the canyon, but it would save an hour's time.

He rode for perhaps another hundred yards, then pulled the horse off the trail behind a tangle of bushes and dismounted.

Swiftly, silently, he worked his way back through the trees, keeping the trail below in sight, and pausing every few moments, ears straining for any betraying sound.

The continued silence began to raise his doubts. Esther Chase had been mistaken . . . She had not seen a second rider coming out of the gap. She had admitted her own doubts.

He came at last to the edge of the clearing. His doubts fell away. Something moved by the gnarled trunk of a huge juniper near the cabin. A shadow angled out from the longer shadow cast by the tree. A man, crouched there, watching the door, waiting in ambush for the kill.

Kirk's eyes measured the distance. He could not hope to get nearer, undiscovered, and he did not dare expose himself to a bullet. Too much was at stake—the lives of the girl and her wounded husband.

Troublesome questions raced through his mind as he waited there. What was the reason behind Clint Sleed's grim determination to destroy this young stranger from the East? The Bar T foreman had lied when he said that Chase was a cow thief. Dunn Harden knew the charge was a lie, a fact that probably explained the cowboy's sardonic amusement. And who was Worden Taylor, the ex-Confederate cavalry officer who had vanished from out of his daughter's life? And why was the daughter so curiously interested in the passing of a notorious border bandit who wore the name of Pecos Jack? And most baffling conundrum of all, Esther Chase's amazing resemblance to the daughter of the man who owned Bar T.

The odd similarity in names was another puzzler. Warde *Taylor—Worden* Taylor. Drop the last syllable and *Word* easily became *Warde*. But Esther Chase's obvious hopes had been quickly dashed by Kirk's description of the big whiskered ranchman. The picture of Worden Taylor certainly bore not the slightest resemblance to Warde Taylor who was known far and wide in the Soledad country, a dominant, aggressive personality. Kirk did not like him overmuch, which was unfortunate because he more than liked Hilda. He had known her since she was a small child.

The shadow suddenly became detached from the larger shadow of the juniper. Kirk tensed. The man crouched there was Clint Sleed's unknown swarthy rider.

Stealthy as a jungle beast the man slipped across the intervening space and pressed close to the cabin door. He stood there and Kirk saw his face swing from side to side in quick furtive glances. There was a gun in his hand, held level at the hip. With his other hand he rapped on the door.

Kirk was already in motion, swift, catlike leaps. He had to cut down the distance between them before risking a shot. The man's hand lifted again. His knock came louder, and then he whirled, saw Kirk.

Sheer astonishment held him rigid for a moment too long. Kirk was now less than forty feet away and coming fast. Smoke and flame belched from the swarthy prowler's gun and then he bolted like a frightened rabbit.

Kirk felt his hat twitch as the bullet tore through the wide brim. He flung two quick shots, saw the fleeing man stagger, then disappear around the corner of the cabin.

Sounds came from inside, quick, light footsteps, and then again the deep silence. Kirk, now close to the door, spoke softly, "Mrs. Chase—"

Her voice answered him, "Yes—yes—"

"I've got a man trapped back of the cabin. I wanted you to know—"

"Shall I open the door?"

Her coolness pleased him. "No," he answered. "Nothing you can do."

Silence fell again. Kirk considered ways and means. He knew there was no escape from behind the cabin. The red cliffs there ran sheer to a height of more than a hundred feet. The man's only chance was to risk a climb down the precipitous bluffs into the canyon, or to make a dash past the corral for the covering juniper scrub. The last alternative would be his likely choice. He would want to get to his concealed horse.

Time, though, was fast becoming a factor. The thing had to be settled before the encroaching shadows deepened into the covering darkness of the night. Already the sun lay close to the western rim.

Kirk threw two fresh shells into his gun, moved stealthily toward the corral side of the cabin. He came to a standstill, gaze fixed on the shadow that lay across the yellowing sunlight. His quarry was standing close to the corner, unaware of the telltale shadow, waiting for the chance to make a break into the junipers beyond the corral.

It was an impasse that held Kirk irresolute for a long moment. He suspected that one of his bullets had scored. How seriously he could not know. The long-reaching shadow in the yellowing sunlight told him that the man was still on his feet—and dangerous. And the precious sunlight was fast fading. It was a problem that only immediate action could solve.

He edged along the wall, felt the toe of his boot come against some object, and glanced down. A tin can.

Kirk's look went apprehensively to the shadow of the man lurking behind the cabin. No stirring there, which meant that his quarry had not heard the sound. In fact there had been no sound.

His reaction to the feel of the can had been too instantaneous.

His lips tightened in a grim smile, and picking up the tin can he tossed it high over the roof, toward the corner behind the shadow. There was a startled grunt, the shadow leaped forward, and behind the shadow the stooping shape of a running man.

Kirk called sharply. The running man's face turned in a look, lips twisted in a vicious snarl. His frantic shot went wild, and the next instant he was down, his body twitching, shuddering.

Kirk holstered his smoking gun. No need for a closer look. He knew the man was already dead—a problem solved. He felt no compunction, no regret—no guilt. This unknown swarthy-faced man had come to do murder—had been sent by Clint Sleed to kill.

His reaction to the sudden and deadly flare of violent action left him dissatisfied. He would have preferred to take the swarthy man alive, force the truth from him. Death had sealed his lips, locked away the secret that had caused Dunn Harden's sinister amusement, the secret that would have explained why Clint Sleed was so resolved it was necessary for Dick Chase to die.

The thought chafed him as he turned sharply and ran with long strides under the shadowed log wall, back to the cabin door. The sound of his booted feet alone disturbed the deep stillness that followed the harsh crackle of gunfire. Esther Chase was waiting, listening—wondering.

He reached the door, pounded with gun-butt. "All right," he called, "it's all right!"

Her voice came, tight with fear. "Mr. Severn—"

"Yes," he called back, "it's all right, Mrs. Chase. Open the door, please."

He heard the scrape of the wooden bar, and the door opened, and he saw her face, pale, eyes wide with shock.

"Those—those shots—" Her voice faded.

Kirk was suddenly reluctant to tell her the truth—tell her that he had just killed a man. He said awkwardly, "I—I came back—but it's all right—"

She seemed to divine the truth, kept her eyes on him steadily. "I know what you mean," she said quietly. "You mean—he's dead—"

"Yes—" Kirk was comfortingly aware of a vast relief. This girl had good, hard metal in her. "He's dead—"

"I counted the shots," Esther Chase told him. She opened the door wide, stepped out to the fading sunlight. "Three shots, the first time, and two more—just now."

"I fired the *last* shot," Kirk said laconically.

She gazed at him, her eyes big, questioning. "Was he—one of them?"

Kirk nodded, and then, inexplicably, he was crowding her back through the door. She uttered a startled cry, beat at him with clenched fists. "No, no! I won't let you harm him!"

He shook his head, quickly closed the door, then threw the bar. "Somebody coming," he said curtly, and then more gently, "I'm sorry I frightened you." He gave her a reassuring smile, pressed close to the log wall and stared intently through a loophole.

She stood watching him, her heart thumping under the tight bodice. His apparent attack had inexpressibly shocked, terrified her. Suddenly she heard the sounds his more alert ears had picked up. The trampling of horses' hoofs.

The color that had drained from her face flooded back, a wave of hot shame at her senseless fright—distrust. The tremble went from her knees and the fear from her eyes. The approaching horsemen meant danger, but a danger she could understand. She moved quickly, snatched up the long-barreled Colt that lay on the table.

To her amazement she saw that Kirk was reaching for the heavy door-bar. He gave her a broad smile. "It's all right," he said, and swung the door wide open and stepped outside to the twilight.

Esther followed, stood framed in the doorway, the gun in lowered hand, mystified eyes fixed on the three men riding into the yard. She stifled an exclamation. She had seen the man on the buckskin horse before.

He gave Kirk an uncertain grin as he pulled his horse to a halt. He was perhaps fifty, long-legged, bony of frame, and wore a drooping sandy mustache. He said laconically, "Hello, Kirk," and unobtrusively holstered the gun ready in his hand, gaze shifting in a brief look at the girl in the cabin doorway.

"Wasn't expecting you, Chuck, but I'm mighty glad to see you." Kirk spoke solemnly, his eyes mirthful. "You always were johnny-on-the-spot."

"Well, Kirk—it's like this—" Chuck's big sandy mustache twitched. "I've knowed you so dog-gone long I've got so I can figger awful close when you get notions."

"Meaning you guessed I'd be heading into Cañon Los Diablos, huh?" Kirk grinned.

"Sure—" Chuck's tone was grim. "That's why I told Justo and Atilano to fork saddle and side me up here. Figgered you'd run into trouble."

"You didn't miss your guess—much," Kirk said dryly.

"If trouble is layin' 'round you're sure to find it," grinned the man on the buckskin horse. His eyes, blue and hard and watchful, took another sidewise look at the girl. "Heard some shootin'," he added casually. "Five shots—"

"That's right," Kirk confirmed. "I fired three of those shots." He was unsmiling now, his voice hard, crisp. "There's trouble on the prod up here,

46

but not the kind of trouble you have in mind. I'm mighty glad you took the notion to trail me, Chuck."

"Who was you shootin' at?" inquired Chuck, his now frankly puzzled look on Esther.

Kirk said dryly, "Mrs. Chase is no nester, Chuck. Her husband is inside the house. He's been shot."

"If he ain't a nester, how come you shot him?" Chuck asked harshly.

"I didn't shoot him," replied Kirk. He smiled at the girl. "This suspicious old-timer is Chuck Rigg, Mrs. Chase. He runs K7 and thinks he runs me. Barks awfully savage, but he's the best cowman in the Territory of New Mexico."

Chuck removed his hat, gave Esther an embarrassed grin. "Don't you believe his loco talk, ma'am"—and then, awkwardly, "I'm sure sorry, ma'am—the way I talked kind of rough the other day." He jerked a thumb over his shoulder at the silent, attentive pair of riders behind him. "These tough-lookin' hombres is Justo and Atilano."

The two Mexicans doffed their hats like one. "Mooch plecz, señora." Teeth gleamed in swarthy faces, two pairs of glistening eyes rolled admiringly.

Kirk saw Esther's astonishment. "Twins," he said, with a chuckle. "Two peas in a pod. The Nueco brothers are Chuck's faithful shadows."

"Sure t'ing," grinned the Mexicans. Their soft voices sounded like one.

47

Esther smiled at them. They were amazingly alike in face and gesture, a fierce-looking pair, with drooping badger-colored mustaches and watchful dark eyes. She backed into the doorway, said to Kirk, "I must tell Dick. He'll be wondering—"

Chuck Rigg's gaze followed her, then shifted inquiringly at Kirk.

"It's quite a story," Kirk said. He gestured. "There's a dead man back of the house, Chuck. Take a look at him. Maybe you know him. I don't."

The lanky K7 foreman sent his horse on a jump that carried him around the side of the cabin. Justo and Atilano spurred after him. Kirk followed, watched in silence while they stared down at the sprawled body.

"Don't know the feller," Chuck Rigg finally announced. His look went interrogatively to the Mexicans. "You boys ever see this hombre before?"

"*Sí!*" Their heads nodded in unison, eyes rolled in a curiously embarrassed look at Kirk.

The K7 foreman regarded them with frowning eyes. "How come?" he demanded; "when and where did you ever see this jasper before?"

Justo and Atilano exchanged glances. Both seemed strangely loath to answer the question. Chuck's blue eyes took on a frosty glint.

"I ain't no mind-reader," he told them, "and I

ain't too deef to hear words when you speak up loud."

"He is one known as Pedro Negro," Justo Nueco finally said in Spanish.

"This Pedro Negro is from *La Topera*," added Atilano. "He is a bad one, and is a man of mixed breeds that began with a white man and a black woman and grew worse with a Mexican father and a low white woman from a Juarez dance hall."

"We know him only by chance," chimed in Justo, with an apologetic gesture. "Is it not true, Atilano?"

"It is very true," confirmed his brother virtuously. "In the *cantina* of Ramon Trevino, which is in the town of Agua Frio below the border." His own gesture was scornful. "*Caramba*! He is a *bandido*."

"From *La Topera*, huh?" Chuck Rigg scowled. "I reckon that places this feller, Kirk. He's an *El Topo* man."

Kirk studied the dead man thoughtfully. *La Topera*—the Mole Hole, secret hideaway of *El Topo*, notorious border *bandido* and rustler, for years a scourge to all cattlemen within a radius of two hundred miles.

"I reckon it answers your question," Chuck said. "Justo and Atilano sure hated to admit they know an *El Topo* skunk, but they don't lie to me no time." He gave the abashed pair a reassuring

49

smile. "You don't need to tell me this feller ain't a friend of yours."

"*Por esta cruz, no!*" exclaimed Justo in a shocked voice and holding up both hands with thumb crossed over forefinger. He kissed the improvised cross.

"*Por esta cruz, no!*" echoed Atilano, making the same pious gesture.

The drooping horns of Chuck's sandy mustache twitched. "I'm believin' you," he said in a kindly voice. His brow furrowed speculatively. "I reckon we ain't got *all* the answer at that."

"No—" Kirk's tone was troubled. "We haven't got the answer—yet. I want to know why this *El Topo* man should be keeping company with Clint Sleed, and why Sleed sent him up here to kill Chase."

The K7 foreman looked thunderstruck. He listened attentively to Kirk's brief story of the encounter in the wash.

"Sure is a queer business," he muttered. "Ain't no savvy to it a-tall, Kirk."

"It's up to us to find out," Kirk said grimly. "I haven't told you the half of it, Chuck." He looked at the foreman thoughtfully. "It's lucky you showed up. I don't like leaving these people without protection."

"Meanin' just what?" asked Chuck Rigg suspiciously.

"Meaning that you and Justo must stick around

50

and keep an eye on things. Chase is in bad shape and I've got to get Doc Williams out here. I'm taking Atilano into town with me. He can bring the doc back."

"You won't be coming with 'em?" asked Chuck.

Kirk shook his head. "The Association has called a meeting. I've got to be there."

"Sure." The K7 foreman nodded. "I savvy." He spoke gloomily. "Hell of a mess—and me snowed under with fixin' for the roundup."

"Can't be helped." Kirk glanced at the dead Pedro Negro. "Get rid of that," he added brusquely.

"Sure," Chuck said again. "I'll have Justo drag the carcass away and bury it."

"There'll be a bronc hid out some place near," Kirk reminded.

"Leave it to Justo." Chuck grinned. "We'll take care of things here. Gettin' dark fast and you've got a hard ride in front of you."

"I'll tell Mrs. Chase—" Kirk swung on his heel. Chuck followed him through the door.

They found the girl waiting as they stepped inside. Her husband was resting easily, she informed them.

"Dick was dreadfully upset by those gun-shots," Esther said. "He—he's so grateful to you, Mr. Severn—"

"Lucky you spotted that man with your glasses," Kirk congratulated. "I'd no idea he was trailing us up the canyon." He told her briefly of

51

the arrangement to leave Chuck and the Mexican on guard.

Esther's relief was enormous. Tears sparkled in her eyes. "I must tell Dick!" She turned swiftly, was held by Kirk's voice.

"Mrs. Chase—can you describe the man you were talking to in Deming?" Kirk broke off, looked at the foreman. "Chuck—tell Atilano to get my horse. I left him in the brush, over where the trail forks into the short cut."

Chuck nodded, gave Kirk a keen look and swung away. Kirk continued in a quick, low voice, "I mean the man who told you about Pecos Jack."

"An old man," Esther said. "Dick bought our horses from him. He had a funny old covered wagon, and quite a lot of horses and mules and burros."

"Mustang Jenns," Kirk guessed. He hesitated, asked abruptly, "Did you show him that picture of your father?"

She stared at him, eyes frightened, dark in a suddenly pale face. The look was answer enough for him. He said gently, "Never mind . . . You needn't say."

The scrape of dragging spurs warned of Chuck Rigg's return. Esther spoke quickly, her low voice steady, curiously hard, almost defiant. "Yes," she said, "I showed him that picture of my father." She turned abruptly, disappeared through the door of the inner room.

52

Chapter IV

DOC WILLIAMS REMEMBERS HIS SHAKESPEARE

The sound of hurried footsteps approaching up the garden walk drew a dismayed grunt from Doctor Williams. He looked up regretfully from his book and listened with growing apprehension to the low murmur of voices at the front door. He was familiar with the signs. His frown deepened and with a gesture of resignation he closed the little book, a well-worn copy of Shakespeare, and laid it down gently on the small table at his elbow.

"The third time tonight," he muttered, and, glancing at the book, quoted grimly, " 'I hope good luck lies in odd numbers.' "

Spurs jingled in the hall, above which sounds lifted the aggrieved voice of Señora Valdez in an outpouring of voluble Spanish. "The poor man can have no peace . . . Always somebody comes with word he is wanted . . . It is too much—"

The door opened, framed the comfortably plump person of the doctor's housekeeper, hands gesticulating, indignation in her handsome dark eyes. Behind her towered Kirk Severn, hat in hand, a somewhat abashed grin on his face.

"Sorry, Doc," he said apologetically. "Concepción's about ready to scratch my eyes out."

"Rascal!" spluttered Señora Valdez. A hint of affection in her voice, her half smile, robbed the word of its sting. "It is not your fault people get hurt and must have a doctor." She vanished down the hall with a soft slapping of sandaled feet.

Doctor Williams chuckled, reached for his pipe. "It's a wonder I have any patients at all, the way Concepción fights 'em off like an old hen with a lone chick." His shaggy, grizzled brows lifted inquiringly. "What's the trouble, Kirk?"

"You won't like it," Kirk answered. "Means a long, tough ride, Doc."

"Now?" Doctor Williams scowled, glanced again at his Shakespeare. " 'A man I am, cross'd with adversity.' "

"Now," Kirk said firmly. "The old cow camp up in Cañon Los Diablos. A shoulder wound and a broken leg."

The doctor got out of his chair. "All right, all right," he grumbled. "A damnable place to get to. I was up there once with your father, years ago." He sighed, shook his head. "I don't sit a saddle so good any more, Kirk—and I'll need somebody with me, or there'll be a doctor lost in the hills."

"I've got it all arranged," Kirk told him. "You'll drive in your buckboard to K7 and pick up Atilano

54

Nueco. He'll have two saddle horses waiting. From there on you can take the old Burro Canyon road to within three miles of the camp."

"Three miles over that confounded ridge," groaned Doctor Williams. He began getting his things together. "Who's the patient, Kirk?"

"An archaeologist, a fellow named Chase," Kirk answered. "His wife is with him."

The doctor looked up from his bag. "Did she do the shooting?"

"She did not."

"You needn't be so close-mouthed," fumed the doctor.

"I haven't got the straight of it myself," Kirk explained. "It's a queer business, Doc." He paused, stared at Doctor Williams thoughtfully. "Any chance of getting a man with a broken leg down that trail to the Burro Canyon road?"

"It's possible—" The doctor's tone was dubious. "Won't be easy. Means using a stretcher." He arched his shaggy bush of brows. "Any good reason why the man can't stay where he is?"

Kirk nodded grimly. "Cañon Los Diablos is a bad place for that pair of tenderfoots. Some devil is gunning for them, Doc. I'd like to get them away from that old cow camp."

"Bring 'em down to my place," suggested the doctor. "Plenty of room." His tired face brightened. "Archaeologist, eh? Sounds interesting."

Kirk shook his head. "Won't do, Doc. I want

55

some place where nobody will think to look for them. I can't think of anything better than the ranch."

"You know best," grunted Doctor Williams.

"I've been thinking it over and K7 is the only solution," Kirk continued. "That's why I asked if it would be safe to move Chase in his present condition."

"I can manage it," promised the doctor.

"That settles it," decided Kirk. "Chuck Rigg and Justo Nueco are up there now. Tell Chuck he's to help you bring Chase and his wife down to the ranch. Justo and Atilano will rig up a stretcher." Kirk paused, regarded the doctor thoughtfully. "Mrs. Chase will want their things brought down. The boys can load the stuff on the burros I saw in the corral." Kirk smiled faintly. "Got it all in your head, Doc?"

Doctor Williams snapped his bag shut, scowled ferociously. "I'm not deaf, young man." He chuckled, "Yes, yes, I understand—and now let me be off."

Kirk accompanied him to the small stable in the rear of the house. An elderly Mexican, a lantern in his hand, greeted them from beside a team of matched bays hitched to a buckboard. Doctor Williams showed no surprise at the preparations for his journey. Señora Valdez too could read the signs.

He climbed into the seat and took the reins. "A

fine time of night to send a worn-out old medico into the remote hills," he groaned.

"The moon will soon be up," comforted Kirk. He added gratefully, "You're a doc to ride the river with, old-timer."

Doctor Williams snorted, remembered his Shakespeare. " 'We have some salt of our youth in us,' " he quoted dryly. The bay team sprang forward and with a muffled rattle of wheels the buckboard vanished into the night.

Chapter V
KIRK FINDS A BOOMERANG

Kirk found the hotel lobby deserted when he descended the stairs from his room. The night clerk, an elderly man, was still on duty. He lifted rheumy eyes from the newspaper spread open on his knees under the desk lamp.

"Dinin' room ain't open yet," he croaked dismally and returned his attention to the newspaper.

Kirk nodded indifferently, stood looking through the open door at the quickening dawn, fingers busy with cigarette paper and tobacco. The clerk broke the silence.

"Says here in the Deming paper the stage was held up ag'in. *El Topo's* gang, I reckon." The newspaper rustled. "Grabbed the payroll for the Santa Rita mines . . . killed the guard."

"How much?" queried Kirk. He lit his cigarette, flicked the burnt match into a cuspidor.

"All of twenty thousand, from what it says here in the paper," answered the clerk with obvious relish. "*El Topo* is sure one smart *bandido*, doggone if he ain't."

Sunlight flowed into the street, pushed back the shadows. Kirk said laconically, "I'll drop over to Moon Yung's for breakfast, Sam."

The night clerk gestured indifferently. "Suit

yourself," he said. "Dinin' room won't be open for mebbe half a hour and that's when I git off duty." He shook his head gloomily. "Ain't likin' this dang job so much. Gits awful dull, settin' here all night."

Kirk studied him without appearing to do so. He said casually, "You could go back to riding for Bar T."

Sam Gaines snorted. "Fat chance, after the way Clint Sleed more or less kicked me off the payroll."

"Why did he fire you?"

"I reckon Clint figgered I'd worked for Bar T too long," grumbled the night clerk. "Told me I was wore out and plumb useless." Sam glowered. "Told me worse than that—said I was a nosey ol' coon."

Kirk smiled sympathetically. "Mighty rough talk, Sam."

"I'll say!" The night clerk lowered his voice, leaned over the desk confidentially. "Clint is upstairs now. Come in after you did last night and stewed to the gills. Said somethin' about he was in town for the Association meetin'. Must have been hittin' it plenty hard over to Samper's Saloon before he landed here."

"Was he alone?" Kirk asked.

"Yeah—and sure fightin' drunk." Sam looked at Kirk sharply. "You in for the Association meetin', Mr. Severn?"

"Yes," Kirk answered briefly.

"Several of the fellers come in yesterday," Sam Gaines informed him. "Mat Dilley of Bar 4, Rock Sledge of the Lazy S, and the feller that runs the Walkin' M outfit."

"Len Matchett," Kirk said.

"Yeah—that's the feller." Sam glanced at the dog-eared register. "Kind of new in the Soledad country. Seemed some peevish 'cause Warde Taylor hadn't got in."

Kirk was careful to hide his quick interest in this bit of gossip about the owner of Walking M. He snubbed his cigarette, tossed it into the cuspidor. "Warde Taylor is the big mogul of the Stockmen's Association," he reminded Sam. "He's sure to be in this morning for the meeting. Len Matchett maybe wants to join up. He isn't a member."

"I reckon," agreed the night clerk. He yawned, glanced at his watch. "Time sure runs slow," he mourned.

"How would you like a job with K7?" queried Kirk.

Sam's face brightened. "Like it fine."

Kirk fumbled in a pocket, drew out two five-dollar gold pieces. "You're hired, Sam, only I want you to stick at the job here for a few days longer." He slid the gold pieces across the desk. "Your first week's pay."

Sam gave him a shrewd look, slowly picked up

the coins. "Mebbe I savvy, and mebbe I don't," he said cautiously.

"You needn't tell anybody you're on K7's payroll," drawled Kirk.

The former Bar T man favored him with a sly grin. "All right, boss, I'll ride this desk nights for as long as you say, and I won't be asleep on the job—if that's what you're drivin' at."

"Figure it out for yourself," smiled Kirk.

"I ain't so old but what I can still see good and hear plenty," assured the desk clerk.

Kirk threw him a nod, sauntered out to the board sidewalk and made his way to Moon Yung's across the street from the Drovers' Hotel. There was little life astir at that early hour, but the Chinese restaurant was already open for business.

Moon Yung, plump and bland, took his order of ham and eggs and vanished into his kitchen. Kirk built a fresh cigarette, his gaze idling around the room. Two other customers were breakfasting at separate tables. One of them was Ben Smithers, the town's barber. Kirk rubbed his bristly chin speculatively. He needed a shave. The signs indicated that Ben would be soon open for business.

His idling gaze came to rest on the second man sitting against the far wall. His eyes narrowed. Dunn Harden.

The Bar T man met his look with an ironical

grin. His hand lifted. "Hello, Kirk," he called; "didn't know *you* was in town."

"Association meeting," Kirk said.

Dunn Harden gulped a swallow of coffee, put the big mug down. "The boss figgers to be in, I reckon. Have to elect a new sheriff to take Jim Shane's place." He fumbled in a pocket for cigarette papers and tobacco. "Goin' to be a hot time, you bet. The boss is sure howlin' loud at the way *El Topo* is rustlin' this Soledad country."

Ben Smithers pushed back his chair, a neat little man with a stiff brush pompadour and trim mustache.

Kirk gave him a nod. "I'll be in for a shave, Ben."

The barber grinned. "Any time, Kirk." He sauntered into the sunlight, chewing daintily on a toothpick.

Moon Yung appeared from the kitchen with the ham and eggs and a mug of coffee. Dunn Harden got out of his chair, paused at Kirk's table. His young face wore a somber look.

"Watch your step, Kirk," he said softly, and moved on toward the door.

Kirk spoke sharply, "What do you mean, Dunn?"

The Bar T cowboy glanced back at him, shook his head. "You can add up the tally for yourself, Kirk." He smiled thinly, pushed into the street.

Kirk's frowning gaze followed him. He was puzzled, vaguely disturbed. He had a liking for

Dunn Harden, his irrepressible gaiety. There was hard steel, though, under that pleasant exterior, and his smiling face masked a shrewd brain. It was a mystery why Dunn Harden was content to be under the ruthless domination of a man like Clint Sleed.

Kirk gave his attention to the ham and eggs. The warning had been unmistakable, and there were two possible explanations. Clint Sleed was one. The Bar T foreman bitterly resented Kirk's interference with his pursuit of the supposed cow thief. Dunn must have known that Sleed had sent Pedro Negro to trail Kirk and Chase up Cañon Los Diablos. Kirk had restrained the impulse to question the Bar T man about the swarthy killer. Questioning would have aroused suspicions. Dunn Harden was smart. He would have correctly guessed as to the fate that had overtaken Pedro Negro.

The second explanation brought a hard glint to Kirk's eyes. He shrewdly suspected that Dunn had certain ideas about Hilda Taylor . . . was warning him to keep away from the girl. The thought of Hilda sent a tingle of excitement through Kirk. She was home again from the school in Santa Fe. He had not seen her for nearly a year. It was possible she would be in town that morning with her father.

He finished his breakfast and made his way across the street to the barber shop, which occupied a small frame building crowded in between Samper's Saloon and the Soledad Emporium. He sank into the gaudy red plush chair, Ben's pride.

"Make it a quick one, Ben," he said.

"Sure," smiled the barber. He whipped a napkin under Kirk's chin and reached for his lather brush.

The street was coming to life. Kirk caught glimpses of passers-by. A pair of cowboys, wide-brimmed hats pushed back on tousled heads, evidently from the hotel and in haste to soothe parched throats. He heard the quick slam of the saloon's swing doors.

A rancher drove past in a light wagon. A small boy sat by his side. The stage whirled up in a cloud of dust and halted in front of Mott Balen's Emporium to pick up the mail. Mott Balen was also the postmaster and Wells-Fargo agent.

Another shape passed the barber shop window. Kirk was aware of a sharp tingle of surprise. Clint Sleed, and obviously showing no signs of the debauch advertised by Sam Gaines. The saloon doors slammed, from which Kirk surmised that the Bar T foreman had dropped in for an eye-opener.

Uneasy thoughts took shape. Why had Sam Gaines lied about Sleed? He began to regret the impulse that had led him to put Sam on the K7 payroll. The idea had seemed good at the time. Sam was inquisitive, nosey, an artful scavenger of gossip. There were things Kirk wanted to know and Sam's job as night clerk offered possibilities as a useful source of information.

Kirk's doubts of Sam began to multiply. Hadn't the former Bar T man gone out of his way to drag Clint Sleed into the conversation? Had Sleed booted him off the Bar T payroll? Still why else would Sam be working at the hotel?

The young cattleman's jaw tensed. Something was going on and he had to find out what.

Ben whisked off the napkin. Kirk got out of the chair, reached for his hat and looked inquiringly down the narrow passage leading to the rear.

"Sure," Ben said. "Help yourself."

Kirk went down the hall to a door marked WASHROOM. He halted, suddenly aware of voices on the other side of the wall that divided saloon from barber shop. Sam Gaines and Clint Sleed, obviously conversing in the similar passage that ran to the rear of the barroom.

The words came distinctly. ". . . sure fell for the talk I give him about you." The night clerk's husky voice, and then Sleed's raspy voice, "Play him along . . . the sucker." A pause, and Sleed's voice again, "Make up to him good, Sam. You can tip me off to plenty." A self-satisfied guffaw from the night clerk. "Serves the skunk right, puttin' me on K7 payroll to spy for him."

The two men moved away, their footsteps fading up the passage to the barroom. Kirk stood for a long moment, digesting the conversation. Sam Gaines was already a spy—but he was spying for Clint Sleed, which meant Warde Taylor. The man had been deliberately planted as night clerk in the Drovers' Hotel to pick up information for Bar T.

Then Kirk Severn grinned.

Ben Smithers looked up from the razor he was honing. "You seem some tickled, Kirk," he observed. "What's the joke?"

Kirk paused by the barber's chair. "Ben—" He spoke solemnly, "ever hear of a boomerang?"

"Sure," answered Ben. "One of them crooked sticks that circles back and hits the fellow that throws it."

"I found one—in there." Kirk gestured at the passage. "A right good boomerang—all ready to use." His eyes danced.

"You're crazy," stuttered the astonished barber. "I ain't never had a boomerang 'round this place."

Kirk grinned, pushed through the door into the street. Ben gazed after him with puzzled eyes. He shook his head. "Boomerang!" he muttered disgustedly. "Now what the hell—"

Chapter VI
A SHERIFF FOR SOLEDAD

The red-wheeled vehicle that rocked along at the heels of the fast-stepping black Morgans had been built to order for Warde Taylor's personal use. It was actually a glorified ranch buckboard with easy-riding springs and soft leather cushions.

The driver, Rincon, was a small, wiry man with a seamed, wizened face poked forward on a turtlelike neck. He wore a red calfskin vest over a blue flannel shirt embellished with large white buttons and a loosely-knotted yellow bandanna. A battered sombrero shadowed restless, watchful eyes.

Warde Taylor and his daughter occupied the back seat. The owner of Bar T towered above the slim girl by his side. He wore a huge white Stetson that shadowed deceptively mild brown eyes. A massive, majestic-looking man with his heavy grizzled beard and air of serenity.

Two riders followed the buckboard, their horses moving at a fast lope to keep up with the Morgans. Rifles peeped from saddle boots and both men wore guns in their holsters. They were a hard-faced pair. Warde Taylor never went to town, or anywhere else, without them. Some said that the owner of Bar T was a show-off, liked display; others suspected more sinister reasons. It was whispered that he went in daily fear for his life— that *El Topo* had sworn to kill Warde Taylor.

The road topped a low ridge and reached away in a beeline down the slope to the little cowtown in the bend of Soledad Creek.

"Four years at that Santa Fe school has changed you a lot, Hilda," Taylor said to the girl. "You're a grown woman, now, and a mighty pretty one." His tone was affectionate, prideful.

"You'll make me vain," laughed the girl. Sunlight flashed tawny glints from a wind-blown curl as she tilted her head in a sidewise look at him. "I've been home every vacation," she pointed out. "I haven't burst out on you all grown up. You've seen it coming, Dad."

"It's this last year," Warde Taylor said. "Maybe I wasn't noticing you so much the other times. You've got style to you, girl. I like it."

"I'm going on twenty," Hilda reminded. She smiled demurely. "We'll have to admit that I'm no longer a little girl, all legs and freckles."

Warde Taylor chuckled in his beard. "Your tomboy days are done, young lady."

"I suppose so." Her tone was rueful.

They were approaching Soledad's wide, main street. The driver snapped his silver-mounted whip and the blacks began to trot. The buck-board whirled into the street, the two cowboys, centaurlike shapes in the dust, following closely, horses on the dead run. It was Warde Taylor's way. Soledad always knew when the owner of Bar T came to town.

Rincon brought the team to a standstill in front of the Drovers' Hotel. Warde Taylor climbed out, reached a helping hand to his daughter. She stepped with a flutter of skirts to the sidewalk, acutely aware of the tall man watching from the wide doorway of the Emporium.

Kirk Severn caught her hesitant smile, but made no attempt to join the group that quickly formed on the hotel porch. Cattlemen, for the most part, in for the Association meeting. In another moment she was the center of a noisily-welcoming crowd.

Warde Taylor towered above them, an impressive figure with his great beard, his huge white Stetson, and the black Prince Albert coat he invariably wore to town. The black trousers that encased his legs were thrust inside soft leather boots, but unlike the other men who openly wore their guns, there was no visible evidence that the Bar T man was armed.

He stood there, benevolent smile on his pretty daughter as she exchanged laughing banter with the admiring cowmen. A soft, drawling voice hailed him. His look went to the speaker, moving toward him from the lobby door, a lean-built man with a keen-cut dark face.

Warde Taylor said genially, "Hello, Len. Glad to see you."

"I thought I'd horn in on your meeting," Len Matchett said. "How about it, Warde?"

"It's all fixed," Taylor assured him.

Hilda disengaged herself from the little group of men and approached her father. "I think I'll do my shopping," she said. Her look went briefly to Kirk Severn, lounging in the doorway of the Emporium.

Len Matchett said, half-reproachfully, "Forgotten me, Miss Hilda?"

She gave him a smile. "How do you do, Mr. Matchett? Of course I haven't."

"You've come home all grown up," chuckled the Walking M man. "I'm going to be camping on your doorstep, along with the other boys."

He spoke teasingly, but the unmistakable challenge in his eyes sent a disquieting prickle through the girl. She forced a light laugh, shook her head at him, and started down the porch steps. The crashing report of a gun brought her to a shocked standstill.

A deep hush followed the shot, and then the street came to life. A man shouted from somewhere and one of the Bar T cowboys slid from his horse, jerked gun from holster, and ran with short, choppy strides to the opposite sidewalk and vanished into the alley between Moon Yung's restaurant and the Soledad County Bank which had a second story used as a hall for meetings and dances.

Men crowded down the porch steps, jostled past Hilda, and fanned out across the street. Two men emerged excitedly from the bank. One of them carried a sawed-off shotgun. Doors slammed up and down the street and voices lifted in a bedlam of excited questions.

Hilda felt a hand on her arm, heard Kirk Severn's voice. "In here," he said. "Might be some more shooting."

She gave him a quick, grateful look and ran by his side into the cool dimness of the Emporium. Mott Balen, a gaunt, stoop-shouldered man with an untidy thatch of badger-gray hair, stood uncertainly by his big iron safe, a shotgun clutched in his hands. He gave the girl a nervous grin.

"Is it a holdup, Kirk?" The storekeeper craned his long neck in a look through the door. "Crowd's all piled up in front of the bank."

"The shot came from the hall upstairs," Kirk answered. "I don't know any more than you do, Mott." He drew Hilda deeper into the long, dimly-lighted store, and suddenly they were behind a stack of shelves filled with a miscellany of hardware, and she was in his arms, soft, warm lips on his.

They drew apart, breathless, shaken, looked into each other's eyes. Kirk said a bit unsteadily, "You

71

stayed so long there, talking with that bunch. It was hard—waiting—"

"I couldn't get away—" Hilda hesitated, "and Father was watching me." A troubled look clouded her eyes. "Kirk—why does Father feel so—so hateful about you?"

Kirk shook his head. "We'll not talk about it *now*." He drew her into his arms again. "It's good to see you, Hilda." His eyes glinted and he added with make-believe jealousy, "Watch out for that Len Matchett hombre. I saw him making eyes at you."

"I can't bear him," Hilda declared. "He—he gives me the creeps."

"He's top man with your father," Kirk commented a bit grimly. His arms tightened hard on her slim waist. "I get to worrying at times, Hilda. Your father likes to have his way, and I've an idea he'll have his way with you."

She gave him a troubled look. "What do you mean?"

"I mean Len Matchett."

"I told you I can't bear the man," retorted the girl.

He saw her distress and dropped the subject. "I wish we could go off for a picnic." His smile was rueful. "Got to attend the Association meeting."

"Tomorrow," Hilda suggested hopefully. "I'm dying for a ride. We could go up Cañon Los Diablos."

Mention of the canyon reminded him of the wounded archaeologist, of Esther Chase. He shook his head. "I can't promise. I've a lot of things on."

"Oh!" She was frankly disappointed, piqued. "Please don't put yourself out on *my* account."

"You little idiot!" Kirk said.

Hilda was suddenly contrite. "Darling—forgive me!" She was in his arms again, clung there, her cheek against his. He said in a low voice, "People coming—" He kissed her hard, and they moved away from behind the screening shelves.

The customers were streaming in from the street, voices clamoring excitedly.

"The feller got clean away, whoever he was," a ranchman told the storekeeper.

Kirk and Hilda approached the group, stood listening. The rancher looked at the girl. "Your dad claims it was an attempt to kill him—says he heard the bullet whiz past his head."

Alarm widened the girl's eyes. The rancher seemed pleased. "Awful close call he had, Hilda. I reckon he's got it figgered right. *El Topo.* That's the answer. Ain't the first time he's been shot at by that *El Topo* gang."

"Anybody see the man?" questioned Kirk.

"Nope." The rancher shook his head. "Sam Gaines was up in the hall, fixin' things for the Association meetin'. Sam says he was back in the storeroom, huntin' for a couple more chairs.

73

He heard the shootin' and started back into the hall but the feller slammed the door on him and turned the key. We found Sam locked up tight and cussin' to beat hell." The ranchman chuckled. "Key was gone. We had to break the lock."

Hilda forgot her shopping. She hurried into the street. Kirk followed her, his expression thoughtful.

Warde Taylor was again on the porch, the center of a group of grave-faced cowmen. He gave Kirk a brief nod, looked keenly at his daughter.

"It's all right," he reassured her. "They didn't get me *this* time." He patted her shoulder.

"It's dreadful," Hilda said, "and so mysterious—"

"Nothing mysterious about it," the Bar T cowman declared grimly. "*El Topo* knows I'm after his scalp. He figures to get mine first." His tone softened. "Run along, girl . . . do your shopping."

Mat Dilley, a compact little man with a red face and angry blue eyes, said heatedly, "We've got to fix this *El Topo* damn quick. A decent cowman ain't safe in this Soledad country with that killin' wolf runnin' loose."

"That's why I called this meeting," Warde Taylor curtly reminded the owner of Bar 4. He gave Kirk a frosty smile. "We're electing you to fill out Jim Shane's unexpired term."

"Elect *me*—" Kirk broke off, acutely aware that the other men were watching him intently.

74

He could read their thoughts. Sheriffs of Soledad County had a way of dying in office, and that did not mean in their beds. Like his two predecessors, Sheriff Shane's bullet-riddled body had been recently found in the chaparral. These hard-boiled cowmen were waiting for his answer. Hilda was watching him, too, from the porch steps where she had halted at her father's words.

The muscles of his jaw tightened. He knew what these tough-minded men would think if he said *no* to Warde Taylor. They would say among themselves that Kirk Severn lacked the guts for a man's job.

Warde Taylor said softly, "Well, Severn—how about it?" There was a hint of mockery in his eyes.

Kirk shook his head. "No sheriff's star for me, Warde. I'm not wanting the job."

There was a hush. Hilda turned abruptly away. Her face was pale. Mat Dilley broke the silence. "Hell," he exclaimed angrily. "I ain't afraid to pick up Jim Shane's star, Warde. I'll take on the job."

"You've got a family," Warde Taylor said. His unsmiling gaze swept the circle of faces. "You're all family men." His voice took on a taunting note. "I don't blame Severn for not wanting to be our sheriff. *El Topo* don't like our sheriffs. We all know what happened to Jim Shane, and to the others before him." He paused, added grimly,

"Just the same, we've got to have a sheriff on the job."

A soft, drawling voice broke in, "What about me, Warde?" Len Matchett smiled at the faces that swung toward him. "I've no family, and I've always kind of liked the idea of a nice shiny star pinned to my shirt."

"You don't belong to the Association, Len," reminded Warde Taylor.

"We sure can soon fix that," loudly declared Rock Sledge, the tall owner of the Lazy S.

"I second the motion," chimed in Mat Dilley. He spat out a brown stream of tobacco juice, flung a scornful look at Kirk.

"That settles it," announced Warde Taylor. "You're elected full member of the Stockmen's Association, Len, and from now on you're sheriff of Soledad." He chuckled in his beard, pulled out a heavy gold watch and looked at it. "Seems to me we've had our meeting right here and now. I vote we call it a day and adjourn."

"I'm buyin' a drink for the new sheriff of Soledad," announced Mat Dilley. "Come on, fellers—"

Kirk was already moving up the board sidewalk. Perhaps Hilda had been watching for him. She appeared in the doorway of the Emporium, stood looking at him. He halted, waited for her to speak.

She said in a low, tight voice, "I don't understand!"

"Don't try." His tone was curt.

"They—they will say you're afraid—a coward." She gave him a piteous look.

"Do *you?*" He asked the question bluntly, unsmilingly.

"I don't know what to think—" She hesitated. "It—it didn't sound like *you.*"

"Listen—" He spoke quietly, "your father had his reasons for wanting to pin Jim Shane's star on me. I have my reason for saying *no.*" His smile came, lingered on her warmly. "It's a very good reason, Hilda. I can't say more—*now.*" He moved on up the sidewalk, left her staring after him, a mixture of bewilderment and relief in her eyes.

Chapter VII

DUNN HARDEN TAKES ORDERS

Kirk lost no time in getting out of town. His friends would be asking difficult questions. He was reluctant to explain why he had refused the nomination that would have made him sheriff of Soledad. Also he was anxious to learn the outcome of his plan to move Dick Chase down to the ranch-house. It was possible that Dick and Esther would balk at the idea. He fervently hoped that Doc Williams would override any objections.

He was too engrossed with his somber thoughts to notice Clint Sleed watching from the corral in the rear of the livery barn. The Bar T foreman's eyes narrowed speculatively. He had already heard of the impromptu meeting held by the Association on the porch of the Drovers' Hotel.

"Severn ain't wastin' time, makin' tracks out of town," he said to his companions. "I reckon he's some sore at the way the boss showed him up in front of the bunch."

"Kirk wasn't likin' the idee a-tall," chortled Sam Gaines. "He sure balked hard agin' steppin' into Jim Shane's boots." The night clerk spat contemptuously. "Chicken-hearted, I reckon."

Dunn Harden looked up from the cigarette he was twisting into shape. "Don't go off half-cock, Sam," he said. "Kirk Severn's got plenty nerve, and then some."

Sleed gave him a hard look. "Meanin' just what?" he asked curtly.

"Meanin' that nerve ain't got a thing to do with Kirk not wanting to play sheriff for this county," Harden replied. "He's got some reason and I reckon it's plenty good."

Sleed's eyes narrowed. He stood silent, lost in thought. It was Harden who spoke.

"Some queer we don't hear from Pedro Negro," he said softly.

"I'll say," muttered the Bar T foreman. He came to a decision. "Fork your bronc, Dunn. I want to know where Severn heads to. Stick to him close, but don't let him know you're trailin' him."

"I'd as lief trail *El Topo*," grumbled Harden. "Be a damn sight easier."

"He mebbe *is El Topo*," chortled Sam Gaines. Malicious amusement lurked in his red-rimmed eyes. "Mebbe that explains the gunplay this mornin'."

"You're loco," scoffed Harden. "Couldn't have been Kirk who took that shot at the boss. Kirk was down on the street when it happened."

"He knowed the boss was due in town for the

Association meetin'," argued the night clerk. "He could have fixed it to have a feller posted up thar in the hall." He gave Sleed a sly wink.

The foreman looked annoyed. "Shut up," he said harshly. "You talk too loose when you get to drinkin'."

"Was only jokin'," mumbled Sam sulkily.

Dunn Harden stared at him intently, then looked curiously at Sleed. "You two fellers know something about this shootin'," he said in a flat voice.

Sleed chose to ignore the accusation. "Fork your bronc like I said, Dunn." His tone was impatient. "Find out what Severn is up to, and don't stand here makin' fool talk."

"I was kind of figgerin' to head back to the ranch," Dunn Harden told him rebelliously.

"Meanin' you figger to see Hilda, huh?" Sleed's tone was biting. "You've got a hell of a nerve—makin' up to the boss's daughter, feller." The fore-man rocked on his heels, hairy hand on the butt of his gun, hard eyes fixed warily on the younger man. "You're takin' my orders, or you're gettin' your time, Dunn." He paused, added softly, "You ain't got a chance at that—not with Kirk Severn swingin' his loop for her."

The Bar T cowboy's face was a cold mask. He said tonelessly, "Sure, Clint . . . I'm on my way—" He swung on his heel, vanished into the barn.

Sleed's sardonic look followed him. "Damn

80

fool," he muttered, "makin' eyes at Hilda. It sure is time he gets wise to himself."

Sam leered at him. "What the hell if the kid *is* sweet on the gal? Won't git him nothin'. . . . and it sure holds him in the Bar T remuda."

"You ain't tellin' me nothin'," countered the foreman gruffly. His face creased in a mirthless smile. "You heard what I said to him about Severn, didn't you?"

"You told him Kirk was swingin' a loop for the gal," grinned Sam. "I savvy—you figger to git the kid green-eyed, huh?"

"You've guessed it," smiled the foreman.

"Dunn has a hair-trigger temper and a hair-trigger finger," Sam said. "You git him worked up good and he'll sure kill Kirk."

"Won't make *me* weep," Sleed said with his bitter smile. He added viciously, "Won't grieve none if Severn gets Dunn in the bargain. Dunn's gettin' too uppity."

"You're a foxy devil," admitted the former Bar T man. He pulled a flask from his hip pocket. "Have a snort?"

Sleed shook his head, watched sourly while the night clerk tipped the flask to his lips. "Go easy on the likker," he warned.

"Likker don't hurt me none," reassured Sam. He returned the flask to his pocket. "That shootin' sure had 'em all guessin'."

"Shut up!" rasped the foreman. He glanced

81

uneasily at the open barn door. "Can never tell who's listenin'." The drunken grin on Sam's face seemed to enrage him. "You damn fool, you'll sure run into trouble if you ain't more careful." He flung an angry look and stalked off toward the barn door.

Sam watched him disappear into the dark interior. His face had a grayish look. He licked his lips as if troubled by a sudden dryness, and after a moment's indecision, fumbled the whiskey flask from his pocket and took another drink. A Mexican, forking manure from the stable door, grinned at him, leaned conversationally on his fork. "You look mooch seek, señor," he began sympathetically.

Sam was annoyed. "You go to hell." He tilted the flask to his lips, swallowed noisily. "It's time I got me some sleep," he told the Mexican haughtily. "Cain't set all night at that damn hotel desk and work all day for Clint Sleed. I ain't sick, Pancho—jest awful sleepy." He looked regretfully at the empty flask, tossed it into the manure pile and moved on unsteady legs toward the corral gate.

Pancho's gaze followed him speculatively. Señor Gaines was drunk . . . *Válgame Dios* . . . a bad one—that hombre. He smelled of evil things. Pancho shook his head, retired with his fork into the stable.

Chapter VIII

MUSTANG JENNS MAKES A PROMISE

The horse was reluctant to obey the signal to halt. He knew that they were pointed for the home ranch and he was eager to cover the distance. Ears laid back in protest he slid to a standstill.

Kirk sat tensely erect in the saddle, ears straining to catch the sound that had made him draw rein. The words came faintly on the wind:

" 'Oh, boys, tell them to stop,'
That was the cry of Mari-er.
But the more she said *whoa,*
They said, 'let her go,'
And the swing went a little
                      bit higher."

A slow smile creased Kirk's tanned face. He swung the horse and rode along the dry wash toward a dense growth of willows and alders. He pushed through the thicket and broke into a small *vega* where a mixed bunch of horses and mules and burros were browsing the short grass.

An ancient canvas-covered wagon stood close to a spring that bubbled from the base of the cliffs. A small, wiry-framed man sat on his heels by a campfire on which stood a battered tin coffee pot. He looked up, jerked a casual nod at Kirk and went on slicing bacon into a frying pan.

Kirk grinned at him. "Hello, Mustang," he said, "when did you get in?"

"Hello, Kirk." The old man methodically wiped the blade of his jackknife, snapped it shut and thrust the knife into a pocket. "Was you lookin' for a trade? Got a span of mules you'd mebbe fancy." He put the pan of bacon on the fire.

Kirk shook his head. "Heard you singing. Thought I'd drop in for a powwow." He slid from his saddle and began to leisurely make a cigarette. "You were singing that song about Maria when I was a kid, Mustang, and that's a lot of years ago."

Mustang Jenns grinned. "I kinder like that song about Marier," he chuckled. "Heerd it one time when a medicine show hit Silver City. The doc always begun his sellin' talk with it . . . used to pluck a banjo and bawl to beat the band until folks crowded 'round his wagon. The words kinder stuck."

"I'll say they stuck," smiled Kirk. "We always know when Mustang Jenns is somewhere close."

The old horsetrader chuckled. "I reckon there

84

ain't no corner in the Soledad whar folks ain't heard about Marier," he admitted. He reached for a fork and turned the sizzling bacon. "What's on your mind, son—if it ain't a trade?"

Kirk found a seat on a boulder. "A question, Mustang. Maybe you have an answer, and maybe you haven't. It was a long time ago."

Mustang Jenns lifted his head in a sharp look. Something like a mask seemed to drop over his lean, leathery face. He was perhaps in his early seventies, sun-dried, and as tough and enduring as mesquite. A battered, wide-brimmed hat shadowed shrewd blue eyes, and he wore a red and white cowhide over a red flannel shirt, and faded blue overalls tucked into dusty leather boots. His motions as he carefully turned the bacon were unhurried. It was apparent he was one who thought before he spoke.

"Waal, son," he drawled, "I got a right smart mem'ry, if the question ain't one I hadn't orter answer." He reached for a tin plate and deftly flicked the crisp bacon from the pan. "How about a cup of cawfee, Kirk?" he added hospitably. "Can throw some more bacon in the pan."

"Already had breakfast," Kirk told him. "Go on and eat, Mustang. You must have slept late."

The horsetrader filled a tin cup from the coffee pot. Kirk watched him speculatively. He knew Mustang well enough to be aware of his peculiarities. The old desert rover was secretive

85

and cautious. His years of wandering had made him a mine of information, some of it apt to be dangerous.

"Should have hit Soledad last night," grumbled Mustang between sips of hot coffee. "Busted a wheel, crossin' Coyote Creek. Took most of last night gettin' the dang thing so's it would hold up. Got bus'ness in Soledad," he added.

"You ought to do some good trading," remarked Kirk. "Lot of cattlemen in town for the Association meeting."

Mustang gave him a sly grin. "Wasn't fixin' to do any tradin', but I'm always ready to dicker," he said. "It's another deal I've got on in Soledad." He carefully placed the tin cup on an upended box. "It's like this, Kirk, I'm done with livin' like a wanderin' Ishmaelite. It's time I settled down. I been rovin' this dang country for nigh on forty years and I reckon I know when it's time to settle down."

"That's right," Kirk said gravely. "You've got me awfully curious, Mustang," he added with a grin.

"I've bought out the Soledad Liv'ry and Feed Stables." Mustang reached into the box, fished out a biscuit and sopped it in the bacon grease. "I'm fixin' to have a new sign painted over the barn door." Mustang swallowed a mouthful of biscuit, grinned triumphantly. "Some sign, Kirk, letters two feet high and says,

THE SOLEDAD FEED AND SALES STABLES
MUSTANG JENNS, PROP."

"Grand news!" congratulated Kirk. He reached out, shook the old man's hand.

"That ain't all of it," chuckled Mustang. "I've bought me a house, up on the slope back of the barn. Come next week I'll have my wife fixed up there all fine." He nodded contentedly. "Yes, sir, I'm sure settlin' down for keeps."

"Your *wife!*" Kirk stared in amazement. "First I've heard of a *wife,* Mustang!"

"Been married most two years . . . got me a real he-man son. A yearlin', next month."

"You close-mouthed old scoundrel!" marveled Kirk. "I wouldn't have believed it of you."

Mustang looked at him suspiciously. "I ain't so dang old," he retorted heatedly. "What's so hard to believe about me havin' a son if I *am* nigh on seventy-three? I'm a awful tough hombre, Kirk."

"I'll say you are," Kirk said with a mollifying grin. "Who's the lady, Mustang?"

"Waal —" The veteran horsetrader hesitated, looked off at the distant hills festooned with fluffy cloud masses, "this here country's in my blood. I've lived here boy and man. I could set 'round all day, lookin' at it—the desert, the hills, the high peaks, the mesquite and cat's-claw, and the junipers and piñons, the blowin' sand, the dunes, the canyons, and—well, dang it all, I sure set a store by this part of New Mexico." He drew a long breath, poured more coffee into the tin cup, looked a bit defiantly at his listener. "That's why Marier and me figgered to git hitched. Marier fits in as natcheral as the mesquite. She's half Apache, Kirk, Mission schooled, and she speaks Spanish good as a grandee." Mustang chuckled. "Got me beat for bang-up American talk. She's fair young, sound in wind and limb, and she's sure give me a he-man son to carry on the name of Jenns."

The two men shook hands solemnly, without words. Mustang picked up his tin cup, lowered it with a startled grunt as one of the burros let out a discordant bray. His keen eyes swept their surroundings suspiciously.

"Lucy's most as good as a watch-dog," he said. "Looks like she's seen some critter out thar in the chaparral." He glanced at the long rifle that leaned against a wagon wheel. "Wouldn't be the first time some stealin' varmint has tried to jump my stock from under my nose. Would have, but for old Lucy soundin' off like she done just now."

They sat motionless for several moments, eyes raking the thicket. Finally Mustang relaxed, fumbled a plug of tobacco from a pocket. He bit off a chew, shrewd eyes fixed inquiringly on Kirk.

"Waal, son," he said, "I'm mebbe ready to

answer that thar question that's on your mind." His lean jaw moved meditatively. "Pervidin' it ain't somethin' I'd ruther keep my mouth shut about."

"What do you remember about Pecos Jack?" asked Kirk.

Mustang looked at him intently. "Waal, now," he said, "I reckon you know what happened to him." His look shifted to the distant mountain peaks, came back to Kirk. "It ain't Pecos Jack you've got on your mind, son."

"You were there when he was hung," Kirk said. "You had a good look at him."

"Must have been all of nineteen or twenty years back," mused the horsetrader. "Weren't a pretty sight, son. No lynchin' is . . . kinder chills the marrer in your bones to see a mob dangle a feller from a tree." He spat a dark brown stream at an investigating fly. "Pecos Jack was one bad hombre and I reckon he got what was due him. Held up the stage, killed the Wells-Fargo man and got away with a big gold shipment."

"Was the money recovered?" Kirk questioned.

"Come to think on it, it weren't," Mustang answered after a moment's cogitation.

"Wasn't that strange?" Kirk arched his brows.

"Oh, Pecos done the job all right," asserted Mustang. "I reckon he cached the loot away some place before they got him."

"Did he deny he was Pecos Jack?"

Mustang nodded. "Any feller would have done the same," he drawled. "Claimed plenty loud he'd never heard of Pecos." The trader spat into the fire. "That was natcheral."

"What did he say about himself?"

"Waal—" Mustang pondered, jaw moving reflectively. "Claimed he was some other feller. Cain't remember the name he called hisself."

"Was it Worden Taylor?"

"*Quien sabe*?" Mustang shrugged a bony shoulder, stared curiously at Kirk. "Could have been." He paused. "What fur you want to know, Kirk?"

Kirk's gaze was on the burro. Lucy's big ears were cocked attentively at something in the thicket. Mustang said with a dry cackle, "She acts like she smells a coyote, or somethin', back thar." He repeated his question. "What fur you want to know about Pecos Jack?"

Kirk hesitated, shook his head. "There's a chance the man you saw lynched wasn't Pecos Jack." His voice was troubled.

"No chance a-tall," asserted Mustang. "I don't hold with lynchin', but the feller was a killer and got what was comin'." He paused, added slowly, "Come to think on it, there was a gal askin' me about Pecos, over to Deming, two or three weeks back."

Kirk made no comment, and after another pause, Mustang continued: "Showed me a pitcher, asked me if it was a pitcher of the feller I saw lynched." He spat again at the buzzing fly.

"Was it?" Kirk narrowed his eyes at him.

"Sure it was," Mustang answered. "The gal acted like she was awful upset." His blue eyes took on a puzzled look. "A purty gal, and so doggone like Hilda Taylor to look at I was knocked all of a heap when I found she weren't Hilda. Saw she weren't when I got to talkin' with her. Some older—more grown up in style and sech." His keen eyes were hard on Kirk, probing, questioning. "Is she back of this talk of yours about Pecos Jack?"

Kirk was silent for a long moment. "I know her," he finally admitted. "The thing has me puzzled, Mustang."

"Seems like it has," Mustang said dryly. His look went off to the hills, and he added softly, "Your dad and me was awful good friends, Kirk." He grinned. "Not that I'm askin' you to talk if you don't want to loosen up."

"You're my friend, too," Kirk said simply. "I need all the help I can get—from my friends."

"My ears is cocked," the horsetrader said laconically.

He listened attentively to Kirk's briefly outlined story of the preceding twenty-four hours, gave him an incredulous look at the account of the Association's impromptu meeting on the porch of the Drovers' Hotel.

"Folks'll say you've got no guts, not wantin' to be sheriff," he muttered worriedly.

Kirk's face darkened. "You know different, Mustang."

"Sure, sure!" Mustang thrust a horny palm at him. "You don't need to tell *me*, son. You have your reasons."

"You bet I have," Kirk said grimly.

Mustang went back to the Chase affair. "You figger the pitcher the gal showed me was her own dad?" He spoke worriedly.

"That's right," Kirk replied gloomily.

The two men were silent for several moments. Mustang's jaw worked vigorously. He shook his head. "Mighty tough on her," he finally commented.

"I've an idea there's been a terrible mistake," Kirk declared. "Doesn't sound reasonable to believe this Worden Taylor could have been Pecos Jack. The man was an ex-Confederate cavalry officer, a cultured gentleman."

"We've had some dang bad hombres that's been them kind . . . fellers that come West and took to robbin' and killin'," reminded the old horse-trader. He scowled. "At that, I ain't likin' the way Clint Sleed is actin' about the Chase feller. Knowin' Clint for the dang scoundrel he is, I'd say there's somethin' awful smelly in the corral."

Kirk looked at him thoughtfully. "You can help, Mustang. You can do a lot for me—in Soledad."

92

Mustang Jenns nodded, his shrewd eyes very bright. "I'll keep a sharp ear cocked for you, son," he promised. "A feller that runs a livery and feed barn can pick up plenty news." He paused, studied the younger man with puzzled eyes. "How come you balked at wearin' Jim Shane's star?"

Kirk was a long time answering. He stared intently at the cigarette stub between his fingers, flipped it into the fire and spoke slowly, as if weighing his words. "I've never been satisfied about the way Jim Shane died," he said.

"Jim was murdered—dry-gulched," Mustang reminded.

"He was murdered all right," Kirk said grimly. "No doubt about that."

"*El Topo's* gang," Mustang said. "Nothin' mysterious about it, Kirk. Jim was after *El Topo's* skelp."

Kirk looked at him hard. "Who is *El Topo*?" He put the question softly. "Have you ever seen this man they call *El Topo*?"

Mustang Jenns pushed back his battered hat, thoughtfully rubbed his badger-colored hair with a horny forefinger. "Come to think on it, I cain't swear I ever laid eyes on the skunk," he admitted. "He—he's jest *El Topo*."

"That is all we know about him," Kirk said with a thin smile. "He's here, there, and everywhere, and nobody seems to have laid eyes on him." His voice hardened. "What's the answer?"

Mustang considered at length. "Adds up to this," he finally said cautiously, "adds up to *El Topo* bein' only a name that some dang wolf is usin' to hide hisself under."

Kirk nodded. "I want to dig him out," he said, his voice grim with implacable purpose. "Jim Shane was my friend. He was shoved into office—just to be murdered."

"I reckon I'm beginnin' to savvy why you wasn't wantin' to pick up his star." Mustang Jenns wagged his head solemnly. "It's a shaddered trail you're fixin' to follow, son."

"I'm following it to the end," Kirk said with a hard smile.

"You and Warde Taylor should orter git together," continued Mustang. "I hear talk that Warde is all set to pay a thousand bucks for *El Topo's* skelp. It's all over the Soledad that Warde is skeered for his life." The old desert man paused, chewed reflectively. "Seems to me Warde had plenty good reason for wantin' you to take up Jim's sheriff job. Warde was pickin' a top-hand man to go after *El Topo*. I reckon he figgered the same way when he got Jim Shane 'lected sheriff."

"I'd like to see it your way, but I don't." Kirk's tone was blunt.

Mustang gave him a shrewd look. "Meanin' you don't think a heap of Warde, huh?"

"I'd rather not say what I think about him—yet," evaded Kirk. "It boils down to this, Mustang— I'm going after *El Topo*, or the man wearing his mask, and I'm going to do it my own way, and no strings to be pulled by Warde Taylor." He scowled, added gloomily, "It's a mess, and the Chase people are mixed up in it. The fact that Clint Sleed did his best to kill Chase hits me hard. Clint is Warde's trusted foreman. The man he sent trailing Chase and me up Cañon Los Diablos was a member of *El Topo's* gang. The Nueco brothers recognized him. What's the answer to that one, Mustang?"

The old horsetrader looked off at the towering peaks darkly massed against the horizon. "It don't listen so good," he said slowly. "Thar's plenty hell, down whar you'll dig up that answer." He wagged his head solemnly, got to his feet. "It's a dark canyon you're headin' into, Kirk, and thar's death lurkin' in that shaddered trail you're all set to ride." He held out his hand. "I'm sidin' you, son. That's a promise."

"Thanks, old-timer." Kirk spoke simply, affectionately. "I don't know any man I'd rather have riding with me." He turned to his horse, swung into saddle. "My regards to the wife, and to the boy." He chuckled. "What's the youngster's name, Mustang?"

"Same as mine," Mustang answered.

"I never did know your name," Kirk said.

The old desert man hesitated, looked off at his beloved mountains, gnarled fingers stroking his grizzled beard reflectively. He turned his head in a curiously shy look at Kirk. "George Washington Jenns," he said with a grin. "That's the kid's name, too, but he won't be like me, Kirk. He's goin' to have a real eddication . . . he's goin' to set astraddle the world when he's growed man-size."

Kirk's hand lifted. It was a salute, as well as a parting gesture.

Chapter IX
THE SPY

Kirk's gaze roved warily as he rode through the willow brakes and headed toward the road. No sound disturbed the stillness. Only the crunch of the bay's shod hoofs as they pushed down the wash.

They cut into the road, and eager for the comforts of the home ranch, the big horse rocked along at his peculiar running-walk. It was a fast, tireless pace he could maintain hour after hour.

The road snaked endlessly through the mesquite, circled around gullies, and swooped over a succession of low ridges. It was a narrow, wheel-rutted, dusty road and Kirk's only reason for not taking the short-cut trail was the fear of missing Doctor Williams who might be on his way back to town. He was anxious to have the doctor's report. Whenever he could keep the road in view he eliminated several long detours by cutting across the mesa.

He forded the sandy shallows of Coyote Creek and forged up the steep slope. It was a climb that took the bay's wind, and Kirk drew to a halt on the summit, slid from the saddle and reached in his pocket for tobacco and cigarette papers.

His keen eyes searched the winding road ahead while he twisted the cigarette into shape. A faint haze of dust lifted in the far distance.

He reached his binoculars down from the saddle and studied the moving black dot. The doctor's buckboard. Kirk placed the glasses on a boulder and put a match to his cigarette, conscious of a vast relief. There was a chance he had missed the doctor while talking to Mustang Jenns.

He picked up the glasses and carefully scrutinized the twistings of the road beyond Coyote Creek. There was a haze of dust down there, a lone horseman. Even as Kirk looked, the rider vanished.

Kirk lowered the glasses, his expression thoughtful. It was in his mind that Lucy's warning had not been in vain. Mustang's surmise about a lurking coyote was wrong. The burro had sensed the presence of a man.

He tried again with the glasses. No dust, now; no movement down there in the mesquite. Kirk's eyes hardened. The signs indicated he was being trailed. The lone rider probably possessed glasses, had picked Kirk up, outlined on the crest of the ridge. He had pulled off the road into the covering mesquite, was waiting for Kirk to move on.

Puzzled, angry, Kirk pinched out his cigarette, swung back to his saddle and rode down the long slope toward the approaching buckboard, bouncing along at reckless speed.

They met at the foot of the grade. Doctor Williams drew hard on the reins, pulled the fast-moving trotters to a standstill.

"You'll break a wheel one of these days," drawled Kirk. "This old wagon road is no race-track, Doc."

"I know every chuckhole in the Soledad," the doctor said dryly. "I wear out a buckboard a year, Kirk." He chuckled. "Chris Joner would likely sell a lot more coffins if I let chuckholes slow me down."

Kirk grinned. "I reckon that's right, Doc." His face sobered. "How did you make out?"

Doctor Williams shook his head. "Wasn't easy, Kirk, what with that trail washed out and the moon lost behind clouds. Must have been a rip-snorter of a cloudburst up in Burro Canyon. The trail is choked with boulders as big as a house."

"I didn't know—" Kirk gave him a concerned look.

Doctor Williams gestured reassuringly. "We made it, boy. Took a long time, that's why I'm so late getting back to town."

"How's Chase?"

"Stood the trip fine," declared the doctor. "Good stuff in that young man. Never let out a whimper . . . must have been hell for him—not that Atilano and Justo didn't do their best to make it easy as possible for him." The doctor's eyes twinkled. " 'Two lovely berries moulded on one stem,' " he quoted. "An interesting pair, those Yaqui twins."

Kirk grinned. "I doubt that Shakespeare had anyone like Justo and Atilano in mind when he got off that line, Doc," he argued. "They're peas in a pod, but those faces they wear can't be called lovely in any language."

The doctor chuckled, then abruptly, "You didn't tell me about Mrs. Chase, Kirk. An unusually attractive young woman." His bushy brows arched questioningly.

"What do you mean, I didn't tell you about her?" Kirk's tone was studiedly casual.

"You know," grumbled the doctor. "That Chase woman is the double for Hilda Taylor. An amazing resemblance." He looked at Kirk searchingly. "You must have noticed it, young man. I know how you feel toward Hilda."

Kirk reddened under his tan. "Well—yes," he admitted. "There is a resemblance. Mrs. Chase is older, though, and—well, there's quite a difference when you talk to her."

"An amazing resemblance," repeated Doctor Williams. "It's very disturbing, Kirk. Can't get her out of my mind. A plucky young woman, cool as ice, coming down that confounded Burro Canyon trail."

Kirk was hardly aware of his words. He was

staring intently up the slope. Something had moved up there. Or was it his imagination? Doctor Williams went on talking. The wounded man's condition was not serious. The broken leg would keep him in bed for several weeks, but the shoulder wound was nothing to worry about.

"He didn't like the idea of leaving the cabin," the doctor said. "Seemed to think it was a dodge to run him out. Mrs. Chase had to talk like a Dutch uncle to him." Doctor Williams paused, gave the K7 man an enigmatical smile. "You certainly managed to win that young woman's confidence, Kirk." He chuckled, continued before Kirk could speak, "Chase was delirious, of course, or he wouldn't have objected."

Kirk nodded. "All right, Doc," he said. "You're a good scout." He paused, added a bit grimly, "It's a secret, Doc. Nobody is to know about them."

"Naturally!" retorted Doctor Williams, acidly. "I'm not a fool, young man."

Kirk was watching up the slope again. "There's a chance you may run into somebody on the ridge," he went on. "Don't answer questions, Doc."

Doctor Williams looked at him sharply. "You are being trailed? Is that what you mean, Kirk?"

Kirk's brief nod answered him.

"He'll get nothing out of me," promised the doctor. His hand tightened on the reins. "I'll have to be moving—"

"*Adiós*, Doc, and a lot of thanks—"

"Forget it," snorted the doctor. "It's what I'm here for, son. My own fault for being a country medico." His eyes twinkled. "You haven't seen the bill—yet."

Kirk's gaze followed him affectionately until the buckboard rattled over the summit in a haze of dust. His expression hardening, he put his impatient horse into motion.

The road made a sharp turn between beetling crags. Kirk risked a backward glance. No sign of the mysterious lone rider. Whoever he was, he was too smart to show himself on the straightaway.

Kirk pushed on between the towering crags, put the horse to a burst of speed, and rounded another sharp turn where the road cut through a dense growth of piñons. He found the place he was looking for and swung behind a cluster of trees.

Approaching hoofbeats touched his ears faintly, the rattle of stones under shod hoofs. The sounds hushed. Grim amusement crinkled Kirk's eyes. His trailer was wary, taking no chances. He kept his gaze hard on the turn where the road broke into the piñons, caught a glimpse of the man, a vague shape behind the screening branches. There was a familiar look about him that brought a frown to Kirk's brow. The shadows there were deep. He could not be sure.

The next moment verified his suspicion. The

man straightened up to his full height, revealed the face of Dunn Harden. The Bar T cowboy stood for a moment, gaze raking the length of the shadowed road. Apparently satisfied, he swung on his heel and vanished around the bend.

Kirk waited, his expression thoughtful. He was finding it difficult to believe the evidence of his own eyes. He had a liking for Dunn Harden. The black-haired young cowboy's one fault was his curious friendship with Clint Sleed. There was good metal under the reckless, devil-may-care exterior. His willingness to take orders from a man like Sleed was the only thing Kirk held against him. Of course, there was Hilda Taylor. It seemed the only answer that explained Dunn Harden. It was an answer that always ruffled Kirk, sent a hot flare of jealousy through him.

His hand tightened hard on gun-butt as he thought it out. There were two reasons that would explain why Dunn Harden was trailing him. Dunn wanted to eliminate him as a rival for the affections of Hilda Taylor, planned to kill him. He feared to have it out, face to face, and was making an opportunity to shoot Kirk in the back. A calculated, cold-blooded murder that would leave him unsuspected. It was an explanation that Kirk found too repugnant to consider more than briefly. Dunn Harden was not of that lowdown killer breed. The alternative explanation seemed more likely. Sleed was worried about the non-return of Pedro Negro and had sent Dunn to trail the man who knew the answer. Not a job that Dunn would relish, but his wish to have a front seat with Hilda Taylor made it difficult to refuse the Bar T foreman's orders. Sleed could fire him from the Bar T payroll, a certainty that Dunn could not endure, especially now that Hilda was home from school again.

The telltale thud of shod hoofs broke the stillness. Kirk tensed in his saddle, alert eyes on the subject of his speculations. The unsuspecting cowboy was gazing watchfully ahead, his horse shuffling along at a fast walk.

Kirk grinned mirthlessly, waited until he had passed, then swung his own horse back to the road. He called softly. "Hello, feller!"

The man in front of him jerked his head around in a shocked look, hand flattening down over the butt of his holstered gun.

Kirk said, in the same soft drawl, "Don't try it, Dunn." His own gun was out, lifted menacingly. He added, with a hint of steel in his voice, "You won't have a chance—"

Dunn Harden hesitated, his eyes stormy. Perhaps what he read in Kirk's implacable face was a warning too grim to ignore. He was fast and deadly with a gun, but if there was one man in the Soledad faster and more deadly, it was Kirk Severn, and Kirk already had the advantage.

Slowly, with obvious reluctance, the Bar T

man's hand fell slack to his side. He gave Kirk a sickly grin, said in an aggrieved voice, "You scared the daylights out of me." He swung his horse to face the other man. "Where in hell did you spring from?"

He saw by Kirk's expression that his attempt at injured innocence was not going well. He spoke again, sullenly, "What about it?"

"That's for you to tell me," Kirk said, harshly.

"This road's free," parried the cowboy. "I can ride this way if I want to—"

Kirk interrupted him. "Don't waste my time. I want to know why you've been trailing me."

Dunn flinched visibly under the other man's eyes. He was trapped, and he knew it. He said haltingly, "Well—it's like this, Kirk—I—Oh, hell, I told Sleed I wasn't caring none for this damn job."

"So Sleed sent you?"

Dunn nodded morosely, fingered in his shirt pocket for tobacco sack.

Kirk studied him curiously. He said with cold finality, "You've got to talk, Dunn. I want the truth from you. Why is Sleed having me watched?"

The cowboy's eyes lifted in a brief look, returned to the cigarette his fingers were swiftly shaping. "Ain't hard for you to savvy that one, Kirk." He lit the cigarette, gave Kirk a satirical smile.

Kirk knew that he was referring to Pedro Negro,

but refused to be drawn. He was not going to admit that he knew anything about Clint Sleed's hired killer. He pondered a moment, frowning gaze on the Bar T man. "Is that all you've got to say?" he asked, finally.

"I reckon," Dunn said. He shrugged a dusty shoulder, flicked his restless smile at his questioner.

Kirk's mind was made up. He said brusquely, "Lift your hands high, Dunn—"

"What the hell—" Dunn broke off, put up his hands, daunted by the other man's hard look, the menacing gun.

Kirk got down from his horse, and careful to keep Dunn covered, moved leisurely to his side and took the gun from his holster.

The cowboy gave him a tight-lipped smile. "You've got a nerve," he said, huskily. "I'll get even with you, Kirk."

"I'm taking you to the ranch," Kirk said. "Your own fault, Dunn, for playing the cards Clint Sleed dealt you."

"It ain't legal," muttered the cowboy. "You ain't no god-a'mighty sheriff. You cain't do this to me, Kirk."

"I'm doing it," retorted Kirk. "Must I rope you to the saddle, or will you ride along—and no tricks?"

Dunn Harden said sullenly, "You ain't puttin' no rope on me. I'll ride along if you're so damn set on it."

Kirk backed away to his horse, stepped quickly into the saddle. "All right, Dunn," he said. "I'll trail you."

Dunn swung his horse and started along the road toward the ranch. Kirk followed, keeping a scant three yards between them. The horses moved along at a fast shuffling walk. No words passed from either of the men. Once Dunn turned his head in a brief backward look that encompassed the gun ready in Kirk's hand. It was a warning that twisted his lips in a sardonic grin.

Chuck Rigg saw them from the doorway of the saddle-room where he was watching an elderly man repair a broken latigo. His sandy brows arched in a surprised look and, with a muttered word to the man, he hurried across the corral.

Kirk threw him a nod, slid from his saddle. "Hello, Chuck." He slipped the bridle from the red bay's head, and, blowing nostrils gustily, the horse moved eagerly to the long watering-trough shaded by a semicircle of aged cottonwood trees.

No response came from the K7 foreman. His frowning gaze was on Kirk's companion. Dunn Harden gave him a grin. "Howdy, Chuck," he drawled. "How's things with you, you ol' buzzard?"

Chuck's look went questioningly to Kirk. "How come?" His tone was puzzled, tinged with dissatisfaction. "Have you hired him away from Bar T?"

Kirk shook his head, stood on wide-apart legs, fingers fumbling in his shirt pocket for tobacco sack. "Dunn's just making us a visit," he said.

Dunn climbed from his saddle and the foreman's sharp eyes now saw the empty gunbelt. Understanding filled his eyes. His face darkened. He said harshly, "What's the trouble, Kirk?"

Kirk put a match to the cigarette. The flame drew hard glints from his eyes. "I've brought Dunn along with me to answer that question," he said. His look went to the Bar T cowboy. "How about it, Dunn? Ready to talk?"

"You go to hell," Dunn said, tersely. He fished tobacco sack from his pocket, gave the two men his reckless smile.

"Tie up that lip, feller!" Chuck Rigg's face reddened.

"I say what I want to say, any time, any place." Dunn Harden spoke coolly. "You don't scare me none, ol'-timer."

"You doggone maverick!" fumed the foreman. Kirk's gesture silenced him.

"Let me handle him, Chuck—" Kirk paused, added thoughtfully, "I'm sorry, Dunn. No hard feelings on my part. I've got to know why Clint Sleed sent you trailing me, and until I find out I'm keeping you here. Savvy?"

"Sure," laconically answered the cowboy. "I savvy." Yellow tobacco flakes spilling from

108

the paper he was twisting betrayed a growing uneasiness.

Kirk was impatient to see Esther Chase. He said curtly, "Keep him safe some place, Chuck." He swung on his heel, halted and looked back. "Take him to your house," he added. "We'll give him all the comforts of home."

Chuck Rigg gave his prisoner a thin smile. "You heard the boss, young feller. You come along with me."

"Takes more'n an ol' mossyhorn like you to hold me," jeered the Bar T man.

"My horns is still plenty sharp," smiled the foreman. His hand was on gun-butt, his eyes watchful, and obeying his gesture, Dunn reluctantly accompanied him across the corral and through a gate into a small yard in which stood a log-walled cabin shaded by two giant cotton-wood trees. Gay flowers bordered the stone-flagged path that led to the door in which suddenly appeared a middle-aged woman. Her pleasant face took on a surprised look as she saw Chuck's companion.

"For heaven's sake!" she exclaimed. "Look what you've brought home!" She added severely, "What brings Dunn Harden to K7?"

Dunn grinned at her. "Howdy, Mrs. Rigg. Don't blame me."

"Dunn figgers to stay with us for a spell," gruffly announced Chuck. Something in his voice apparently warned his wife. She nodded in a matter-of-fact way as if it were a common occurrence to have Bar T riders in the role of guests. "Dinner's most ready," she said.

"That's fine, Martha." Chuck was looking back at the yard gate. Justo suddenly appeared. He halted at the gate, caught Chuck's beckoning look and came clattering up the walk.

"Boss say you want me," he said to the foreman.

"Yeah—that's right." Chuck's tone was grim.

The three men followed Mrs. Rigg inside. Dunn Harden sniffed appreciatively, "Smells like apple pie." His brown face lighted. "Ain't sure but what I'm glad to be here."

Mrs. Rigg beamed at him. "Now I call that real nice of you." She went briskly into the kitchen.

There was an awkward silence, Chuck obviously making his plans, Dunn Harden as obviously uneasy under the foreman's scrutiny, Justo politely attentive but frankly hostile.

Chuck broke the silence. "Keep your gun on him, Justo," he said.

"*Sí*." The Mexican's big Colt leaped from holster. Chuck motioned his prisoner to follow him down a narrow hall. Dunn obeyed without protest, Justo, close at his heels, gun in lifted hand.

The foreman opened a door and the three men trooped into a small bedroom lighted by a window overlooking a vista of grassy woodland that reached away to the main ranch-house.

"I'm keepin' you here," Chuck said to Dunn. "Won't be no trouble if you make none, young feller."

"Suits me," Dunn said, with a careless grin. He moved to the small wooden bed and sat down. "What if I bust out through the window? This ain't no kind of jail for *me*, Chuck."

"Don't try it," Chuck warned. "I'm plantin' Justo outside that window." He threw the Mexican a nod. Justo opened the window and went out with the agility of a great cat.

"Watch him close, Justo," the foreman instructed. "Empty your gun into him if he makes a move to climb out."

"*Si!*" Justo grinned, waggled his Colt. "Thees hombre die queek eef he make try."

Chuck nodded, looked at his prisoner. "You heard him, mister. Justo will sure kill you if you get wrong notions." He backed into the hall. "I'm keepin' this door locked. No chance for you to break out this way—not without plenty noise."

Dunn smiled insolently from the bed. "Don't forget that apple pie," he said.

The door closed with a bang. The key grated in the lock. The Bar T man continued to sit on the edge of the bed, gazing idly around the room. A washstand stood in one corner. There was a lone, homemade chair, and a looking glass on the wall, above a homemade table. A bare little room, evidently seldom used.

Dunn Harden yawned, felt in his pocket for tobacco sack. His look went to the open window, met Justo's watchful eyes. He gave the Yaqui a lazy smile.

"Which one of the Nuecos are you?" he asked. "Never could tell you hombres apart."

"Me Justo," replied the Yaqui. His tone was reproving. "You no hear boss say me Justo?"

"Sure, sure—that's right. Chuck *did* call you Justo awhile back." Dunn watched him from narrowed eyes, hand busy with tobacco sack. It gently collapsed, dribbling grains of fine yellow tobacco into the palm of his other hand. His voice droned on, low, amiable. "Was hearin' some talk you're a friend of Pedro Negro. Haven't seen Pedro for a long time. You see him around, Justo?"

The Yaqui shook his head, his face expressionless. "No see thees Pedro Negro hombre," he replied, blandly.

"My mistake," Dunn Harden said, with a careless gesture of the hand that had palmed the tobacco. With the fingers of his other hand he was leisurely shaping a cigarette. He put it between his lips, fumbled in his pockets, gave the Yaqui a dismayed look. "Got a match on you, Justo?" He spoke casually. "Seems like I ain't got a match left."

"*Si.*" Justo felt in a pocket, fished out a block of sulphur matches.

"*Gracias.*" Dunn got up from the sagging bed

112

and moving to the open window, reached out a hand. He muttered a startled exclamation. "Look out, feller—that snake—" As the Yaqui involuntarily turned his head, the Bar T man flung the palmed tobacco dust into his eyes. Justo uttered a stifled groan of pain. The gun slipped from his grasp as he clapped both hands to his tortured eyes.

It was the brief moment Dunn had gambled on. He drove through the window with the impact of a battering ram. One hand caught Justo a dazing blow that left him groggy, his other hand snatched up the fallen gun. An infuriated gurgle came from the Yaqui's throat. He lunged forward, went down with a groan as the gun crashed hard on his skull.

Chapter X
"POR ESTA CRUZ . . ."

Dunn Harden stood rigid for a moment, his breath coming in gulps, gun clutched in hand. His quick look reassured him. There still was life in the sprawled body. The Yaqui's heavy sombrero had saved him a fatally broken skull.

Voices came from the kitchen, the slam of the oven door. Dunn wasted no more time. So far the element of surprise had been in his favor. He had seen and grasped the one chance, caught Chuck Rigg and the Yaqui off guard.

It had not entered the K7 foreman's head that his prisoner would so swiftly attempt an escape. But the moments were perilously few. Dunn had good reason to suspect that he would all too soon be missed. The telltale slam of the oven door meant that the apple pie was ready for the table, and Mrs. Rigg would be remembering him. She would want to serve it warm and juicy and fragrant. The thought made his mouth water, also sent him on swift, soundless feet into the cover of the trees.

Midway between the foreman's cottage and the big ranch-house he halted to take stock of his bearings. Much as he yearned for his horse, he knew it was impossible to get to the barn unseen. He was in for a long walk. The thought made him wince. Walking was meant for sheepherders, not for cowboys.

Crouched low behind a bush, he studied his surroundings and mulled over Chuck Rigg's likely reactions when he discovered his prisoner's escape. The foreman's first thought would be the horses. He would head for the barn to make sure the fugitive had not managed to get a horse, perhaps waste time in searching the arroyo beyond the corrals.

Dunn came to a swift decision. His best chance was to keep as close to the house as possible, work his way through the tangle of brush and trees that reached down to the road less than half a mile distant. Once in the open country he could elude pursuit by taking cover in the numerous arroyos, lie low until it was dark.

Reassured by the continued silence, he crawled stealthily through the undergrowth and reached an adobe wall at the back of the rambling old house.

Dunn halted again, screened by the bushes at his back, and hidden from the house by the patio wall, which was higher than a tall man. He listened intently. Still no sound of alarm. Only the muted splash of a fountain somewhere in the patio, and then the light slam of a door, the tread of feet in the *galeria*. The cowboy held his breath. Kirk Severn's voice, and the softer, hardly audible tones of a woman.

A puzzled frown furrowed the Bar T man's brow. He had always understood that the K7 ranch-house was womanless. Kirk's domestic needs were taken care of by an ancient Chinese who had been there for years. The soft-voiced speaker certainly was not Mrs. Rigg. She was back in the Rigg cottage, putting a hot apple pie on the table for her husband's dinner.

The thought spurred Dunn. He could not hope for many more minutes before his escape was discovered. He moved on cautiously and suddenly came to a gate of Spanish iron grill.

He halted, dismayed, for the first time aware of a feeling of panic. He could not retrace his steps. Time was too short, and he dared not risk passing the gate with Kirk Severn so close on the other side of the wall.

Hand gripped hard over the butt of Justo's Colt, now in his holster, Dunn's lips hardened in a bleak smile. He could get the drop on Kirk, kill him, but killing him would not help his own escape. A half score K7 men would have a rope on his neck before he could reach the road.

He ventured a cautious peep through the grill-work of the gate, drew his head back with a jerk, an incredulous, startled look in his eyes. The blood drained from his face, left the mask of a man in a killing rage. The knuckles of the hand that gripped gun-butt stood out starkly.

He let out a long breath that was near to a groan, forced himself to look again. His eyes had not fooled him. The girl standing so close to Kirk Severn was Hilda Taylor. She was not in the dress she had been wearing a few hours earlier in town, a somewhat puzzling circumstance, if his distraught mind had given the matter a thought. He saw only Hilda, the filtered sunlight striking tawny glints from her chestnut hair as she stood there, face lifted to the tall man in front of her.

A loud shout from somewhere back in the corral brought Dunn to his senses, cleared the rage from his eyes. He flattened close to the wall, saw Kirk Severn spin on his heel and start running toward the gate that led to the ranch yard. More shouts continued to come from the corral, a chorus of excited voices. Booted feet slammed out of the bunkhouse, went racing toward the barn.

The girl stood there, watching Kirk until he vanished through the gate. She seemed momentarily paralyzed, as if held in the thrall of a great fear. Suddenly she was running, feet beating like castanets on the stone floor of the long *galeria.* Before Dunn Harden's hand could find the gate-catch she had disappeared inside the house.

Dunn abandoned the impulse to follow her. Also the gate was locked. It was a high gate, surmounted with wicked iron spears. With danger reaching for his heels, he was again cool, resourceful. He slid past the gate and hurried along the wall. In another moment he was in the cover of the close-growing trees. He pushed on toward the road, careful of twigs and branches that would crackle underfoot. The uproar had hushed, but he knew the chase was on in earnest. He was a range man himself and knew the ways of range men. They would hunt in silence, stalk their victim with the stealth of an Apache.

He came to the narrow, dusty road, took a cautious look up and down, then crossed over, carefully finding stones on which to step. His pursuers would not pick up his tracks in the dust of the road.

In a few moments more he was working his way along the tortuous twistings of a dry wash. Sweat streamed down his face. He felt heartsick, was still inclined to doubt his senses. How was it possible for Hilda Taylor to be at Kirk Severn's ranch? Dunn could find only one explanation. Hilda had given her father the slip in town and made her way to the ranch alone. Which meant that the meeting had been prearranged. Kirk was the girl's lover. The thing must have been going on for a long time, while he, Dunn Harden, humiliated himself for her sake, taking orders from Clint Sleed, doing his dirty work and asking no questions.

Swearing bitterly, the disillusioned cowboy

dropped on a hillock of sand under the covering branches of a mesquite. One thing became fixed in his mind. He would not return to Bar T, not unless it was to kill Clint Sleed. He began to regret his break from Chuck Rigg's cottage, the blow that had struck down the unsuspecting Justo Nueco. Chuck Rigg was a squareshooter, and so was Kirk Severn. Both were men to tie to, to ride the river with; and then, there was Hilda. . . . His love for her was a sacred thing, a young, clean love that asked for nothing, that wanted only to serve. To be near her, serve her, seemed the biggest thing in life to young Dunn Harden.

He sat there, despondent, despairing, his good-looking young face set in hard lines of grief, his eyes perplexed, troubled. Shadows crept unnoticed down the wash. A coyote drifted in close to the mesquite, sensed the cowboy's presence and went like a gray streak up the bank. Something else stirred on the opposite bank where the sunlight still lay. A shadow that moved imperceptibly closer to the mesquite. A voice spoke quietly, warningly.

"Come out of there, Dunn, and keep your hands up."

Dunn's head lifted. He said wearily, "Sure, Kirk—" He got to his feet, pushed his way through the branches, saw Kirk Severn in the fading light, his face set in hard lines, a gun in lifted hand. The cowboy gave him a bleak smile. "You

119

don't need to hold that gun on me, Kirk. I've been doin' some thinkin'. The way it works out in my mind I've been a damn fool."

"Did you have to nearly kill Justo Nueco to find that out?" Kirk flung the question harshly.

"That was Chuck Rigg's fault," Dunn said. "Chuck didn't use good savvy, shovin' me into that room. You'd have busted out yourself if you'd been me—and God help the feller that stood in your way."

Kirk was silent. He knew that Dunn spoke the truth. In the same position he would have used any means possible to contrive an escape. Chuck Rigg had woefully underestimated Dunn's nerve—his resourcefulness.

The young cowboy spoke again, his tone bitter. "I've finished with Bar T, Kirk. I'm done with doin' dirty work for Clint Sleed."

Quick interest flared in Kirk's eyes. He said quietly, "You've been thinking to some purpose, Dunn." He frowned, pushed the gun into its holster. "What puzzles me is the why of it."

Dunn stood there, staring at him, lips set in a tight line, his eyes hot with the jealousy that suddenly waved over him.

"You ain't needin' to ask me that," he answered in a stifled voice. "You know what's bitin' me, Kirk Severn." He gulped. "I could have killed you—back there at the patio gate."

A hint of the truth came to Kirk. He said in

a low, incredulous voice, "So that's the reason!"

"It's plenty reason," muttered Dunn. "I saw her there, talkin' to you. Knocked me silly." He gulped again. "I could have killed you."

Kirk shook his head. "You're all wrong about what you saw, Dunn. You thought the girl was Hilda Taylor. Is that right?"

Dunn began to shake. He clenched his fists. "Don't try to pull that stuff on me. I won't stand for your lyin' to me."

"It wasn't Hilda you saw," Kirk said, curtly.

"I won't stand for your lyin' to me," repeated Dunn in a thick voice. "I saw her with my own eyes. She sneaked away from her dad in town—come out to be alone with you at the ranch. If anybody had told me that, I'd have killed him, but I saw her, and I ain't takin' your lies about it."

"You're wrong, Dunn. Hilda didn't come to the ranch." Kirk's tone was impatient, touched with amusement. "I don't blame you for being fooled."

"I warned you!" shouted the infuriated cowboy. "I won't stand for your lies." He lunged forward, fists swinging.

Kirk sidestepped the blow, and a shape moved suddenly from the brush-covered slope, slid between the two men. A voice said sharply, "*Basta!*"

The harsh, swarthy face of the speaker, the

121

leveled gun, was like a bucket of cold water in Dunn's face. He froze to immobility and a slow grin relaxed his tight-set lips.

"I reckon you're the other Nueco," he said. "Atilano, huh?"

"*Sí*." Atilano's tone, his look was fierce. "*Por Dios*—I like cut your t'roat."

Kirk shook his head. "Keep out of this, Atilano. Get back to the horses." A smile touched his lips. "Dunn Harden is my good friend. Keep that fact in your head."

"*Sí*." Atilano looked dubious. "This man was rough with Justo," he said in Spanish. "He threw tobacco in Justo's eyes—knocked him sense-less with Justo's own gun." His glittering look fastened on the Colt in Dunn's holster. He snatched it. "*Por Dios!*" His fierce expression relaxed. "Justo mooch like thees gun back."

Dunn grinned, offered his hand. "I'm sure sorry I treated Justo rough," he told the Yaqui. "You tell him for me, Atilano."

"*Sí*." Atilano was frankly puzzled. He looked questioningly at Kirk. "You say he good friend, no?"

"Good friend," confirmed Kirk. He added sternly, "Don't forget, Atilano. My friends are your friends, and Justo's friends. It was all a mistake."

Atilano nodded, soberly. "*Sí*," he said, "I no forget." He held up both hands, with thumb crossed over forefinger.

122

"*Por esta cruz*, I no forget!" He kissed the improvised cross.

They watched him face back into the brush. Dunn said admiringly, "Them Mexican Yaquis are sure fightin' wildcats."

"They'll die for a friend," Kirk said simply.

The tension between them had relaxed. They stood for a brief space, fingers busy with cigarette papers and tobacco.

Dunn put a match to his cigarette, broke the silence. "Thought I'd covered my tracks plenty good," he said. "How come you hit my trail so quick?"

"Atilano can follow a wood tick in the dark of the moon," drawled Kirk.

"I reckon." Dunn grinned. "At that, I'd have made a clean getaway if I hadn't got all hobbled thinkin' about what I saw back at the patio gate."

"What you *thought* you saw," mildly corrected Kirk.

"I'm takin' your word for it," Dunn said. He scowled. "I'm all haywire about it. Cain't do no more thinkin'." He smiled, unhappily. "Where do we go from here?"

"Back to the ranch," Kirk told him. "I want to prove how wrong you were."

Dunn followed him up the bank of the dry wash. Atilano was waiting with the horses. The twilight was fading fast and a new moon made a faint silver scimitar above the black mass of the western hills.

Kirk swung into his saddle. "Climb up behind me, Dunn," he invited. "It's ride double—or foot it."

"Never did fancy usin' my feet like a sheep-herder," grinned the cowboy. He made a spring that placed him behind Kirk and in a moment they were moving through the gathering darkness.

Kirk's voice sounded above the crunch of hoofs. "Mighty glad it turned out this way, Dunn."

"I reckon," Dunn said, laconically.

"Never could see you with that Bar T outfit—not under Clint Sleed," Kirk went on. "I think I understand, Dunn." He hesitated, "I—I don't blame you."

"I've been loco," Dunn said bitterly. He thought a moment. "I mean I was loco—the way I went about it . . . thinkin' it would do any good stickin' to the Bar T payroll the way I done."

"What do you figure to do—that is when you've answered some questions I've got for you?"

"What's it to you what I do?" Dunn's tone was sulky, resentful.

"I've an idea we can get together," Kirk said in a quietly confident voice. "You're just the man I want siding me, Dunn. You know things about Clint Sleed."

Dunn thought it over at some length before

he replied. "You're maybe right at that, Kirk. I dunno, though—" He paused. "Clint Sleed will be gunnin' for me when he knows I've quit him."

"He's gunning for me already," Kirk said, mildly.

"That's right." Dunn hesitated, added in a hard voice, "There's more'n him behind what's goin' on in the Soledad."

"You're getting close to *El Topo*," commented Kirk.

"I ain't sayin'," Dunn's tone was cautious.

The silvered scimitar moon dropped behind the mountains, stars made bright splinters in the night sky. Dunn spoke again, his voice resolute, touched with a hint of shyness.

"You said back there to Atilano that I was your good friend. I kinder liked it. I'm awful short on friends. They don't run that way over at Bar T. A no-'count outfit, that bunch, even if Hilda's dad *is* the boss."

Kirk turned his head in a brief look at him. "You can count on me, Dunn," he said simply.

"I'd like it first-rate to side you," Dunn continued. "Any old way you want, on the payroll or off. I'm all set to nail some hides to the barn door."

Kirk chuckled. "You're hired, Dunn. You can have anything K7's got for the job."

"I'd as lief Sleed don't hear of it for a while,"

Dunn said. "Seems like I could do more, kinder workin' under cover."

"We'll keep it quiet you're with K7," Kirk promised. "You have a head on you, feller."

"*Gracias.*" Dunn gave the straight back in front of him a mirthless smile.

The ranch lights glimmered through the darkness, made twinkling yellow stars through the trees. Dunn broke the silence.

"Hope Ma Rigg has some of that apple pie left," he said wistfully. His tough young body shook with sudden inward merriment. "I'll sure make away with a man-size hunk—if Chuck Rigg don't kill me first."

"He won't," Kirk said.

"I reckon," agreed Dunn. He was silent for a brief space, then soberly, "I won't forget this, Kirk. *Por esta cruz, no!*"

Chapter XI

HILDA

Warde Taylor looked at his daughter with disapproving eyes. "I don't know that I like it," he said. "Nice girls don't go 'round in men's pants. You aren't a kid any more, Hilda. It was all right when you were in pigtails, but you're a grown woman now." His voice took on an aggrieved note. "Where's that riding habit we sent all the way to New York for?"

The girl looked down at the overalls that incased her legs. "Skirts are too tiresome for riding," she argued. "Don't be silly, Dad. You'll see the day when it will be the smart thing for women to ride astride."

"I don't like it," repeated the big cattleman. "It isn't decent. You're no Cactus Kate living 'round with an outlaw gang."

She made a face at him. Slim fingers toyed with the silver-plated butt of the thirty-two Colt holstered in her Mexican leather belt. "You'll have to get used to it, Dad. It was sweet of you to give me the riding habit, but I much prefer my Levi Straus overalls, copper rivets and all."

Warde Taylor chuckled. "You're as stubborn as a mule," he told her indulgently. "Have it

127

your own way, girl. Wear pants, if that's how you feel."

"If I'm stubborn, it's because I'm your daughter," laughed Hilda.

"Yeah—I reckon that's it." Taylor looked at her, unsmilingly. "Comes natural for you to be stubborn." He moved on past her, a hint of a frown in the arrogant eyes shadowed by the huge white hat.

Hilda stood watching him from the back veranda steps, disturbingly aware of a vague uneasiness. She shook off the feeling, thinking herself too prone to silly imaginings. It was not difficult to guess the cause of her father's attitude. He did not approve of her continued friendship with Kirk Severn, perhaps suspected that her feeling for Kirk was something more serious. He was not wrong there. She loved Kirk, and Kirk loved her. It had always been that way with them—always would be, and not even her father's disapproval could change it.

Her eyes clouded as she thought of Kirk, her father's dislike of him. For that matter, Kirk disliked her father. The enmity between them was inexplicable, had its roots in ground unknown to her. Curiously enough, her father had wanted Kirk to succeed the late Jim Shane as the sheriff of Soledad, and, even more strange, Kirk had refused. She recalled his words, the last time she had seen him, in front of the Emporium. *I have*

128

my reason for saying no. It's a very good reason, Hilda.

She became aware of voices in the kitchen at the far end of the long veranda, the shrill tones of the cook in loud denunciations. Something had upset Mercedes, and when she was angry, Mercedes had a way of speaking her mind.

"*Qué animal*! Peeg! *Quita*! You go from here queek, you beeg no-good hombre!"

"Quit your yellin'." Clint Sleed's rasping voice. "What's got into you, Mercedes, layin' your ears back at me like a damn outlaw bronco?"

"You play beeg fool weeth me!" scolded the cook. "You go town and make loave weeth *cantina* girls, then try for come kees me so smar-rt, you no good *ladron*. You go from here queek before I keel you weeth meat knife."

There was an amused laugh from the foreman, the sound of a brief struggle, the hard slap of the cook's hand—a prolonged stillness, broken by a giggle from Mercedes.

"*Basta*! Enough, greedy peeg. You get out. I 'ave mooch wor-rk."

The kitchen door slammed, the clatter of bootheels, the jingle of spurs, told Hilda that Sleed was coming around the side of the house. He stopped short at the sight of her on the veranda steps, grinned uncertainly, obviously wondering how much the girl had overheard.

Hilda returned his look unsmilingly. She was

129

not going to oblige his curiosity. Apparently reassured, Sleed approached her, his protruding blue eyes ogling her insolently. He halted, stood staring at her, thumbs hooked over gunbelt.

"You sure look purty in them pants," he said. "You could pass for a boy, settin' a saddle in that rig."

Hilda ignored the remark. "I think dad is looking for you," she said. She looked at him intently. "How did you get that scratch on your face, Clint?"

His grin widened. "Wildcat clawed me." He rocked on his heels, greedy eyes frankly feasting on the girl. She was wearing a white Stetson, an apricot-colored silk blouse tucked inside the hand-carved Mexican leather belt, and the snug-fitting blue overalls over high-heeled boots on which shone small-roweled silver-mounted spurs.

Hilda stirred resentfully under his devouring scrutiny. She disliked the carroty-haired fore-man, his saturnine face, his evil eyes. Instinct warned her against the man. He had no respect for women, and she had a shrewd suspicion that Mercedes was only one more unfortunate victim.

The disdain in her eyes, her mounting annoyance, seemed to amuse the foreman. He laughed softly. "Wildcats is my meat," he said. "I tame 'em awful fast."

"You leave Mercedes alone," she said fiercely. "I'll tell Dad!"

His eyes went the color of pale blue marbles, and as hard. "Go ahaid," he answered indifferently. "Tell him. I ain't carin' a damn." He went on down the garden walk toward the yard gate, spurs rasping at boot-heels.

Hilda watched him, her lips compressed in a tight, angry line, and thought helplessly that Sleed was speaking the truth. He would not in the least mind any accusations she brought against him. He was too secure in her father's confidence— a fact that more and more was the cause of a growing perturbation within her. She could not understand what her father saw in Clint Sleed, or why such a man should be Bar T's foreman. Now that she had returned from school, she realized, she disliked and distrusted all the men on the Bar T payroll. With one exception—Dunn Harden.

A faint color touched her cheeks as she considered Dunn Harden. She was not blind to the reason that kept him at Bar T. It was a reason that worried her. She had a fondness for him, sensing the good metal under his reckless, hard exterior. Dunn was different. Clint Sleed and the others were really all of them hard men, a ruthless and tough outfit. She was mystified at her father's blindness to the character of his men. Only last night, when she had hesitatingly brought up the subject, Warde Taylor had merely looked away from her and said, "Running a cattle ranch isn't a parlor game, child. A cow outfit is none the worse for being hardy." His explanation had left her vaguely dissatisfied. *Hardy* did not describe the Bar T outfit.

Troubled by the brief encounter with the foreman, Hilda went into the house and made her way to the kitchen. Mercedes gave her a sidewise look from the big brick range where she was emptying a bowl of cut vegetables into an iron kettle. Her smooth brown cheeks were flushed, her eyes excited.

Hilda addressed her in Spanish. She had grown up with Mexican servants and spoke the language fluently. "I want a sandwich," she said.

"You go for a ride?" Mercedes placed the bowl on the table. "There is the cold chicken," she suggested.

"I'll fix them myself," Hilda said. She went out to the back porch, to the cooler. The cook had a loaf of bread on the board when she returned with the chicken. Hilda fished out a knife from a drawer and began slicing the chicken. Mercedes watched her for a moment, a curiously knowing smile on her full lips. She was a large, buxom woman in her late twenties, with liquid brown, cowlike eyes and a sulky mouth. Her broad, rather flat face betrayed a touch of Indian blood.

"You are cutting enough chicken for two people," she commented. Her smile was faintly malicious. "One of them a man."

Hilda said nothing, but her heightened

132

color betrayed annoyance. Mercedes laughed unpleasantly, looked appraisingly at the plate of chicken and expertly cut six slices from the big homemade loaf. "I know who the extra sandwiches are for," she said. "I know where you are going—but I won't tell the señor. Oh, no, not me!"

"Don't be impudent." Hilda gave the cook an unsmiling look. "You seem very curious about what I do, and where I go."

The Mexican woman's brown eyes went glassy, her lower lip sagged sullenly. "I am not a fool," she said. "I have eyes and ears. I see and hear a lot of things." Her voice lowered to a whisper. "Listen, señorita, the old señor is smart. He is not fooled. He is watching you, always. It is not safe for you to have these secret meetings with Señor Severn. There will be trouble."

"I'd rather you didn't interfere in my affairs," Hilda rebuked. She studied the buxom cook thoughtfully. "Do you get all this nonsense from Clint Sleed?"

"I will talk no more," grumbled Mercedes. Her eyes lowered before the girl's probing gaze. "I was only being a friend and you start asking questions about Señor Sleed. He is a good man, a smart man. I trust him."

"I suppose that is why you scratched his face just before I came in," Hilda said, too sweetly.

Mercedes stared at her, mouth open, her face flaming. Mumbling under her breath, she flounced out to the back porch. Hilda, her face pale, finished making the sandwiches, wrapped them in paper, and hurriedly returned to the garden, more disturbed than she cared to admit. She did not like Mercedes. The woman was too sure of herself, too openly interested in Hilda's affairs. She was not to be trusted. Her pretence of warning Hilda against her father was for the purpose of gaining her confidence. She was Clint Sleed's woman—his spy, and Clint Sleed was Kirk Severn's enemy.

Hilda halted midway down the path. She must do nothing that would bring added danger to Kirk. It was quite possible that Sleed would have her followed, hoping the trail would lead to Kirk. The thought sent a cold wave over her. Actually her plans were somewhat vague, for she was not sure that Kirk would be waiting for her at the mouth of Cañon Los Diablos. He had not promised, but she had resolved to go anyway. The extra sandwiches were for him in the event he met her. She would ride as far as the old line camp with or without him. She was determined to go. That is, she *had* been determined to go. She was not sure now.

She moved on, hesitant, debating with herself, paused again at the yard gate. Len Matchett was dismounting at the hitch-rail. He caught sight of her, swept off his hat in a bow.

Hilda bit her lip with vexation. The debonair

owner of the Walking M was another of her father's friends she found disturbing to her peace of mind. He had tried to make love to her during her last vacation home from school, and it was obvious that he intended to continue the courtship, of which her father apparently approved. Len Matchett had not been in the Soledad long, less than two years, but he was already her father's friend. She did not like the man. He was handsome enough, tall, dark-haired, self-assured. She resented his easy familiarity, his assumption that his attentions were pleasing, an honor to be gratefully received. She disliked his swagger, his suave talk. Instinctively she sensed insincerity in him a latent cruelty.

She watched him approach, lean and graceful, spurs dragging, white teeth gleaming under trim black mustache—a range dandy in white silk shirt and black cord trousers and hand-carved black leather boots. The high-peaked black hat he wore was embellished with silver braid.

Distaste filled the girl's eyes. She was suddenly acutely aware of a change in her. Things she had not noticed as a girl were taking unpleasant form in her mind. She had come home from school a woman in thought and understanding. She was no longer a carefree child. She was a grown woman and she was seeing things for the first time in their true perspective. And what she saw disturbed her. She was not finding the old pleasure in her father. There were things about him that puzzled and worried her. Like Len Matchett, he did not ring true.

Matchett halted, hand extended, his smile glittering. "I promised I'd be over soon," he said. His voice was rich and vibrant and hearty. "You're going to see a lot of me, Hilda, now you're back for keeps."

Her hand lay in his for a brief space, limp, unresponsive. She withdrew it quickly. "You and Dad are such good friends," she said. "Dad is always talking about you."

Matchett looked pleased, also reproachful. "It isn't Warde who is going to make me camp on Bar T's doorstep," he countered banteringly. "Going for a ride?" His bold eyes were avid, absorbed her from head to foot.

Hilda felt her color rise under his appraising look. She knew the die had been cast for her. Her one thought now was to get away, put a lot of distance between them.

"Yes," she answered. "I'm going for a ride—a long ride. I'm wild to get out, see the range—the cattle."

Matchett's expression showed regret. "I'd give a lot to be with you," he said. "Got some business with Warde that won't keep."

Hilda gave him a demure smile. "I thought you came to see me."

"You're unkind," he laughed. It was a laugh

136

that did not reach to his eyes. They were suddenly cold. "You don't like me," he charged with an unexpectedness that startled her.

She stiffened. "It's too nice a day to quarrel," she rejoined icily.

Warde Taylor's booming voice broke in from the ranch-office, a squat adobe building at the far end of the patio wall and overlooking the corral. "Hello, Len! Come on over. Clint's got some news."

Matchett turned his head in a look. "With you in a minute," he answered. His look came back to Hilda. "That settles it." His tone was rueful. "I'd about made up my mind to side you on your ride." His smile enveloped her. "You'll like me better when you get to know me." He swung on his heel. "So long for now, señorita. Good riding."

Hilda waited until he vanished into the office with her father, then she almost ran to the barn and into the stables. Her mare was waiting in the stall, saddled and ready except for the bridle. She snatched it from the horn and hastily crushed the bit into the mare's mouth and buckled the latchet. She was in a hurry to be gone before Len Matchett could change his mind. It would be impossible to be rid of him if he forced his company on her.

A raw-boned, elderly man with shaggy gray hair under a battered sombrero, appeared from a stall, a pitchfork in his hand. He looked at her with red-rimmed eyes.

"Goin' fur, Miss Hilda?" he inquired.

"I don't know, Pete." She jerked at the latigo, made sure it was secure.

"The mare's some skittish," Pete said, leaning on his fork. "I rode her some this mornin' to git the buck out of her."

"You needn't," Hilda said sharply. "Castaña never bucks with me. I like her lively."

The choreman grinned, showed tobacco-stained teeth. "Sleed told me to bust her some," he said.

Hilda flung him an angry glance. "Castaña is *my* mare," she retorted sharply. "I'm the boss when it comes to her."

Peter mumbled something under his breath and shuffled away with his pitchfork. Hilda's indignant gaze followed him. She was angry, and worried. Too many people on the ranch were interfering in her affairs. Even old Pete wanted to know where she was going. She detested the choreman. She had the uneasy feeling that he had been told to watch her. The suspicion in his rheumy eyes had been plain enough.

She led the chestnut mare outside and got into the saddle. The door of the ranch-office was closed, she saw, and with a sigh of relief she rode the mare at a walk down the corral. In another moment the trees of the long winding avenue hid her from view. She shook the reins and Castaña moved into a fast, easy lope. She was a beautiful mare, and Hilda's pride and joy. Her father would

138

have been startled, even angry, could he have known the truth about her. He thought Hilda had purchased her from Mustang Jenns, which was only part of the truth. The mare had been born and bred on the K7 ranch and was a birthday gift from Kirk. They knew that Warde Taylor would never have consented to such a gift to his daughter from the man he hated, and so Kirk had arranged the make-believe purchase from Mustang, first swearing the old trader to secrecy.

The fact that the mare was full sister to Kirk's own big red horse, and his gift to her, added to the girl's satisfaction and pleasure. It had been Kirk's suggestion that she name the mare Castaña, Spanish for her rich chestnut color.

The ranch-house faded back behind the low hills. Almost unconsciously, Hilda headed the mare in the direction of Cañon Los Diablos. In a way, her decision had been forced by Len Matchett's presence at the ranch. She had almost decided to abandon her plans, for fear of being trailed. Len Matchett's arrival had temporarily driven thoughts of danger to Kirk from her mind. Her one impulse was to get away from the ranch as quickly as possible. And now—well, she might as well keep going until she reached the canyon.

She pulled to a standstill twice, and carefully scrutinized the back trail. Apparently her fears were groundless. She could see nothing suspicious—only cattle browsing in the chaparral.

She became aware of low, menacing mutterings as she neared the top of a rise. Hilda was range-bred. The sound was familiar, the angry mutterings of a great range bull.

She topped the rise and halted the mare. Below her was a roundish basin, almost an amphitheater, set in the encircling hills. In the center of the amphitheater was a huge bull, down on his knees, great horns savagely spiking the earth and sending clouds of dust over his shoulders.

It was from a second bull that the blood-curdling rumbles came as he deliberately descended the slope. He reached the bottom, halted and pawed the dust, went down on his knees and tore at the ground with his horns. He was an old lord of the range, prepared to accept the challenge of the younger bull now calmly awaiting his advance. Hilda could see his harem on the far side of the basin, a score or more cows with their calves. Apparently none of them took the least interest in the impending duel. They continued to browse placidly, indifferent to the fact that their lord's rule had been challenged by a bold young stranger.

For a long moment the two bulls stood motionless, shaggy white heads lowered stiffly, angry rumbles in their throats, then slowly, deliberately, they moved closer until lowered heads almost touched. Hilda held her breath, heard the sharp click of horns as they locked in battle.

Churning feet sent up clouds of dust as the straining, infuriated animals pivoted round and round. The young challenger was lighter than the big herd bull, also less experienced. He began to give ground, found himself suddenly helpless before the mighty battering-ram rush of the old bull. With a quick sidewise leap he disengaged his horns and fled, flank torn and bloody from a lunging horn that caught him as he swerved away.

The victorious herd bull made no attempt to pursue. He stood there, pawing the earth, showering massive shoulders with dust and bellowing his triumph.

Hilda rode on her way, her expression thoughtful. She was vaguely conscious of a feeling of depression. The two great range bulls, battling for supremacy, the younger one against the veteran. She wondered if there was anything symbolic in the struggle she had just witnessed. Kirk Severn against Warde Taylor. But the old bull had won. The thought troubled her. She was too honest ith herself not to know on whose side she would be if and when it came to a crisis between the two men, one her father—the other the man she loved. She would want Kirk to win, would desperately want him to win. She could not bear for him to lose.

She fervently hoped that Kirk would be waiting for her in Cañon Los Diablos. There were so many questions she wanted to ask him—so much she *must* know.

Chapter XII
THREE WORRIED MEN

Bar T's ranch-office made a fitting background for its big-framed, bearded owner. Warde Taylor liked space and solidity and splendor. Frescoes adorned the adobe walls and the high ceiling, supported by massive beams of virgin yellow pine. The frescoes were the work of a wandering penniless artist from Mexico City. Taylor had given him a free hand and the result was a series of scenes of the bullring done in gay reds and yellows and blues. There were bright Navajo rugs on the floor, and huge homemade chairs built to withstand the cattleman's two hundred and twenty pounds. There were guns of various makes on the walls, and a big silver-mounted Mexican saddle. A pair of huge spurs dangled from the horn of the saddle, and a silver-encrusted bridle with a savage-looking spade bit. The room was some twenty by thirty feet, with deeply embrasured windows that failed to let in enough light. The result was an impression of perpetual twilight, which Taylor sometimes heightened by lighting the two fat candles in the tall candlesticks on the table he used as a desk.

Clint Sleed never felt at ease in the place. He

despised such foolish elegancies. They did not belong on a cattle ranch. He felt outraged every time business took him into the office. It might be all right for some female, but it was no fit place for a hard-bitten cowman.

He sat stiffly in a straight-backed chair, thumb of one hand hooked in his belt, the other hand fingering the protruding strings of the tobacco sack in his shirt pocket. His face was expressionless as he listened to the heated argument going on between Taylor and Matchett. He played his cards close to his chest, kept his private thoughts to himself. He did not like Len Matchett. The dandified owner of the Walking M spread was a show-off. At the same time, the Bar T foreman was not deceived by the man's flamboyant manner. His smooth exterior was the sleekness of a panther. Len Matchett was dangerous. And the big, bearded man sprawled loosely in the desk chair was dangerous. Clint Sleed was perhaps the only man in the Soledad who knew how completely dangerous they were. He had good reason to wear a poker face when in their company, measure his words with care, and keep a tight lock on his lips at all times. There were dark secrets he could divulge if he wanted to make sure of his own swift and sudden end, find his long, lean body dangling and jerking in the noose of a rope.

"We've got to do something, and do it quick,"

Warde Taylor said angrily. "There's nothing to stop you from going any place you want, Len. Why do you suppose I fixed it for you to be sheriff?"

"I don't think Kirk Severn was fooled a minute," Len Matchett declared. His voice had lost its smooth drawl. He spoke raspingly. "Severn knew that *you* knew he wouldn't fall for the bluff. He knew too, how long he would have lasted as sheriff of Soledad. No longer than Jim Shane."

Sleed broke his silence. "No sense trying to get Severn with poison bait," he said. "He's too damn smart."

Taylor grunted, combed his heavy grizzled beard with long, thick fingers. "I know he's smart," he rejoined irritably. "That's why I want action." He began again on Matchett. "You're sheriff. Nothing to stop you from going over to Severn's place and combing the house from end to end. Easy enough to fix up a search warrant. It's going to be just too bad if Severn gets hold of that girl. Like Clint says, he's smart. He'll smell a rat."

"She's enough like Hilda to be her own sister," Matchett said. He grinned.

Taylor's face purpled. "You talk too much," he said coldly.

"I'm just saying what Severn, or anybody else, will say," muttered the Walking M man. He paused, added thoughtfully, "We don't know for certain that Severn has run into her."

144

"Only one way to find out," grumbled Taylor. "You fix up a search warrant and ride out to K7 for a good look." He got heavily out of his chair and went to the table in the center of the room. "Have a drink, boys," he invited. He poured whiskey into a glass and drank without waiting for them. The two men joined him and poured drinks.

"You keep good stuff, Warde," Matchett said. He put down his empty glass and reached for the bottle.

Taylor stood glowering at him. "Wish I'd been the one to see her in Deming, instead of you," he grumbled. "She wouldn't have got away from *me*, Len."

"We're maybe all wrong about her," argued Matchett.

"Not if she looks enough like Hilda to be her own sister. I don't like it, Len. I haven't been so scared since the thing began, twenty years back."

"Don't be a damn fool," exclaimed Matchett. He poured another drink. His hand was not quite steady.

Clint Sleed spoke again, fingers toying with his empty glass. "There's a chance she an' the feller are still up in Cañon Los Diablos," he said. "I don't often miss my shots. That feller took my bullet all right. Come close to pitchin' from his saddle. I was sure we'd find him layin' down in the gully."

"You didn't," reminded Taylor in a surly voice.

"I told you how we run into Severn. He got awful stiff-lipped, claimed we was trespassin' on his range." Sleed poured another drink. "Would have meant a fight—"

"Well?" Taylor's tone was sarcastic.

The lanky foreman stared at him fixedly. "You know Kirk Severn." His tone was grim. "Kirk ain't so easy to kill. He was all fixed to take us to Boothill with him."

Taylor grunted again, shook his massive head like an angry range bull. "You let him bluff you," he fumed.

"You wasn't there," Sleed rejoined laconically. He lifted his glass, bleak look challenging the other men.

Len Matchett said softly, "The best way for his kind is a shot in the back."

"You've said it," grinned the foreman. Matchett's words seemed to mollify him, remove the sting from Taylor's thinly-veiled charge of cowardice. "You cain't give Kirk Severn an even break no time."

There was a silence, and then Taylor spoke again, worriedly, "What about Pedro Negro?"

"Pedro ain't showed up," admitted the foreman. "Don't look so good, him not showin' up."

Warde Taylor picked up bottle and glass and went back to his desk. He refilled the glass, drained it, looked at the bottle as if considering another drink, then pushed it back on the desk with an impatient gesture. "Only two answers," he said. "Pedro either ran into Severn, or he followed Chase up to the cabin and Chase nabbed him—probably killed him."

Sleed shook his head. "Ain't so simple as that," he demurred. "The way I see it, Severn had the feller hid out when we come along. The feller was hurt, and Severn got him back to the cabin." He gestured grimly. "Pedro got as far as the cabin all right, but it was Severn that killed him. Severn is smart. He'd figger he'd be trailed—was on the lookout."

"You mean that Chase and the woman are still at the cabin?" Taylor's voice was suddenly hopeful.

"It's my notion that Chase would be too bad hurt for Severn to move him away from there," Sleed replied. "Awful rough country. He couldn't do it hisself." The foreman frowned, went on thoughtfully, "Doc Williams was out to K7. I had Sam Gaines kind of pump him. Doc claimed he was out there to fix the Chink cook's hand. Cut hisself with his meat cleaver, Doc said."

"Sounds suspicious," muttered Taylor. "The Chinaman could have gone into town for the doc to fix a cut hand. Doc Williams wouldn't likely take a twenty-mile trip just to fix a cut hand."

"That's right," agreed Matchett. "Sounds fishy."

"I ain't finished," Sleed told them with a grin. "I figgered the same way, sent Dunn Harden trailin' Severn when he left town after the

Association meetin'. Told Dunn to do some scoutin', find out what was goin' on at the ranch."

"What did Dunn find out?" questioned Taylor.

"Waal, Dunn ain't got in, yet," admitted the foreman. He fingered the dangling string of his tobacco sack. "Ain't likin' him bein' so long," he added uneasily.

Len Matchett's smile was unpleasant. "Played your cards wrong again, huh, Sleed?"

"What the hell are you drivin' at?" flared the foreman. "If you're so damn smart why don't you do what the boss says an' go look K7 over your own self? I ain't the sheriff."

"I'll swear you in to go along with the posse," smiled Matchett.

"Suits me," grunted Sleed. His angry look shifted to the door. His face brightened. "Here's Dunn now," he added in a relieved voice.

The hurrying footsteps halted outside. Taylor called out impatiently, "Come in, Dunn."

The cowboy stepped inside, closed the door behind him. His gaze settled on Sleed. "Got news," he said. "Plenty news."

"Let's have it," growled Taylor. His fingers combed his beard nervously. "What did you find out, Dunn?"

"Kirk nabbed me, back in the chaparral," Dunn told them with a grin. "Took me along and turned me over to Justo Nueco." He rolled amused eyes at his impatient but attentive listeners. "That

Yaqui sure is dumb. Wasn't no trouble a-tall to pump him. He told me the feller is still up there in Cañon Los Diablos, too shot up to be moved."

Nobody spoke for a moment, then Taylor asked, his voice gruff with anxiety, "The girl with him?"

"Sure she is," answered the cowboy. "Justo said she told Kirk to get to hell out of there. Didn't want him bustin' into their affairs. Said he heard Kirk tellin' Chuck Rigg about it." Dunn's look went longingly to the bottle on Taylor's desk.

"Help yourself," Taylor invited.

Dunn found a glass, filled it and drank. "From what Justo told me, Kirk was plenty peeved at the Chase outfit. Wasn't likin' them nestin' up in the old line-house. I reckon he told 'em to clear out quick as she could move Chase."

The other men exchanged looks. Taylor said in a relieved voice, "Should be an easy job, Clint."

"If we work fast," agreed the foreman. He stared hard at Dunn. "How did you pull off your break from there?" he wanted to know.

Dunn grinned. "You'll laugh," he said complacently. "All I done was fill the Yaqui's eyes with tobacco dust, take his gun away and smack him down." He gestured. "Wasn't no more reason for me to stick 'round, so I walked out on 'em." He swore feelingly. "Couldn't risk lookin' for my bronc. Had to use my own laigs over to Mat Dilley's. Mat loaned me a Bar 4 bronc." The cowboy sensed the satisfaction caused by his story. Not waiting for an invitation, he coolly poured another drink. "I reckon you was doin' some wonderin', me not showin' up sooner," he said to Sleed.

"You're lucky," the foreman said grimly. "I'd say Severn acted loco, lettin' you break away so easy."

Dunn Harden emptied his glass, laughed softly. "I ain't seen the hole yet I cain't wriggle loose from," he boasted. He yawned widely. "I'm dead on my feet for some shut-eye. I got to hit the hay."

Steed hesitated, looked questioningly at the other men. "Don't seem like it's good sense for us to wait for him," he said. "I say we hit the trail for Cañon Los Diablos pronto."

"Not me!" Dunn declared heatedly. "I got to get me some sleep."

Warde Taylor's gesture silenced an annoyed rejoinder from the foreman. "I've been doing some thinking," he said. His look fastened on Matchett. "Len, you're heading for the canyon with a posse. You can swear in Clint and some of the boys."

"Yeah?" Matchett arched his brows, shook his head. "I'm not so sure I want the job."

Taylor frowningly ignored the interruption. "You will take a warrant along, arrest Chase and his woman for the murder of Pedro Negro."

"We don't know for sure that Pedro is dead," objected the sheriff.

"Of course he's dead," rumbled the cattleman. "Anyway, it makes a good excuse to arrest them." He paused, added with sinister emphasis, "It's possible they will make a break—try to escape. Be their own fault if they get killed."

Dunn Harden's skin prickled. He was afraid to look at Taylor, afraid the cattleman would correctly interpret the contempt and anger that burned his eyes.

Taylor continued in the same deadly voice, "You are the Law. Nobody could touch you for it, Len."

Matchett nodded. "Sounds like a good idea," he reluctantly conceded. His sardonic smile swept their faces. "For that matter, we don't need to make it a law job. We can leave *El Topo's* card pinned on 'em."

Warde Taylor's big body stiffened, then he slowly nodded his massive head. "Not bad," he said softly. "Not bad, Len." His voice became crisply impatient. "On your way, Clint. You won't need more than a couple of the boys with you."

"I'll take Rincon and Tate along," decided the foreman. He looked at Matchett. "You'll side us, Len?"

"Just to be sure you don't make any more mistakes, I think I'll do that little thing," Matchett told him with an insolent smile.

The foreman reddened, jerked at the door angrily, paused and looked back at Dunn. "You can head for the bunkhouse and get some sleep," he said gruffly. "Stick 'round close, feller. I'll be needin' you, when we get back."

Dunn said sulkily, "I was figgerin' to head for town, come sundown."

Sleed considered him, a hint of suspicion in his pale eyes. He nodded, assented with some reluctance. "All right, but keep in touch with Sam Gaines."

"Sure," agreed the cowboy. He followed the foreman into the sun-baked corral. Sleed said over his shoulder as they moved away, "That damn place the boss calls an office gets me sick at the stummick. All them fool fixin's." He spat contemptuously, halted and carefully scrutinized the roan horse tied to the hitch-rail. The horse wore Mat Dilley's Bar 4 brand, a fact that seemed to allay any lingering doubt in the foreman's mind.

"Mat must have been some surprised, you showin' up on foot," he commented. "What kind of song and dance did you give him?"

"Told him my bronc got to pitchin' when I wasn't lookin', and left me flat in the chaparral."

A bleak smile creased Sleed's hard face. "I'll bet Mat give you the laugh," he chuckled. "He'll sure spread it 'round."

"I promised I'd buy him a drink if he didn't," Dunn said with a rueful grin. "That's one reason I'm headin' for town. I aim to keep Mat's mouth shut if it takes a dozen drinks."

Sleed guffawed. "Don't blame you none." His

quick look at the office door told him that Matchett and Taylor were coming out. "All right, Dunn," he added hurriedly, "you beat it for the bunkhouse and ketch up on your sleep." He moved on toward the barn, spurs rasping quick time to his short, choppy stride.

Dunn called out, "I'll see if Mercedes can fix me up some chow. I ain't et since last night." He pushed through the garden gate and made his way to the back of the house.

The cook gave him a smile as he stepped inside the kitchen. He said ingratiatingly, "How about some chow, Mercedes?"

Mercedes tossed her head. "You no fool me, *muchacho.* You no wan' food . . . you wan' see the señorita."

"Where do you get that *muchacho* stuff?" retorted the cowboy. "I ain't no kid, Mercedes."

"You mooch same as kid if you theenk the señorita wan' see you any time." Mercedes snapped thumb and forefinger. "She no care that mooch." With a derisive sniff she got out of her chair. "I feex you cold meat and bread," she added ungraciously.

Dunn watched her glumly as she sliced some bread. She caught his frequent glances at the hall door, said spitefully, "She 'ave gone r-ride. Maybe go for meet some hombre, no? She take plenty san'wich weeth her."

Dunn made no response, silently took the cold

meat sandwich and stalked out. Mercedes shrilled at his back, "You no like, no?"

Sandwich in hand, the cowboy made his way to the bunkhouse. It was deserted. He went to one of the murky windows and stood there, chewing the bread and meat, watchful gaze on the scene in the corral.

In a few minutes Sleed and Matchett rode away, followed by Tate and Rincon. There was grim satisfaction in Dunn's eyes as he watched.

He saw Warde Taylor slowly cross the corral and disappear through the garden gate, pausing for a brief glance at the brand on the roan horse. Dunn hastily swallowed the remainder of the sandwich and went to the bunkhouse door.

He stood there for a long moment, wary eyes roving around the big corral, then he went swiftly to the roan horse, slipped the tie-rope and stepped into the saddle. Only the choreman, appearing suddenly in the stable door, saw him ride away. It meant nothing to Peter. He knew that Sleed was off on a mission. Dunn Harden always went with him. Dunn was the foreman's right bower.

Chapter XIII
PIECES OF A PUZZLE

Justo Nueco hesitated inside the kitchen door and smiled ingratiatingly at the elderly Chinese cook who was stirring batter in a large bowl. Gin Suey slanted a brief questioning look at the intruder, returned his attention to the batter, nodded satis-faction, and reached for a large cake pan.

The Yaqui cleared his throat nervously. He knew how the old cook resented any invasion of his domain. Gin Suey was notorious for his short temper, his readiness to brandish his meat cleaver.

"*Por favor, señor,*" Justo began humbly. He removed his enormous high-peaked sombrero. "*Por favor, señor,*" he repeated.

Gin Suey put down the cake pan and faced him, annoyance in his eyes. "Wha' foh you come makee talk?" he asked impatiently.

"Me wan' see boss," Justo explained. He touched the soiled bandage that wrapped his head. "Boss say he wan' feex thees."

Something that resembled a smile flickered across the cook's wrinkled poker face. He nodded. "You catchee bad knock . . . you look allee same hell."

Justo gestured indifference. "Thees no bad. Br-reak skeen . . . no br-reak bone."

"Your head heap tough—allee same bull," chuckled Gin Suey. He waved a skinny hand at the door. "Boss in office. You go see." He turned back to the pan. "I got no time fool away. I makee cake foh Missy Chase."

Justo, sombrero clutched in hand, tiptoed across the kitchen and disappeared into the hall. He passed the dining room and halted at the open door of the ranch-office.

Kirk was sitting on the arm of his desk chair, talking to Esther Chase who stood slim and straight on a worn old bearskin rug in front of the fireplace in which redly glowed the remains of a mesquite log. Kirk broke off in the middle of a sentence as he caught sight of the hesitant Yaqui.

"Well," he greeted. "How's the head, Justo?"

"Mooch good," replied the Yaqui. He returned Esther's smile with a bashful grin, added in Spanish, "The pain is gone. I have come because Señor Rigg said you wanted to look at my head."

"That's right," Kirk said. He went to a closet and opened the door. "I'll put on a fresh bandage."

"It was a shame," Esther Chase sympathized. "I'm awfully sorry, Justo."

156

Justo rolled pleased eyes at her. "*Gracias, señora.*"

Kirk removed the soiled bandage, tossed it on the red coals and expertly appraised the gash. He nodded satisfaction. "Fine," he ejaculated. "You'll be as good as new in a day or two."

He dressed the wound and adjusted a fresh bandage. "You've had a good lesson, Justo," he said. "You won't fall for such tricks again."

"No, señor." The Yaqui looked embarrassed.

"You and Atilano are on special duty," Kirk continued in Spanish. "Day and night you must keep close watch on this house." He spoke gravely. "You must not let harm come to the señora and her sick husband."

"We will guard them with our life's blood," promised Justo. His dark eyes glowed fiercely. "*Por esta cruz, sí!*"

"I'm trusting you," Kirk said soberly. He thought for a moment. "Tell Kansas to throw my saddle on Pancho," he added.

"*Sí.*" Justo backed toward the veranda door, paused and gave Esther Chase a bashful smile. "*Adiós, señora,*" he said politely.

He vanished outside, his feet as soundless as a cat's. Esther Chase let out a little sigh. "His savage face is quite frightening, until he smiles," she commented. "He is almost beautiful, when he smiles like that."

"He likes you, Kirk said. "It's lucky."

"*Por esta cruz*," she murmured. "What does it mean, Mr. Severn?" She shook her head. "I don't need to ask. He means *by this cross,* doesn't he?"

"The Nueco twins' most solemn oath," Kirk told her. "Justo and Atilano would die—before they'd dishonor that oath."

"I'm glad they are my friends," Mrs. Chase declared. She paused, then worriedly, "You think you can trust Dunn Harden? Are you sure he's not playing you a trick? It was really his only chance to get away from here."

"I'm not worried about Dunn," reassured Kirk. He chuckled. "Dunn has picked up the Nueco oath and has sworn by it. He'll stick, Mrs. Chase."

"When will he be back?" she queried. She repressed a shiver. "What you propose to do seems so fantastic. How do you know they'll take the bait?"

"I *don't* know," confessed Kirk. "It's a tough problem, and one that involves you and your husband." He paused, added significantly, "*You*—mostly."

She gestured hopelessly, moved slowly to a chair and sat down. "You mean it has something to do with my—my father?"

Kirk nodded. "He's mixed up in it—in some way."

Esther was pale. "How can it be possible? He—he was—" She brought out the words with an effort, "—was hung."

158

"We don't know the truth—yet," Kirk said.

"The photograph," she said piteously, "the one I showed the old horsetrader. It was a photograph of my father. Mustang Jenns said it was Pecos Jack—and he was there—saw Pecos Jack hung—by a mob."

"I don't think they hung Pecos Jack." Kirk's tone was harsh.

Her puzzled eyes clung to his. "But—but the old horsetrader said he saw—"

"Mustang saw them hang a man," Kirk said. "He was told that the man was Pecos Jack. He had no reason to disbelieve. He'd never seen Pecos Jack."

"I don't understand," Esther said wearily. "Why should something that happened twenty years ago make those men want to kill Dick?" Anger darkened her hazel eyes. "Dick has never been in this country before, nor have I."

"I was saying that you are more directly concerned than your husband," Kirk reminded. He was looking at her intently. "Somebody must have seen you in Soledad—somebody who guessed who you were—and was frightened."

"I've never been in Soledad," protested the girl.

"In Deming, then," persisted Kirk. "That is where you ran into Mustang Jenns and showed him your father's picture." His eyes narrowed thoughtfully. "Do you remember noticing anybody in particular, anybody who seemed curious about you?"

She sat silent, brows furrowed as she ransacked her memory. "I don't know," she finally answered. "It's so hard to think back. Dick and I were so busy, getting our supplies. It wasn't in our minds to notice if people were curious about us."

Kirk kept on at her. "You didn't notice any man looking at you?"

She colored, made a grimace. "Well—men do look at a girl—sometimes. We get used to it. We don't think anything of it."

"That's right." His tone was amused, and then, half-impatiently, "It would have helped if you'd noticed any man in particular—could describe him."

She considered this, asked speculatively, "What might he look like—this man you have in mind?"

"A big man, with a long grizzled beard, a white hat and—"

Esther interrupted him. "I would have remembered, if I'd seen him."

Kirk tried again. He described Clint Sleed. She shook her head. "So many men could answer that description," she pointed out. "Deming was full of cowmen with drooping mustaches and hard faces and boots and spurs." Her half-smile came again. "So many of them are bowlegged. Why are they bowlegged?"

160

"They spend most of their years in a saddle," explained Kirk with a grin. "They start young, almost before they're weaned. They get that way."

Esther smiled faintly. "Who are the two men you described?" she asked abruptly.

"Warde Taylor and his foreman, Clint Sleed," Kirk answered, after a momentary hesitation. "Sleed is the man who was trailing your husband."

"Oh!" She was visibly startled. "I don't remember noticing anybody like them in Deming." She shook her head. "I couldn't be sure."

He continued to press her, carefully described Len Matchett. Esther puckered her brows, showed excitement.

"I seem to recall somebody who looks like that," she exclaimed. "A tall man, dark, small black mustache, and, quite a dandy—for a cowman."

"That's Matchett," exclaimed Kirk. "He owns the Walking M ranch." His lip curled. "Looks more like a tin-horn gambler than a decent cowman."

"I seem to remember him," the girl continued. "Dick and I were in the store, looking at pack-saddles. This man spoke to me, asked if we were strangers and could he help us."

"He didn't give his name?"

Esther shook her head. "No—it was only for a moment. Dick called for me to join him. The man didn't follow."

"You didn't tell him where you were going . . . mention Cañon Los Diablos?"

"I'm sure I didn't," Esther assured him. "We didn't see him again, at least I didn't notice him."

"Think hard," Kirk urged. "Did you speak of Cañon Los Diablos to anybody?"

"Oh, yes—to the storekeeper. He told us about the trails." She smiled ruefully. "He didn't tell us we'd be trespassing on your ranch. In fact we didn't know of the cabin until we stumbled on it."

"Forget it," Kirk said with an embarrassed grin.

Esther went back to the stranger. "He was smoking a long, brown cigarette. It had a different smell from the kind most of you smoke."

"Not homemade," smiled Kirk.

"I'd know that smell anywhere. Not a bit like your Bull Durham."

Kirk's expression was grim. "Matchett gets his cigarettes from Mexico City," he said. "I know the cigarettes you mean. He smokes them, and he's the man who spoke to you, Mrs. Chase."

"It doesn't explain much to me," the girl rejoined. "Why should he want to harm Dick?"

Kirk considered her for a long moment before answering. He said slowly, "You reminded him of somebody he knew. In fact he probably was fooled for a second or two . . . thought you were this other girl—until he spoke to you."

She wrinkled her brows at him. "I remember," she said. "You told me up there at the cabin that I reminded you of a girl you know."

"The resemblance is amazing," admitted Kirk. "Doctor Williams couldn't get over it. I can't either," he added frowningly.

"Who is she?" Esther asked the question in a perplexed voice. And when he did not immediately answer, "It's really frightening, to think that somebody wants to kill my husband just because I resemble a girl I never even knew existed." She paused, her eyes on him, miserable, panicky. "Who is she—this girl?" she repeated.

"Warde Taylor's daughter," Kirk said in a strained voice. His moody gaze was on the window. "I've known her since—since she was so high." He gestured. "I put her on her first horse." He added softly, "Hilda isn't like her father. She—she is *nice*—"

Esther was staring at him, a fascinated look in her eyes. "Hilda was my mother's name." Her voice was husky. "It is very strange."

"Yes," Kirk said gravely. "It is more than strange." His eyes were hard. "Warde Taylor is mixed up in this business. That man who spoke to you in Deming, Len Matchett, is his close friend."

Her eyes widened. "Warde Taylor," she echoed. "I told you that Taylor was my name before I married Dick."

163

"Yes," he said. "I remember."

"Father's name was Worden Taylor." She was very pale. "Something dreadful has happened. Why should this Warde Taylor have a daughter who so closely resembles me, and who has the same name as my mother?"

"It's a mystery I'm going to solve," Kirk said quietly. "Until it is solved, there is danger for all of us, for you and your husband—for Hilda—for myself."

"Why for you?" Esther asked.

"Because I'm too inquisitive about *El Topo*, for one thing," Kirk told her grimly.

"You have mentioned him before. Who is *El Topo*?"

"It's one of the things I'm going to find out," Kirk replied. He spoke gloomily. "I wish I could tell you more. The pieces are too jumbled."

She saw the pain in his eyes. "You are in love with her—this Hilda Taylor?" She asked the question gently.

Kirk nodded. "I'm afraid for her," he said simply.

Esther got out of her chair, stood looking at him. Sunlight streamed through the window, drew ruddy glints from his dark hair. There was maturity and resoluteness in the strong lines of his tanned face. His enemies would respect him— and all the more fear him.

His look went to the window. Kansas was

tying the red horse to the hitch-rail under the umbrella tree. He said hastily, "I have to go, Mrs. Chase."

She touched his arm gently. "Call me Esther," she said. "You are wonderful to me—and to Dick—" Her voice was suddenly unsteady. "I—I think we wouldn't be alive—if you hadn't been such a good friend."

He was touched. "You're a brave girl, Esther," he said. "Doc Williams said you were brave, and Dick, too."

She smiled. "You have a moment to spare? Dick would like to see you, before you go."

Kirk followed her from the office and down the hall to the bedroom. Dick Chase grinned at them from his pillows. His face was haggard, showed the strain of mingled anxiety and pain.

"Hello, people." He spoke with forced cheerfulness. "Am I still being hunted for a rustler?" He directed the question at Kirk.

Kirk returned the grin. "I shouldn't wonder," he answered. "You must have been swinging a wide loop, young feller." His tone sobered. "The thing is still a mystery, Chase. It's tough on you, but you're lucky at that."

"I'll declare out loud that I'm lucky," Dick Chase said fervently. His eyes clouded. "I'm stumped. The whole thing is crazy. Anybody could take one look at me and know I'm no cow thief. I've got greenhorn written all over me."

Esther shook her head. "There's more to it than that, Dick," she told him.

"What do you mean?" His tone was puzzled.

"Apparently it started a long time ago, twenty years ago," Esther said gravely. "At least, that is what Kirk thinks, and I'm inclined to agree with him."

"I don't know what you are talking about," complained her husband.

"I think you should tell him all that we know," Kirk suggested to the girl. "Tell him about the man who spoke to you in the Deming store." He turned to the door, looked back at their troubled faces. "*Adiós*, and don't worry."

Dick Chase's eyes followed him through the door. "I don't like it," he muttered. His gaze shifted to his wife. "What does he mean? He said something about some man who spoke to you in Deming."

She looked at him compassionately. "He is the direct cause of what happened to you," she answered. "But Dick—" There was a curious horror in her hazel eyes. "It really began twenty years ago, as I told you, and it's dreadful—"

"Twenty years ago?" He stared up in bewilderment from the pillows. "Go on—"

"Yes, twenty years ago—when—when my father was murdered—" Her voice broke.

"Murdered?"

Esther nodded, her eyes wet. "I'm quite sure

166

now, that he was murdered." She turned away, faced the window and dabbed at her eyes with a handkerchief. She could see the corral. Kirk Severn was on his horse, was riding away. He drew rein at the avenue gate and spoke to a man standing there. Atilano Nueco, a rifle in his hand.

Her look drew in, slowly swept the garden. Another man sat on a bench inside the high wall. He wore a bandage on his head, and a rifle lay across his knees. Justo Nueco, his watchful eyes unceasingly vigilant.

The sight of those two fierce-looking Yaquis sent a thrill of apprehension through her, also a certain comfort. They were on guard, had sworn their most solemn oath.

Chapter XIV
THE FIGHT AT THE CABIN

Uneasy forebodings put a somber look on Kirk's face as he rode out of the yard. He was worried about Hilda Taylor. They had spoken of a picnic in Cañon Los Diablos, but the thing had been left somewhat in the air, and there had been no chance to get word to her since those brief moments with her in town. It was possible she would go anyway, thinking he would be waiting at the old meeting place. Hilda was that way, inclined to follow where impulse led.

The thought increased his uneasiness. He had told Esther the truth. He *was* afraid for Hilda. Behind the shadowy shape of the mysterious *El Topo* lurked danger for Warde Taylor's daughter.

His face set in hard, grim lines. No turning back, now. He had to go on, follow the trail to the abominable end. A shadowed trail, old Mustang Jenns had warned, a crooked trail, marked with dishonor and blood down the length of its twenty years.

He reached the wash below the canyon's portal. There were fresh hoofprints in the sand. The signs indicated that Hilda would be waiting. There were no returning tracks.

Disappointment met him when he broke through the willow brakes. The girl was nowhere in sight. He saw imprints of her boot heels, and got down from the horse and studied them. The tracks led to a large boulder on which lay three stones piled on top of each other, an old sign he had taught her to use. He grinned, moved on, eyes alert, and came to a bit of smooth sand on which was traced the outline of an arrow. It pointed into the canyon.

He stared at the arrow with growing dismay. Cañon Los Diablos was no place for Hilda Taylor. If his carefully concocted plans matured, there would soon be plenty of excitement in the remote upper reaches.

With an impatient gesture he swung back to his saddle and sent the horse up the steep incline that led into the dark gorge.

Clouds had piled behind the mountains, were spreading a gray blanket across the heavens. The sun disappeared. Sudden thunder cracked like a bullwhip over his head. Kirk felt a splash of rain on his face. He reached for his slicker and pulled it on.

It was raining hard by the time he reached the fork where the trail to the cabin began its twisting ascent up the slope.

He kept the horse moving at a jog trot, reckless of the slippery trail, the clawing, dripping branches of the junipers.

The horse was blowing hard by the time they came to the flats. Kirk got a glimpse of the cabin through the dripping trees, saw a blue haze of smoke whipping from the chimney.

Another minute brought him to the door. He slid down and with a loud announcing knock, pushed inside.

Hilda was sitting on a chair drawn close to the stove. She sprang up, stared at him, delight and relief in her eyes. She gave him a rueful smile. "One grand day for a picnic—but I'd given you up."

"The picnic is out," Kirk said a bit grimly.

Hilda shook her head. "Oh, no, it isn't. Now we are both here, we are going to enjoy the lunch I brought." She pointed at a shelf. "Look—there's coffee in that can, mister. We're in luck."

"You're getting away from here pronto," Kirk said. "Where's your mare?"

"I'd like to know." Her tone was chagrined.

"What do you mean?" drawled Kirk.

"Castaña didn't like that crack of thunder." Hilda gestured disgustedly. "I was just opening the door to have a peep inside when the most awful clap of thunder I ever heard scared the wits out of her. She went away from here fast and probably is still running her legs off. That's all I can tell you."

"She'll likely make for K7," Kirk said.

"You needn't look so cross," Hilda said. She

170

made a grimace. "It's not my fault, and you should be very glad I had a nice dry roof to shelter me from the storm."

Kirk grinned, pulled off his dripping hat and shook it. "Could have been worse," he admitted.

"You needn't be so gloomy about it," she complained. There was a hint of concern in her bantering voice. "What's on your mind, mister?"

He gestured at the white Stetson on the table. "Put it on," he said. "We're leaving here."

Something in his voice made her obey. She reached for the hat, pulled it over her warm chestnut hair, adjusted the chin strap, her eyes on him, big, questioning. Her look went to the packet of sandwiches on the table. She said rebelliously, "At least we can stay long enough to eat the lunch."

Kirk shook his head. "You'll have to ride double," he said. "Where's your slicker?"

"Castaña took it away with her," Hilda replied. "Find Castaña and you'll find my slicker, properly tied to my saddle."

Kirk was tugging at his own slicker while she talked. "Put it on," he ordered. He gave the slicker a vigorous shake that sent drops of water hissing against the hot stove.

The girl was staring at him, growing perplexity in her eyes. She exclaimed petulantly, "Do tell me what it is all about! Why must we go off in a pouring rain when we have this nice dry roof over our heads?" Exasperation sharpened her voice. "You're acting so strangely, Kirk."

"We haven't time for explanations," Kirk said briefly. "Get into this slicker."

Hilda hesitated, her expression still rebellious. "But why—"

"There's a chance of a lot of trouble here," Kirk explained. "Clint Sleed thinks a cow thief is using this camp for a hide-out. I've reason to believe Sleed is headed this way."

"Clint Sleed—coming here!" Consternation swept her face. "He mustn't find me here—alone with *you!*" She paused, added in a troubled voice, "A cow thief, Kirk? You wouldn't be hiding a cow thief—a rustler."

"The man is not a rustler," answered Kirk. "Sleed knows he is not."

"Then why does Sleed pretend he is?" asked the girl in a puzzled voice.

"It's all part of a long story," Kirk said. "No time now, to tell you about it." He turned to the door, went rigid. Slowly his face came round in a warning look.

Hilda heard the sounds, faintly at first above the rain pelting on the roof, the dull thud of hoofs, the jingle of spurs and creak of saddle leathers. The wet slicker fell from her hands.

Kirk put finger to lips in a warning for silence, then to her shocked amazement he opened the door and stepped outside.

172

She stifled a cry, stood there, dismayed eyes on the closed door. She heard Sleed's startled voice and went on swift soundless feet to one of the small windows and parted the cowhide curtain.

Kirk stood close to his horse, his back to the door. Some ten or fifteen feet beyond him clustered a group of horsemen. Rain dripped from hat brims, drew steely glints from wet slickers.

Sleed said angrily, "What the hell—"

"That's right—" Kirk's voice was thin edged. "I thought I warned you to keep off K7 range, Sleed. What's the idea?"

Another voice answered him. "You're talking to the Law, Severn. This is a sheriff's posse."

Hilda's mouth formed an incredulous *Oh!* She pressed closer to the window, stared with dismayed eyes through the blurring rain at the speaker. *Len Matchett.* His smile was unpleasant—mocking.

"The Law can have no business up here, Matchett," Kirk rejoined harshly.

"*Sheriff* Matchett, if you please."

"Anything you say, Sheriff." Kirk's tone was contemptuous. He waited, his eyes watchful.

"I've got a warrant," Matchett continued smoothly. "I'm arresting the man you are hiding out in this cabin. I want the woman, too."

"You're crazy," drawled Kirk.

"I'm arresting them for the murder of Pedro Negro." Matchett's voice showed a growing

173

impatience. "Stand away from that door, Severn."

"You've been eating loco weed," Kirk jeered. "I'm hiding nobody here."

"Stand away from that door!" shouted Matchett. "I'm sending my men inside."

"You heard the sheriff," interjected Sleed. His grin was malevolent. "Ain't healthy for a feller to buck the Law. You cain't bluff our guns with fool talk, Severn."

"Listen—all of you—" Kirk's drawl hardened, slashed at them like cold steel. "Keep your guns out of it."

"Yeah?" The Bar T foreman's grin widened. He glanced significantly at his companions.

Kirk studied their hard faces attentively. He sensed an impending crisis. These men were hungry for an excuse to kill him, providing they could do it without any risk. He said quietly, "You can kill me, but two of you will die first. You, Matchett, and you, Sleed. That's a promise, if it is the last one I make."

Silence settled over them. Only the swishing sound of the rain. They knew him, knew he spoke the truth.

Matchett broke the silence, his voice uneasy. "You're going too fast for us, Severn. We've got nothing against you. Our business here is to arrest a murderer, and his accomplice. Don't play the fool, man."

"I told you they are not here," reiterated Kirk.

174

His cool smile swept the glowering faces. "Go back the way you came, and take your fake posse with you."

Clint Sleed stirred restlessly in his saddle. "You're a damn liar!" he shouted. "We seen smoke comin' from the chimney. You ain't bluffin' us."

"It's my stove," countered Kirk. "How do you know I didn't light a fire?"

"You couldn't have," jeered Sleed. "We sighted you down in the gorge. Ain't been time for you to get a fire started." His hand lowered to his gun.

"Don't try it!" Kirk said sharply.

Sleed hesitated, impotent rage in his eyes. His hand came away from the gun reluctantly.

Matchett said crisply, "It's a crime to obstruct the Law, Severn. You'll be sorry for this." His lips twisted in a crooked smile. "You can get jail for this."

Kirk studied him intently and was about to speak when the door behind him suddenly jerked open. It required all his resolution to refrain from a backward glance. He dared not take his eyes from the men in front of him. Their thunderstruck faces told him enough. He heard Hilda's indignant voice:

"You should be ashamed—threatening to put Kirk in jail!"

She came on from the door, stood close to Kirk, gaze fixed angrily on Matchett. He stared back at her dumbly.

Sleed muttered something under his breath. Hilda looked at him. "You, too, Clint. You have no business doubting Kirk's word, calling him a liar."

"He's hidin' a rustler on us," grumbled the Bar T foreman defensively. "We figgered to get him."

"It's not true," Hilda declared. "Anyway, the man is not a rustler. Kirk said so, and said you know it."

Sleed and Matchett exchanged uneasy looks. It was apparent that they were disturbed, thrown off balance by the girl's presence at the camp.

"You don't need to stay any longer," Hilda said. "You'd better go home and let me finish my picnic." She gave Matchett a scornful smile. "I'm sure you must be quite satisfied *now,* Mister Sheriff."

He looked at her, an unpleasant leer in his eyes. "I must apologize for butting into your little love nest," he retorted. "It's lucky your father isn't along, to find you with your—your lover."

"That's enough from you," Kirk said quietly. "Shut your foul mouth, Matchett." His hand was on gun-butt. "I should kill you."

One of the riders flanking Sleed, said softly, "I got the girl covered, Clint."

Kirk's look leaped to the speaker, saw the leveled gun. He said in a low aside to Hilda, "Don't move—"

A jeering laugh came from Sleed. "Looks like we got you, Severn. You won't want harm to come to her." His voice held a brutal threat that sent a chill through Kirk.

"You—you wouldn't—" Hilda faltered, looked appealingly at Matchett. "It—it's murder—"

His sardonic smile was on her, triumphant, almost gloating. "I can't be responsible," he said smoothly. "These men are on your father's payroll. They take orders from Sleed, not from me."

"You're the sheriff," the girl said between stiff lips. "These men are members of your posse."

Matchett shook his head. "Not exactly. They've not been sworn in."

Kirk said contemptuously, "For a very good reason, Matchett. I said your posse was a fake. You haven't been sworn in as sheriff yourself. You have no authority to arrest even a sheep tick."

"Unfortunately for you," sneered Matchett.

Sleed muttered an oath. "Quit stallin', Severn. Get your hands up. Be too bad for the girl if you start trouble."

"You beast!" Hilda lashed at him angrily. "I'll tell father—"

The Bar T foreman smirked at her. "I reckon not. He won't like it much, us catchin' you up here alone with Kirk Severn."

Kirk felt the press of her against him. She was trembling. He flicked a glance at the man with the leveled gun. There was no mercy in that hard face, the narrow-slitted eyes, the thin lips drawn back in a blood-lusting grin. He would shoot the girl down without the least compunction. He was a killer.

Sleed and Matchett were watching him closely. He sensed that their impatience was tempered by fear—fear of instant death. The man could send his bullet into the girl, but it would not save them. They would die in their saddles. Kirk read their minds, knew they dare not give the signal to the killer with the leveled gun.

The fourth man, flanking Matchett, had both hands resting on his saddle horn, in plain sight. He was taking no chances, was waiting for the right break. He was a chunky man, with slate-cold watchful eyes.

Their plight was desperate. Kirk's thoughts raced, seized and examined each possibility with lightning speed. He spoke quietly, his voice devoid of expression. "Looks like you win, Sleed."

"Now you're talkin' sense," chortled the foreman. "All right, feller, get your hands up—"

Kirk's swift, encompassing look saw a lessening of the tension that held them rigid in their saddles. For a moment, guards were down. His left arm brushed in front of the girl, swept her back so violently that she staggered and fell. Even before she struck the ground, Kirk's gun was out of its holster, pouring flame and smoke. The man with the gun pitched from his saddle, gun exploding harmlessly as he fell.

The chunky rider flanking Matchett made a grab for his gun, uttered a groan as Kirk's second bullet smashed into his chest. His horse reared, whirled and the man toppled sideways. He screamed as he hit the ground. His foot caught in the stirrup and in a moment the horse was in panic-stricken flight, the helpless man dragging and bumping at the end of the stirrup.

Kirk made no attempt to look. His gun was boring at the two men in front of him. He had never seen anything like the sheer horror that froze their faces. He said curtly, "Get your hands up—quick!"

Sleed was the first to obey. Matchett took more time. He was in the thrall of a paralyzing fear. He was shaking. His hands went up slowly, with an effort, and his lips mouthed unintelligible words.

Kirk gave them a bitter smile. He said contemptuously to Matchett, "You damn coward."

Hilda was on her feet again. There was mud on her face, on her clothes, but her eyes were brilliant in her pale face. She stood there, staring at the two men so rigid in their saddles, their hands lifted above their heads.

Kirk spoke quietly. "Take their guns, Hilda."

She started, as if his words shook her out of a dream, went slowly past him and reached up

179

and snatched the guns out of their holsters. She stepped back, a heavy Colt forty-five in each hand, and looked inquiringly at Kirk.

He spoke again. "Get down," he said.

They obeyed, wordless. Sleed's face was a mask of balked fury. Matchett was still shaking, but his mouthing lips now formed words.

"It's murder, Severn. You'll hang for this."

Kirk ignored him. There were sounds back in the junipers that interested him more. He said to Hilda, "Somebody headed this way. Take a look—"

She was already gazing off past the corral. A rider pushed into view from the trees. Hilda uttered an alarmed cry. "Dunn Harden!" she said frantically. "It's Dunn Harden coming!"

Kirk, watching the two disarmed men in front of him, saw quick relief in their eyes. His mirthless smile covered them. "Don't get your hopes up," he warned.

Hilda spoke again, excitedly, relief in her voice. "Chuck Rigg, too! A lot of men—*your* men, Kirk."

Dunn pulled his sweat-lathered horse to a plunging halt. He slid from his saddle, gave Hilda an agonized look, and jerked his gun from its holster. "Heard the shootin' when we was back of the ridge," he said to Kirk. He gave the girl another incredulous look and fastened hard eyes on Sleed.

The Bar T foreman said bitterly, "You damn sneakin' coyote! I savvy your play now."

Dunn grinned. "Looks like you run into plenty trouble, Clint."

Sleed's gaze was on the riders streaming in past the corral. One of them had Hilda's mare on a lead-rope. The Bar T foreman's look went back to Dunn. "It was a frame-up," he snarled. "You rigged that damn story just to get us up here. You figgered to ambush us."

Chuck Rigg heard him. He swung from his horse and with a brief, incredulous look at Hilda, said to Kirk, "Our timin' was sure off schedule, Kirk. These jaspers got up here awful fast." His tone was rueful. "We was waitin' at the Burro Mesa camp like we planned. Dunn come on the jump with the news that Sleed had snapped the bait like a starvin' wolf and was headed this way."

Sleed glowered at Dunn Harden. "You lyin' coyote," he said venomously. "I checked up on that horse when we passed Mat Dilley's place. He said he loaned the bronc to you, same as you told us."

"I figgered you'd do just that," grinned Dunn. "It was Kirk's idea, me footin' it in to Dilley's and getting him to loan me that roan bronc. I was sure you'd check up on me . . . figger that all the rest of the story I spilled to you was gospel true."

Sleed cursed him. Dunn threw an apprehensive glance at Hilda and stepped toward the

181

man with menacing fists. "Shut your mouth," he warned. "There's a lady here, you goddam snake!" He broke off, reddened, flung Hilda an imploring look.

"Don't mind me, Dunn." She smiled at him. "Call him all the names you can think of. I can think of a lot myself."

Several K7 riders slid from saddles and took charge of the prisoners. Chuck Rigg slanted a look at the sprawled body of the dead Bar man. "You've been right busy," he said laconically to Kirk. He scowled at Sleed. "Kind of queer he'd pull off any rough stuff with her on hand to see his play." He nodded at Hilda, curiosity in his eyes. "Did she come with 'em?"

"I did not!" Hilda's voice held a touch of defiance. "I was up here to picnic. It began to storm and Castaña got away from me." She threw the chestnut mare an indignant look. "The wretch!"

"We run into her down in Burro Cañon," Chuck said. "Headin' for the old home ranch—where she was born." He looked at the dead man. "We met up with another bronc, back in the junipers," he continued. "Was draggin' a feller."

"Dead?" Kirk's tone was indifferent.

"Won't never be more dead. Head busted open. Was dragged over the rocks, I reckon." The K7 foreman paused, added laconically, "Bullet hole in him."

Hilda shuddered and went to the chestnut mare and hid her face against the thick bright mane.

Dunn Harden's gaze followed her. His face was white and drawn. He said to Kirk, "Did you know she was up here?"

Kirk nodded. "I thought there was a chance she'd ride this way." He hesitated. "We'd been talking about a picnic."

"I savvy." Dunn scowled. "Mercedes told me she'd gone off ridin' some place." His fists clenched as he recalled the cook's sly insinuations. "Wish I'd knowed. I'd have got here some sooner."

"I'll bet you would," Kirk said. His tone was warm, sympathetic. He added softly, "Go talk to her, Dunn. She's been through a lot of hell—more than you know."

"Sure." The cowboy flicked him a grateful look and moved toward the girl. She lifted her head from Castaña's mane and gave him a tired little smile. "My legs feel like rubber," she confessed.

Kirk was watching them. He called out, "Take her into the shack, Dunn. There's some coffee in that can on the shelf."

"A right smart notion," approved Dunn. "You come along with me, Hilda. I'll fix up a pot of hot coffee."

She smiled gratefully and followed him into the cabin. Kirk returned his attention to the prisoners. His eyes were hard, full of purpose.

Chuck Rigg and the half-score K7 riders watched him in silence. They sensed an unexpected crisis.

Len Matchett also sensed that something was up. His first panic had left him. The presence of the K7 men seemed to give him courage. He was safer with them, than alone with this man who could shoot with such deadly accuracy. He said insolently, "Plenty of witnesses here, Severn. I'll have them on the stand, force them to swear that you killed two harmless men in cold blood."

"Harmless?" Kirk's smile was ironic. "Do you claim it was harmless for that man to hold a gun on Miss Taylor—threaten to kill her?"

"It was only a bluff," Sleed blustered. "Tate was just foolin'. He wouldn't have done nothin'."

Kirk's eyes scorched him. Sleed's face went ashen. He said hoarsely, "Turn us loose, Severn. You ain't got no right to hold us. We was up here lookin' for rustlers. Ain't our fault you and the girl butted into the play."

"I'll turn you loose," agreed Kirk. He was unbuckling his gun-belt. He handed it to the K7 foreman. "Hold it for me, Chuck. I've got a little bill to collect from Matchett before I turn 'em loose."

Matchett showed growing uneasiness. "You can do your talking in court, Severn," he said. "You've got to answer for the killing of these men."

"My business with you is going to be settled right now," Kirk told him. "You insulted Miss

Taylor and you're going to pay plenty." He gestured to the interested cowboys. "Give us room."

Matchett took a backward step and put up his fists. He was breathing hard, a curiously triumphant gleam in his eyes. He was a powerful man, fully as tall as Kirk and several pounds heavier. From the way he fell into a natural crouch, Kirk correctly guessed the reason for that triumphant gleam. The man was a trained boxer.

Matchett charged him, feinted with his right hand and swung a left upper-cut that just missed Kirk. Kirk grinned, smashed a right into his opponent's face. Matchett's head jerked back. Kirk followed the blow with a terrific left to the stomach. Matchett doubled up, face contorted with pain. Another blow landed flush on his nose, sent him reeling on his heels. Kirk pressed in, whipped rights and lefts to bloody face and body. Matchett whimpered, and was suddenly sprawled facedown in the mud.

Dunn Harden, startled by the commotion outside, hastily put the coffee pot down and ran to the door. Hilda overtook him. Dunn jerked at his gun, felt the girl's restraining hand on his arm.

"Don't!" she exclaimed. "He had it coming—for what he said to me."

"Huh?" The cowboy gave her an uncomprehending look. She continued to clutch his arm. "He said hateful things about me—and Kirk—because we were alone in the cabin."

Dunn suddenly saw light. He reddened, then turned pale. "I'll kill him!" he gasped.

She shook her head. "Leave it to Kirk. He's doing a good job." She suddenly shuddered, pulled the cowboy back into the cabin, and shut the door.

"You've killed him," hoarsely muttered Sleed. "My gawd, you've killed him." He gave Kirk a dazed, horrified look and licked dry lips.

"He'll come out of it," Kirk said. He wiped a cut on his cheek with his shirtsleeve. "You can go now, Sleed." He smiled bleakly at the Bar T foreman. "Next time I tell you to keep off K7 range you'll know I mean it."

Chapter XV
THE CHALLENGE

The sign drew a grin from Kirk. He reined in from the dusty street and halted under the interlacing branches of the two huge cottonwood trees in front of the big livery barn. An armchair of polished manzanita wood stood under the trees. Kirk eyed it admiringly. It was a new chair, obviously homemade by skillful hands.

From somewhere in the cavernous depths of the barn drifted the unmelodious voice of Mustang Jenns. Kirk's smile widened as he listened.

" 'Oh, boys, tell them to stop,'
That was the cry of Mari-er.
But the more she said *whoa,*
They said, 'let her go,'
And the swing went a little
bit higher."

The old horsetrader's voice died away in a grunt. He stood in the doorway, delight in his eyes as he saw Kirk. "Howdy, young feller." He jerked a thumb at the big sign over his head. "How does she look, son?" He grinned.

"A humdinger." Kirk cocked properly appreciative eyes at the two-foot red and black letters.

THE SOLEDAD FEED AND SALES STABLES
MUSTANG JENNS, PROP.

"A humdinger," Kirk repeated gravely. He chuckled, swung from his saddle. "You're telling them in a big way, Mustang."

Mustang nodded contentedly. "I figger folks is goin' to know I'm runnin' this outfit." He limped slowly to the manzanita chair and lowered himself with a grunt. "That doggone arrer wound gits to actin' up on me," he grumbled. He fished in a pocket, drew out his tobacco plug and reminiscently gnawed off a chew. "I reckon I was some lucky at that. Come awful close to losin my ha'r that time." He chuckled. "Been totin' that pesky redskin's skelp for more'n thirty years. He weren't so lucky."

His keen blue eyes studied Kirk curiously. "How's it comin', son?"

"Not so good," confided Kirk soberly. He frowned, thumbnailed a match and lit a cigarette.

"I been keepin' my ears cocked," Mustang said. "Pick up anything?"

"It's kind of scrambled," Mustang said. "Mebbe you can do some unscramblin' an' make sense of it." His voice lifted in a shout. "Pancho!"

The Mexican made a hurried appearance, gave

188

Kirk a grin of pleased recognition. Mustang gestured at the horse.

"Fix up a good feed for the bronc," he ordered. "Treat him like he was your own *muchacho*. We aim to give Kirk the best any time he hits town." Mustang grinned. "That goes for the hull doggone K7 outfit. Savvy?"

"*Sí, señor.*" Pancho treated Kirk to a broad, reassuring smile. "Señor Severn my good frien' long time."

"A good hombre," commented Mustang as the Mexican led the horse off to the barn. He gestured at a wooden bench propped against the tree. "Set yourself an' we'll palaver."

Kirk accepted the invitation, said interestedly, "That's a fine chair, Mustang. Looks comfortable enough to catnap in."

"Marier give it to me," Mustang informed him. "Made it herself. Went foragin' up in the hills for the manzanita an' fashioned it herself. Marier's awful smart," he added contentedly.

"It's sure a fine chair," admired Kirk. "How's the youngster, Mustang?"

The proprietor of the Soledad Feed and Sales Stables beamed. "That kid is sure one he-man," he chuckled. "You should orter hear him yell, Kirk. Kin make noise enough for a Comanche war party."

"Takes after his dad," smiled Kirk. His face sobered. "Can we talk here?"

"Ain't no walls 'round us for long ears to hide behind. Sure we can talk." Mustang's keen gaze raked up and down the street. "Like to set here under the tree. Kin see the hull Soledad go by . . . pick up plenty gossip, jest settin' here."

"You'll get fat and lazy, loafing in that chair," jeered Kirk.

"I aim to take life some easy," rejoined Mustang equably. "Set here an' swap lies . . . do a bit of hoss tradin' an' keep a eye on the stable hands." He grinned. "All right, son, unload what's on your mind."

He listened attentively to Kirk's story, wagged his head dubiously. "Looks like you misplayed your cards," he commented. "What fur did you frame to git Sleed up at the ol' camp?"

"The thing went off half-cock," grumbled Kirk. "We weren't expecting that Sleed would act so quickly. I was hoping that somebody else would be along with him and planned to have Chuck and the boys staked out in the junipers. I'd have gathered in plenty proof—proof we need."

Mustang was silent for a moment, jaws moving meditatively. "You mean—" He lowered his voice.

"Sleed and his gang were up there to kill Chase," Kirk went on. "The fact that Len Matchett was with them means that Warde Taylor must have been aware of their intentions. From Matchett he must have learned about the Chase girl. Matchett spoke to her in Deming. He found out from the storekeeper that they were planning to camp up in Cañon Los Diablos." Kirk leaned toward the older man. "Why is Taylor so interested in the Chase woman? Answer that one, Mustang."

"She looks so doggone like Hilda she could be her own sister," Mustang said slowly. "I told you 'bout me runnin' into her in Deming—when she showed me that pitcher of Pecos Jack." He spat out a dark stream, settled back in his chair and stared at Kirk from narrowed eyes. "Mighty cur'us bus'ness, son." His eyes suddenly widened, and he added worriedly, "Did Hilda go back to the ranch, after the ruckus up thar in the canyon?"

Kirk nodded, his expression troubled. "I couldn't stop her, not without telling her things I couldn't prove."

"Sleed will likely tell on her," mused the liveryman. "Won't listen good to her dad . . . her an' you, alone at the camp."

Kirk shook his head. "Hilda thinks Sleed will keep quiet about it. He won't want Taylor to know that he threatened to kill her."

"I wouldn't gamble on it he won't," Mustang said dubiously. He looked at Kirk worriedly. "Matchett is goin' to lay for you, him an' Sleed both. It's my notion you signed your death warrant, son."

Kirk shrugged. "I'm not worrying about myself."

"They'll lay for you in the brush—unload some lead in your back," Mustang warned.

Kirk grinned. "I'm not betting you're wrong," he said. He paused, eyes questioning the other man. "What's this scrambled gossip you mentioned?"

"Waal—" Mustang was watching a haze of dust in the road beyond the town. "Sam Gaines was over, gittin' the lowdown on my notions of runnin' a livery bus'ness. He's doggone nosey, that feller . . . loose with his tongue. Got to gabbin' 'bout Warde Taylor gittin' shot at the time he was in town for the Association meetin'." Mustang paused, looked hard at his listener. "What fur the grin?" he asked suspiciously.

Kirk's smile widened. "What did Sam tell you?"

"Weren't what he told me, so much as the *way* he told me," Mustang paused again. "Mebbe I'm wastin' my breath tellin' you," he grumbled.

"Taylor was plenty worked up about it," Kirk went on. "Something had to be done about *El Topo*. The man had dared a cold-blooded killing right in their own town." Kirk's voice hardened. "It was high time to elect a new sheriff to go after *El Topo*. Jim Shane and two of his predecessors had tried to get him and been killed for their pains."

"So he fixes on you to pick up Jim's star, huh?" rasped Mustang. He scowled, his blue eyes hard and bright.

"*El Topo* likes to kill sheriffs," Kirk said dryly.

The two men stared at each other in grim silence. Kirk was the first to speak. "I must have a talk with Mat Dilley and Rock Sledge. We can't have a man like Matchett the sheriff of Soledad."

"Taylor has them two cowmen eatin' out of his hand," Mustang declared. "Ain't much you can do with 'em, Kirk. Right now your stock don't rate good with folks, from what Sam Gaines says. Sam picks up plenty gossip at the hotel desk." Mustang broke off, gestured up the street at the rapidly approaching cloud of dust. "Looks like Taylor headin' in now from the way that buckboard's churnin' dust." He craned his neck. "Yeah, it's him, by the looks of them two fellers ridin' herd on him. Warde never goes fur without 'em."

The black Morgans whirled the glittering buckboard up the street, closely trailed by the pair of hard-faced riders.

"Don't give a damn how much dust he starts to flyin'," complained Mustang. "Sure acts like he owns the town."

To Kirk's surprise, the buckboard drew to a halt. The big, bearded cattleman peered at him, lifted a hand in recognition. "Hello, Severn. Want to talk to you."

Kirk made no move to leave the bench. "Hello, Taylor." His tone was frosty.

Warde Taylor hesitated, frowned, combed his beard thoughtfully, then with a low word to the heavily armed riders he climbed out. One of the riders slid from his saddle and followed him, watchful gaze on Kirk.

"Don't blame you for staying in the shade." Taylor's smile radiated friendliness. "Sun's hot enough to fry an egg."

"Sure is," grunted Mustang. Kirk offered no comment. He was intent on the man who had halted a few paces behind Taylor. A pair of wicked-roweled Mexican spurs dragged at his boot-heels. There was efficiency in his lean, hard body, the alert eyes that gave back a frankly hostile look. Kirk guessed he had heard of the affair in the canyon, the swift death that had overtaken two members of the Bar T outfit.

Warde Taylor rumbled on, addressing the new owner of the Soledad Feed and Sales Stables. "Handsome sign, Mustang. I'm mighty glad to have you settle down in our town. We need good citizens like you."

"*Gracias*." Mustang ejected a dark brown stream from the corner of his mouth. "I figger to run a good barn—treat my friends right."

Taylor nodded, smiled genially. "You'll maybe do some tradin', huh?"

"Always ready to dicker," Mustang answered with a dry grin. "Got somethin' to trade?"

"Huh?" Taylor's tone was vague. He was frowning slightly, his look fastened on Kirk. It was apparent that Kirk's frigid silence worried him. "I'll speak to Clint," he said. "I leave the tradin' to Clint." His rumbling voice took on a sudden crispness. "That was bad business yesterday, Severn. I'm eternally grateful for what you did for my girl."

"She told you?" Kirk's tone was cautious.

"A damnable outrage," continued Taylor. "It was lucky Clint and Len Matchett turned up in time to take a hand." He paused, added gruffly, "I called the sheriff in to help Clint catch a rustler, one of *El Topo's* gang. They picked up his trail in Cañon Los Diablos."

Kirk managed to hide his astonishment. He nodded, waited in silence for Taylor to continue.

"Clint didn't want to follow the trail into the canyon," Taylor went on. "He said you'd warned him to keep off K7 range. Matchett was bound to go. He's the sheriff—the Law. He'd a right to go any place on law business." The cattleman was watching Kirk intently. "You know the rest of it. I don't need to tell you."

"Two of your men were killed," Kirk said. "Yes, it was bad business, Taylor."

"That's right." Taylor spoke angrily. "It's evident that *El Topo's* gang is using your old line camp as a hidcout." He shook his massive head. "God knows what might have happencd to my little girl if you hadn't turned up. As it was, things would have been worse if Clint and Matchett hadn't come along to drive the scoundrels away."

Kirk studied him curiously. It was possible that Sleed and Matchett had concealed the facts from Taylor. It was more probable that he knew the truth of the affair, and for some reason was pretending ignorance. He wanted Kirk to believe that he was not personally involved. He said cautiously, "I hope Hilda is none the worse for it."

"She's all right," Taylor assured him. "Nervous shock, of course. She's quite repentant for disobeying my wishes." The cattleman smiled thinly. "She knows I don't like her riding alone so far from the ranch. Not with *El Topo's* desperados on the loose."

Kirk said bluntly, "We'd planned a picnic—"

"She told me." Taylor fingered his beard, gave him a frosty look. "Len Matchett didn't get off so easy," he went on. "Got his face cut on the rocks when his horse threw him."

"I saw the accident," Kirk said laconically. The corners of his mouth twitched.

"He's in bad shape, went back to his ranch to lay up for a few days." Taylor shook his head gravely. "Nose broken, one of his eyes closed tight and a two-inch gash under the other. Some of his teeth knocked loose. I've never seen a man so messed up."

"Soledad sheriffs seem to have a rough time," Kirk drawled.

Taylor frowned, stared at him suspiciously. "It ain't funny," he snapped.

"You should know." Kirk's voice hardened. "At that, Len Matchett is no friend of mine. As a member of the Stockmen's Association, he doesn't get my vote for sheriff."

"Len is a friend of *mine*." Taylor's shaggy brows lowered ominously. "I have vouched for him, his honesty and courage. Be careful, young man. Your word doesn't go far against mine."

"Is that a challenge?" drawled Kirk.

The big cattleman glowered, fingers combing his beard. He met Mustang's quizzical look, frowned. He said in a surprisingly quiet voice, "I've known you since you were a youngster, Kirk . . . knew your father when he was running the K7. He was a friend of mine. I don't understand your antagonism."

"Think it over," Kirk said bleakly.

There was no geniality left in Taylor, no pretence of friendliness. His eyes went cold, wary. "I will." His voice was a deep-throated growl. "In the meantime—keep away from my girl." He swung on his heel. "Come on, Fargo," he said to the silently attentive man at his back.

The two under the cottonwood watched the buckboard rattle up the street. Mustang was the first to speak. "Mind your step, son," he said solemnly. "That buzzard figgers to lift your ha'r when you ain't lookin'."

Kirk nodded, said thoughtfully, "He's scared, Mustang."

"All the worser for you," warned the old man. "A cornered wolf gits pizen mean."

"You called him a buzzard just now," grinned Kirk.

Mustang chuckled. "When I don't like a hombre, I ain't choosy in the names I call him." He spat contemptuously. "Come to think on it, I'd say Warde Taylor has the instincts of a pizen sidewinder." He leaned back in the manzanita chair, hat tipped over half-closed eyes. "His talk didn't fool you none."

"He knows exactly what happened up in Cañon Los Diablos," Kirk said. "He wants me to believe that he knows only what he's been told by Sleed and Matchett."

"Playin' innercent, huh? The mangy coyote!" Mustang's narrow-slitted eyes gleamed angrily. "Do you figger he knows that Sleed was all set to kill the gal?"

"I'm certain of it," Kirk said. He shook his head gloomily. "I wish Hilda were a long way from there. I don't like it."

"Taylor knowed you was there, saw the hull play," mused the liveryman. He straightened up, stared fixedly at the younger man. "Him wantin' folks to think he don't know what went on up in the canyon sure proves you're on the right trail. You're readin' sign on him, and the doggone old wolf is scared, like you say." Mustang reached in his pocket, agitatedly gnawed off a chew of tobacco.

"It's a long trail," Kirk said soberly. "A lot of

198

years have traveled it . . . makes it hard to read sign."

"You've got the mind for it, son," encouraged the old man. "You're doin' fine. I seen the look he give you. He's all set to stampede." Mustang paused, added grimly, "Mind he don't stampede right over you. You'll be a hunk of buzzard's meat."

"*Gracias* for the tip." Kirk got to his feet. "I'll push along. Want to see Doc Williams."

"I was fixin' to have you over to the house," protested Mustang. "Marier has 'em all beat when it comes to fryin' a steak." He grinned, added shyly, "Kind of wanted you to see the boy."

"Some other day," promised Kirk. "I've got to see the doc for a minute, then I'm heading for Mesquite Springs to meet Dunn Harden. He's on a scout for me." His eyes twinkled. "We'll put that boy of yours on the payroll when he's big enough to sit a saddle, Mustang. We'll make a cowman out of him."

"The kid's goin' to collidge," declared Mustang. "He's goin' to have a bang-up eddication." He nodded solemnly. "He'll likely grow to be president—same as the other George Washington feller."

"*Quien sabe?*" Kirk chuckled. "He can have my vote right now."

Chapter XVI

DUNN HARDEN BRINGS NEWS

The doctor was climbing from his dusty buckboard when Kirk reached the neat brick and adobe house set back on the bank of the creek that skirted the town. He gave Kirk a wary look.

"Don't get scared," chuckled Kirk. "I'm not sending you on another fifty-mile trip."

"Wild horses couldn't drag me away from home right now," asserted the doctor with considerable vehemence. "I'm worn out, Kirk. Serves me right for being a country doctor." He tugged off his long dust-coat and tossed it to the old Mexican who gave it a shake and placed it on the seat of the buckboard.

"You wouldn't be anything else," Kirk said. "You don't fool me, Doc. If I told you that Chuck Rigg was laid up with a broken leg you'd climb right back into your rig and make dust for the ranch."

Doctor Williams attempted a ferocious scowl. He gave up, smiled instead. It was a warming smile that illuminated his tired face. His keen eyes probed the younger man. "You didn't come here just to show me up. What's on your mind?"

"Need medical advice," Kirk answered.

"Nonsense! You're the picture of health. Not an ache in your body by the look of you."

"It's for Chase. He's full of aches." Kirk shrugged. "Nerves all shot to pieces."

The doctor considered a moment. "I'll make up a prescription for him. Won't take five minutes." He shook his head ruefully. "I'll drop over tomorrow and look him over."

"*Gracias.*" Kirk followed the doctor up the porch steps where Señora Valdez greeted them with a protesting outburst at Kirk.

"He does not go out again," she said in Spanish. "No—not if every man in your outfit is dying. Have some pity for the man. He wears himself out, saving your worthless lives."

"Be quiet," reproved the doctor. "You will ruin my practice." He chuckled, trotted into the office.

The señora glared at Kirk. He said solemnly, "It's a mighty good thing the doc has you to look after him, señora."

"His heart is too big," she declared. "The work he does for poor ones who cannot pay and never will." An affectionate smile softened her lips. "I would not have him different."

"You won't," Kirk assured her.

Señora Valdez smiled, nodded, and bustled off to the kitchen. Kirk went into the office and stood watching while the doctor counted little brown pills into a bottle.

"Just got in from the Bar T," the doctor said as he pasted a label on the bottle. "Nasty accident . . . a man thrown from his horse and dragged. Never saw such a messed-up face."

"The Bar T?" Kirk arched his brows.

Doctor Williams nodded. "You know the man. Len Matchett." He frowned, shook his head. "His nose will never be quite the same."

"You mean you've been out to the Walking M, don't you?" asked Kirk.

"I mean nothing of the kind," snapped the doctor. "I said the Bar T—the Taylor ranch."

"My mistake," Kirk murmured. "Naturally, I thought you meant Matchett's ranch." His thoughts raced, tried to find an answer to Warde Taylor's statement that Matchett had returned to his own ranch. Only one fact was clear. Taylor had deliberately lied.

Doctor Williams broke into his reflections. "The directions are on the bottle," he said. "The pills will quieten his nerves. I'll be out tomorrow," he added.

"Thanks, Doc." Kirk went down the porch steps, hardly aware of the doctor's parting words. The news that Soledad's sheriff-elect was at the Taylor ranch disturbed him. It was also a bit of useful information that called for certain changes in his plans.

He closed the gate and stood for a moment, absorbed with his thoughts, then turned into the path that led through the crowding junipers to the town almost a quarter of a mile away. His alertness was temporarily at low ebb, or he would have noticed the sudden agitation of the brush rabbit as it scurried across the trail a hundred paces ahead.

He moved along with lagging steps, eyes moodily downcast, oblivious of the sign that ordinarily would have challenged his caution. It was the faint crackle of brush that warned him. He reacted automatically, flung himself sideways in a leap that landed him sprawling behind a buckthorn. He heard the spat of a bullet, the sharp bark of a Colt forty-five.

Stillness settled down. Kirk held his breath, cautiously pulled his gun from its holster. His assailant was somewhere in the bend of the trail less than twenty yards distant. He would be uncertain as to the result of his shot. Kirk's plunging fall had the look of a suddenly stricken man.

Using infinite stealth, he crawled deeper into the brush and flattened behind a jutting upthrust of rock. Still no sound came from down the trail. He lifted his head, glimpsed a shape, the glint of sunlight on metal. With lightning speed he flung two shots.

He peered through drifting gun-smoke, heard the crackle of brush, the quick pound of running feet as the man fled. It was obvious he was not caring to shoot it out in the open. His attempt at murder had failed and he was in a hurry to remove himself from the scene.

Kirk resisted the impulse to follow in pursuit. It was likely he would run into another ambush.

He finally went back to the trail, eyes alert now, searching for possible clues to his attacker's identity. He reached the spot where he had glimpsed the lurking shape, the glint of sunlight on metal.

The ground was still wet from the previous day's thunder shower. Kirk studied the imprints left by the man's boots. The tracks made when he fled almost paralleled the incoming impressions. Kirk guessed he had made for a concealed horse.

His surmise was immediately confirmed by the sound of receding hoofbeats that drifted up through the junipers. Whoever he was, the man was in full flight. It was equally apparent that he was anxious not to be seen, which indicated he was some person who knew that to be seen was to be recognized.

Kirk gazed around disappointedly. One thing was a certainty. His bullets had gone wild. There were no evidences of a wound, no trail of blood. Only the deep imprints of boot-heels made when the man fled.

Something that sent back a dull gleam suddenly caught his questing eyes. A piece of metal, caught in a thornbush as if flung there by a careless hand.

Kirk hurriedly retrieved it, turned it over in his fingers curiously. He was at a loss for a moment. It was a broken piece of plated silver from which protruded two blunt spikes.

A picture took shape in his mind as he stood there, frowning gaze on his find. The lean-faced man who had waited during the conversation under Mustang's cottonwood tree in front of the livery barn. The efficient look of him had drawn Kirk's attention. He had been wearing a pair of silver-mounted Mexican spurs. Warde Taylor had spoken his name. *Fargo*.

Enlightenment filled Kirk's eyes. The fragment in his fingers was a bit of rowel broken from a spur. He had not missed both his shots. One bullet had struck the man's spur and hurled the torn fragment of rowel into the thornbush.

He slowly pushed the broken rowel deep into a pocket. His eyes were hard, angry. The attack on him was no longer a mystery. Warde Taylor had set a hired killer on him, proof that the cattleman was growing panicky. Taylor's failure to get his hands on the girl who so startlingly resembled Hilda was a threat to his own safety.

Bit by bit the pieces were falling into place, forming a picture that sent a chill through Kirk. They were bloodstained pieces, stamped with inhuman cruelty and ruthless purpose.

He moved along the trail, eyes wary, hand

on gun-butt. Esther Chase held a key. She was unaware that the faded daguerreotype which she treasured, and which she had shown to Mustang Jenns, could unlock the door behind which lurked the secret of twenty dark years.

Kirk came to a standstill, his thoughts seizing fiercely on Len Matchett, his part in the mystery. The man's close friendship with Warde Taylor was suspicious. Len Matchett, too, had a reason for wanting to destroy Esther Chase and her archaeologist husband. He also held a key that could open the door to those closely guarded years.

Grim purpose took shape in Kirk's mind as he pondered about Len Matchett. His eyes gleamed. The owner of Walking M was still at the Taylor ranch, resting his wounds, lolling in fancied security—perhaps attempting to make love to Hilda. The last thought put bleakness into Kirk's face.

He turned into Soledad's one dusty street. The customary Saturday crowd jammed the side-walks. Sunburned ranchers, with their women and children; lean-hipped cowboys and burly miners; trim cavalrymen from the fort; sun-dried, bewhiskered prospectors and freighters; an impassive Navajo, trailed by his squaw.

Kirk passed the hotel. Warde Taylor's buckboard had been there an hour earlier. It was gone. The drift of dust beyond the town told Kirk the cattleman had left in a hurry.

He turned into the store. Mott Balen saw him. "A couple of letters for you, Kirk," he greeted, and went inside the wire cage on which a sign read, U.S. POST OFFICE.

He fumbled the letters from a pigeonhole and pushed them through the wicket. "How's things at the ranch, Kirk?" His eyes were brightly inquisitive behind steel-rimmed glasses.

"Fine, Mott. No complaints." Kirk wondered how much the long-necked storekeeper knew about the affair in the canyon.

Balen leaned toward him, his voice lowered confidentially. "There's talk goin' 'round that Taylor claims you're hidin' out a cow thief."

"Who told you?" demanded Kirk.

"Sam Gaines. He picks up a lot of news when he's clerkin' nights at the hotel desk. Sam says he heard that Mat Dilley and some fellers are some worked up about it." The storekeeper hesitated. "I thought I'd tip you off, Kirk. From what Sam says, it looks like they plan to make a personal call out to K7 most any time."

"It's all right with me," grinned Kirk. "Thanks for the tip. I'll fix up a barbecue." He thought for a moment. "Give me a couple of stamped envelopes, Mott."

The postmaster reached inside a drawer. "You don't seem much worried," he commented. He dropped the coin Kirk handed him into the drawer. "It's serious business, Kirk."

207

"I'm not worried." Kirk made his way to the door, pausing several times to greet friends he recognized among the customers lined up at the long counters piled with assorted merchandise. He caught sight of Mat Dilley. The choleric little cowman gave him a blank stare and turned his back.

His smile a trifle bitter, Kirk continued down the street toward the livery barn.

The sun was low when he reached Mesquite Springs. A voice hailed him guardedly from somewhere inside the dense mass of the mesquite. Kirk rode around the thickly clustered branches and came to a small, tunnel-like opening. He got down from his saddle and led the horse under the prickly thatch.

Indians, and later, desert prospectors, had used the place for years because of the several little springs of cool water hidden under the spreading tangle of branches. Usage had in time made a clearing around the huge gnarled bole, a sanctuary in a storm, a hiding-place, a camp for the wearied and thirsting traveler.

Dunn Harden sat on his heels near his horse. He was munching a meat sandwich, slowly, as if without relish, and his eyes were troubled.

Kirk dropped the bridle reins and bent down for the dipper some long-gone prospector had fashioned from a tin can. He filled it at the little pool and drank thirstily. The horse took a few steps, lowered his head to the overflow and supped with noisy mouthings of the bit.

Kirk sank on his heels opposite the cowboy. He said softly, "Well—"

Dunn leaned toward him. "We've got to get her away from there." He spoke in a curiously tight voice, the words hard as bullets. "No tellin' what will happen if we don't get her away fast."

"What did you find out?"

"Plenty," answered Dunn. "She's a prisoner, locked in her room."

"How do you know she's a prisoner?" asked Kirk.

"It's like this," Dunn went on, "I hit the ranch about an hour before sunup. Still plenty dark. There's an arroyo that cuts across the horse pasture back of the barn. I staked my bronc down there in the brush and found me a nice place to hide where my ears would do me the most good."

"Where is this place?" Kirk's eyes narrowed thoughtfully.

"You know the fancy ranch-office Taylor fixed up?"

Kirk nodded. "What about it?"

"There's a cellar underneath. I reckon Taylor had some notion of usin' it for a likker cellar when he had the hole dug and lined with adobe brick." Dunn's grin was rueful. "He must have changed his mind. Wasn't nothin' but cobwebs in that cellar. I should know, after layin' there for most four hours."

"How did you get in?"

Kirk's interest in the cellar drew a sharp glance from the cowboy. "Figgerin' to use it?" His tone was dubious.

"It's a useful thing to know about," Kirk said.

"I'm goin' along with you," Dunn said vehemently. He glowered, then, "The office backs up close to the patio wall. There's mebbe a couple of feet between it and the wall, all kind of closed in with grapevine branches that have climbed over. I squeezed in through the brush tangle to a window that sets near the ground. Ain't no glass, just boards nailed up. The nails was loose and it wasn't no trick to pry the boards out. I slid down into the cellar quick as a shake of a dogie's tail."

"You took a long chance," Kirk commented.

"Only chance there was to pick up some news about Hilda," Dunn said with a shrug. "I figgered right at that. Clint and Taylor showed up in about an hour. There's a trapdoor in the floor . . . it don't fit close, and I was able to hear most of their talk. Taylor cussed Clint plenty for messin' the play up in the canyon—gave him hell. Clint talked back. I reckon from what he said he's got something on Taylor."

Dunn paused, his eyes grim. "One thing is mighty sure. The both of 'em is scared. They figger there's plenty trouble on the prod if they don't fix you pronto."

Kirk gestured impatiently. "What about Hilda?"

"Wasn't much talk about her. I heard Clint tell Taylor he was scared she'd make trouble on account of the way she felt about you." Dunn stared gloomily at his dozing horse, went on with an effort, "Clint said she—she was in love with you."

Kirk reached out, gripped the cowboy's hand. "*Gracias*, Dunn." His tone was warm. "Hilda thinks the world of you. She talks about you a lot, says you've been the one man on Bar T she could trust."

Dunn's head lifted in a look that was a mingling of pride and bitterness. "Ain't nothin' I wouldn't do for her," he said in a low voice. "You know that, Kirk."

"She knows it too," Kirk told him.

"We've got to get her away awful quick," Dunn went on. "Taylor told Clint he needn't worry, said he was keeping her locked up in her room and that Mercedes was watchin' her. Old Pete, too. He's got Pete staked outside her window. She's a prisoner, all right." He gestured impotently. "We're wastin' time, settin' here."

"Let's have the rest of it," urged Kirk. "Doc Williams told me that Len Matchett is there."

"Len is laid up in the house," Dunn confirmed. He grinned. "You sure beat him up good, Kirk. Taylor was talkin' about him, said he was

211

sending for the doc to come and fix him up. Didn't hear much more, only that Taylor was headin' for town. He told Clint to stick close to the house and make sure Hilda didn't get away." The cowboy scowled. "I sure hated to leave her there—all alone. Wasn't nothin' I could do—not in broad daylight."

"You'd have only got yourself killed," Kirk said.

"Wouldn't mind that, if it would help her," muttered Dunn. He questioned the older man with hot, impatient eyes. "What do you figger to do, Kirk?"

"I'm heading for Bar T now," Kirk answered.

"*Bueno.* Let's get goin'." Dunn was on his feet, hard, lean body tense with excitement.

Kirk shook his head. "You have another job to do."

Disappointment and anger darkened the cowboy's face. Kirk gave him no time to speak. "You're starting out for Deming, with a couple of telegrams I want put on the wire. I'd planned to write, but things are moving too fast." He fished out the two envelopes he had bought from Mott Balen and hastily scribbled a message on the back of each. "It's important, Dunn, or I wouldn't ask you."

Dunn took the envelopes and read the messages. They were both addressed to United States Marshal Holden.

Dunn's gaze lifted in a surprised look. "Goin' to the same feller, but one says Santa Fe and the other says Albuquerque. How come?"

"Holden told me to try both places if I needed him in a hurry," Kirk explained.

"I savvy." Dunn folded the envelopes and tucked them in a pocket. He looked at his friend resentfully. "You're the boss, but I ain't ever took on a job I like less. The trail don't head in the right direction—for *me*."

"You'll be doing Hilda a service," Kirk said soberly. "More than you know."

The cowboy's gloom lifted, but he was still dubious. "You'll run into plenty trouble," he said. "You know Clint Sleed. He's tough as they come. I don't figger how you can get Hilda away from there by your lonesome."

Kirk made no comment. He turned to his horse. "Let's go," he said.

Chapter XVII
THE PRISONER

Hilda stood at her bedroom window, a pale slim shape in the veiling gray mantle of early dawn. The chill air bit through the thin nightdress, drew a little shiver from her. She had slept badly, her thoughts a maddening maelstrom of conflicting hopes and fears. She was glad enough to leave her bed and run to the beckoning pale fingers at the window.

She found hope in the pink flush that slowly stained the dark saw-toothed peaks. She was always stirred by the coming of dawn to the desert. Never the same—always a thrill.

Vague thoughts crystallized into steely determination as she watched the swiftly spreading splendor of the sun's rising. She became fiercely aware of what she must do.

She bathed and dressed in feverish haste. Warde Taylor had always been generous, gone out of his way to give her the best. His pride in her material comforts was enormous. No other girl in the Soledad had a real bathroom all to herself. The great bed, in which she had tossed through the long, dark night, had come from Mexico City. She had always loved her bedroom, its rich beauty. At this moment she felt a dread of it. She knew only one thing. She must get away.

She pulled on the brown pigskin boots made for her by a skilled craftsman of Santa Fe, tugged her white Stetson over warm chestnut hair and reached the silver-buckled gunbelt from its peg. Something was wrong with the gunbelt. The thirty-two was not in its holster.

She stared at the belt dangling from her hand, a startled, incredulous look in her eyes. She could have sworn the gun was in the holster when she hooked the belt on the peg the night before.

She was bewildered, vaguely frightened. There could be only one explanation. Somebody had been in her room during the night—had stolen her gun.

The thought sent a hot wave of anger through her. She buckled on the belt, picked up her quirt, and went to the door. The knob turned, but the door did not open at her pull. It was stuck. She gave it a harder tug, was suddenly aware of a surging panic, an impulse to scream. The door was locked.

She fought off the panic, the impulse to scream; grew angry instead. She stepped back from the door, forced herself to think the thing out. Her gun had been stolen, surreptitiously removed, her door locked on the outside. Only one person in the house could possibly be responsible. *Her own father.*

The thought chilled her, but did not lessen her mounting anger, her indignation, her determination to immediately leave the house. She went swiftly to the window. She could climb down from the little balcony. There were vines, strong enough to support her.

Her first look warned her there could be no escape by way of the window. A man leaned against a tree down in the garden. Pete, and there was a knowing grin on his face when he caught sight of her.

Hilda drew back. The glimpse of the choreman made her feel a bit giddy. She actually was a prisoner. She was not having a bad dream. Her gun really had been removed, her door really was locked, and it really was Pete down in the garden, stationed there to prevent her escape by way of the window.

She went unsteadily to a chair. Her legs felt oddly weak. She sat there, struggling for composure. She had never been so frightened.

Footsteps approached the door. Her father's heavy tread. Hilda heard the rasp of the key in the lock. The door opened, revealed Warde Taylor.

He came in, closed the door, stood looking at her, fingers combing his great beard. "Well, daughter," he said. His voice was a kindly rumble, his smile affectionate. His eyes, though, were cold, sharply scrutinizing. "Were you planning to ride so early?"

Hilda gazed at him. She said unsmilingly, "Why am I locked up in my own room? Who stole my gun? Why is Pete down there, watching my window?"

Warde Taylor rocked gently on his heels, his smile still urbane, kindly. "Come, come," he said. "So many questions all at once!"

"Answer me," she flared.

"It's for your own good," he said. "After what happened yesterday I am reluctant for you to continue this undesirable friendship with Kirk Severn."

Hilda only looked at him, her mouth hard and angry.

Taylor continued in the same restrained voice, "You might have come to serious harm. It is fortunate that Clint and Len Matchett arrived in time."

Hilda spoke desperately, "They have been telling you lies!" She sprang to her feet, faced him with clenched hands. "Clint Sleed threatened to kill me. Len Matchett wouldn't have stopped him."

Taylor shook his head sadly. "You must be out of your mind, daughter."

She brushed his words aside with an angry gesture. "If harm had come to me it wouldn't have been from Kirk Severn. Kirk saved me from harm." She paused, added more quietly, "Kirk said you sent them to murder friends of his."

"Dangerous rustlers, my dear," corrected Taylor.

217

His smile was thinning, his voice harder. "I sent the sheriff to arrest them."

Hilda shook her head. "I don't know what it all means. Only that you hate Kirk Severn."

He was studying her intently. "Have you seen these people he calls his friends?"

"No." Hilda kept her voice steady. "I want my gun back. I'm going out of this room. I'm going over to Kirk's place and ask him what you have against him."

Taylor shook his head slowly. "I think not, daughter."

Hilda said furiously, "Let me pass!"

He pointed at the chair. "Sit down!"

His tone terrified her. She slowly obeyed, fixed wide eyes on him.

"I want you to answer a few questions," Taylor continued. "Has Severn talked to you about this woman?"

Hilda shook her head, said helplessly, "I don't understand."

"The woman Severn has been hiding out in Cañon Los Diablos." Taylor's eyes probed her suspiciously. "Don't lie to me."

"I don't know what you are talking about. Kirk has not mentioned any woman. He only spoke of friends. He didn't say who they were—only friends."

Her complete bewilderment, her growing agitation, seemed to satisfy him. He nodded slowly.

"Naturally he wouldn't talk about her to *you*. He wouldn't want you to know about this woman."

The sneering implication drew no retort from her. She gazed at him, wordless, a curious horror in her eyes.

"You see—" Taylor's smile was unpleasant, "it is very necessary for me to protect you from this unscrupulous man, even if it means locking you up in your own room, placing a guard under your window."

Hilda found her tongue. "I don't believe what you are trying to make me believe." The words came stumblingly from stiff lips. "I—I'll *never* believe anything like that about Kirk."

"That is unfortunate." Taylor fingered his beard reflectively. "It forces me to send you away for a few weeks."

"You—you wouldn't!" she exclaimed frantically.

"A little trip to a place in Mexico." Taylor's eyes glinted wickedly. "An interesting old *pueblo*—where I have good friends who will be glad to look after my daughter."

Hilda was conscious of terrifying thoughts as she looked at him. This big, benevolent father was suddenly a stranger, a harsh, sinister man she had never seen before. She stared at him dumbly.

He turned to the door. "I'll send Mercedes up with your breakfast."

She heard the rasp of the key turning in lock,

his footsteps, fading down the hall, and then another sound—the quick beat of her own heart. It disturbed her, made her think of a frightened animal caught in a trap.

She jumped from the chair and went to the window. The choreman sent up another of his unpleasant grins. The sight of him enraged her. She moved to one side, out of his range, and looked despairingly at the distant saw-toothed ridge of hills. Kirk's ranch was somewhere over there. He would have no way of knowing of her dreadful predicament.

Her mind began to clear and she found herself thinking of her father, coolly, dispassionately, seeing him for the first time as perhaps Kirk Severn saw him. It came as a shock for her to realize that she had never felt any deep affection for him. He had always been generous to her, never spared expense for clothes, schools, all the things a normal, healthy-minded girl demanded from life. She had responded dutifully, given him what she had thought was real affection. She knew now that her feelings toward him were not the feelings of a daughter for her father. There always had been an indefinable chasm between them. She could find no explanation that would explain. The knowledge of such a chasm had been more in her consciousness of late. She was no longer a child. She saw things as a woman and instinctively sensed that her father was not the genial, benevolent cattleman he pretended to be. There was something sinister about the ranch, about all the men on the payroll. Excepting of course, Dunn Harden. She believed she understood why Dunn had stayed on. Dunn was in love with her. She was sorry for that, but grateful in a way for his nearness.

A sickening loneliness waved over Hilda as she thought of Dunn. He was gone now—had thrown in his lot with Kirk. She was entirely alone, helpless to protest against her father's plan to send her below the border—to this unnamed hamlet in Mexico.

The prospect appalled her, grew all the more horrifying as she recalled the look in her father's eyes. She had gazed for a moment into the blackness of a pit, a slimy sink of infamy.

Her heart thumped maddeningly. She felt as if her head would burst. She wanted to cry out that it was all a hideous lie and that she was quite mad to have such terrible thoughts about her father. But she knew with sickening sureness that she was not mad—that she had seen beneath the mask—seen a thing unspeakably vile.

The key again rasped in the lock. Mercedes came in with a tray. Hilda glimpsed the shape of a man lurking in the hall. She was to have no chance to force her way past the Mexican woman.

Mercedes placed the tray on a table. She said

to Hilda's stiff back, *"Buenos dias, señorita."* There was a touch of mockery in her voice.

Hilda refused to look at her. Mercedes laughed softly. The door closed behind her, the key clicked in the lock. Hilda slowly turned and stared at the tray. Fruit, ham and eggs, delicate biscuit—fragrant coffee. Mercedes was an excellent cook, but the best breakfast on earth could not at that moment have tempted the girl to eat.

Anger filled her eyes. She wanted relief in action. She *must* do something to express herself. With a fierce little gesture she picked up the loaded tray and went to the window. Pete was still loafing down by the tree, his attention momentarily occupied with a plug of tobacco he was shaving with a knife.

Hilda leaned out with the tray, flung it with a wild swing at the unsuspecting choreman. His outraged yell was the first incident of the morning that brought a smile to her lips. She watched with grave satisfaction while the cursing choreman wiped ham and eggs and coffee from his face, felt the bump on his head.

"You wait till yore dad gits back from town," he shouted furiously. "He'll fix you for what you done."

Hilda drew back from the window. So her father had gone to Soledad. The knowledge gave her some relief. She was not to be immediately hurried across the border. The day was still young, and it was in her mind that Kirk Severn was not forgetting her.

Kirk was a comforting thought. His quiet efficiency, his unfaltering courage. He had not wanted her to return to the ranch. She had thought at the time that his fears were due to a possible unpleasant scene between herself and Warde Taylor because of the meeting in the canyon. She had told Clint Sleed she was at the cabin to picnic with Kirk. Her father was certain to be furious with her. She knew now that Kirk's reluctance had deeper roots. There were things that Kirk knew, or suspected about her father, things that mysteriously concerned her, threatened her.

It was a thought that fanned the embers of her courage, gave her fresh hope. The cheering fact that Kirk *knew*.

She moved about the room, restless, her mind seething with plans. She must use her wits—be ready when the time came. She would leave in the clothes she wore—take nothing with her.

Hilda came to a standstill. There was *one* thing she would take. Not even her father had a greater right to it.

She went swiftly to a massive chest of drawers, a hand-carved Spanish piece from Santa Fe. She sank on her knees, pulled open the lower drawer and took out a small box of hammered Navajo silver.

Her hands trembled as she opened the lid and lifted out a tissue-wrapped object. She carefully undid the soft paper and gazed for a long time at the disclosed faded daguerreotype.

The mother she had never known, who had not lived to hold her baby in her arms.

Hilda blinked suddenly wet eyes. She would take the little picture with her. She had found it in an old trunk years earlier when she was a child. The picture had fascinated her and her father had good-naturedly told her she could keep it for her own. "A picture of your mother," Warde Taylor had said. "She died when you were born." He had never spoken of it again, never asked what she had done with it, had apparently forgotten its existence. Years later, when at school in Santa Fe, she had seen the Navajo silver box in a shop window. The box was just the little shrine she wanted for the picture.

She replaced the box in the chest and got to her feet. She was reluctant to leave it behind, but she must. It was too awkward to carry. She must take nothing that would hamper escape when Kirk Severn came for her. Perhaps she was crazy, holding to the thought that Kirk would come for her. She resolutely pushed the doubt away. He *would* come. She knew him too well to doubt.

She carefully rewrapped the daguerreotype in the tissue paper, and after some deliberation found needle and thread and sewed a little pocket inside her blouse. It made a safe hiding place for the picture. The feel of it against her breast cheered her.

With her rise in spirits she became acutely aware of a clamoring appetite. She was in a mood now to relish the good food so angrily tossed out of the window. She made a little grimace. The memory of the choreman's egg-smeared face was worth the loss of her breakfast.

The hours dragged, heartless, torturing, never-ending. Hilda could hardly hold her impatience in check. She wanted to scream at the man lounging under her window, wanted to pound on the door with her fists. She knew that to give way to hysteria was a waste of strength. She must conserve her strength, keep her mind cool—*be ready.*

Mercedes brought in another tray. Soup, a steak and fried potatoes, pie and coffee. The cook gave the girl a resentful look as she placed the tray on the table.

"Pete ees mad as hell," she said. "The coffee pot made hees head hurt."

"He shouldn't have been standing under my window," smiled Hilda.

"Throwing away my good food," grumbled the cook in Spanish. "I would let you starve, but the señor told me to feed you." She slammed out of the room.

Hilda looked at the loaded tray with sudden

distaste. The shadow of the man lurking in the hall had done something to her appetite. She felt miserably helpless—afraid.

She scolded herself. It was no time to give way to nerves. *I'm a little fool . . . frightened of shadows . . . a child in the dark.* But the shadows were very real, and the hours so long—so dark with unknown terrors to come.

She forced herself to eat; valiantly swallowed the steak and potatoes and pie, drank the coffee, and felt the better for the effort.

She lay down on the bed. The strain of the long morning had wearied her. She felt completely undone.

It was with some amazement that she found twilight creeping into the room when she awoke. She must have slept for hours.

She sprang from the bed and ran to the window, looked down at the long, crawling shadows of the trees. Another man had taken Pete's place, a quick glance told her.

She went to the mirror and passed the comb hurriedly through her tumbled curls. The sleep had refreshed her, relaxed tense nerves. She was conscious of excitement tingling through her. Things were going to happen. *Kirk Severn— deliverance. Time wouldn't wait on her much longer.*

Footsteps approached the door. The key rasped and Warde Taylor stood in the entrance. There was no smile on his face. He seemed terrifyingly enormous, standing there in the vague evening light, his big white hat pulled low over his eyes, fingers slowly combing his great beard.

He was silent for a long moment, cold eyes appraising her. He said in his rumbling voice, "You'll do as you are. Don't need to change your clothes."

Hilda found her voice. "What do you mean?"

"You are starting for the border tonight," he answered. "It's a long ride. That man's rig you've got on will be fine."

Her heart sank. *"Tonight?"*

"Yes," Taylor said curtly. "Tonight." He turned away, glanced back at her white face. "Bundle some clothes into a bag. I'll have 'em loaded on a packhorse." The door closed behind him, the key clicked.

Hilda stood transfixed, the heart within her like a cold stone. *Tonight.* The word beat at her ears like the roaring of great seas. *Tonight . . . tonight.* There was to be no escape . . . no Kirk Severn.

Chapter XVIII
THE BLACK NIGHT

Kirk got down from his saddle and tied the horse to a scrubby oak that leaned from the crevice of a split boulder. He recognized the place from Dunn's description. The scrub oak, the big split boulder, the concealing growth of thornbush. He was in the loop of the arroyo where it thrust within fifty yards of the corrals.

Climbing the steep slope was slow work. Heavy clouds blanketed the stars and he had to feel his way through an inky blackness. Despite his caution he bumped into something that clattered. Startled snorts told him he had reached the gate of the horse corral in the rear of the barn.

The gate was the hingeless affair common on ranches. Two posts held it in place at either end, with a chain hooked around one end, securing it to the posts.

The invitation was irresistible. Kirk unhooked the chain, quietly slid the gate back a few inches and dragged it wide open. A horse drifted up, a vague shape in the darkness. More shapes crowded in and with a flurry of heels the first horse tore into the pasture. In another moment the score or more horses poured out of the corral, stampeded with thundering hoofs into the night.

Kirk began to half regret his impulse to open the gate. Turning the horses loose was a sound idea, would put his enemies on foot. However, the sudden uproar in the corral was sure to result in unpleasant complications.

A shout from somewhere in the big yard told him that his fears were realized. He heard the quick pounding of booted feet, glimpsed a man's shape. There was a brief silence, broken by a loud, heartfelt curse.

"Hell! The cavvy's bust out!"

More shouts drifted up from the bunkhouse. Kirk heard the door slam open, the hurrying stamp of running feet. He started to sidle along the split-rail fence, halted as he heard the first man's voice.

"That you, Pete?"

Kirk realized he had been seen. He answered in a muffled voice, "Sure . . . Heard 'em stampedin' . . . Got here too late."

"Looks like some damn fool left the chain unhooked," grumbled the man. "You git a bronc from the barn, Pete. There'll be hell to pay if we don't git that cavvy back in the corral awful quick."

"Sure," mumbled Kirk. He slid along the fence and found the rear door to the stable. He went inside. His lips were set in a hard smile. Luck was still with him. He would do the job right.

He made out the shapes of three horses in the

long line of stalls. One of them wore a saddle. It was often customary to keep a horse saddled, ready for an emergency.

The rising clamor of excited voices in the yard warned him that the moments were few. He slipped the tie-ropes and led the horses outside through the door that opened directly into the big pasture.

He turned them loose with a slap on each flank that sent them off in a dead run. In another moment they were lost in the night's blanketing darkness.

A man shouted as the hoofbeats faded into the distance. "Pete's hightailin' it after 'em!"

Kirk grinned, went stealthily around the side of the barn. He heard another voice, suspicious, uneasy. "Seems like it was more'n one bronc headin' out of the stable."

There followed a brief silence, then the first man's voice. "Pete was standin' over by the gate when I got here. I yelled for him to git the cavvy horse an' go chase the bunch."

Another voice broke in wrathfully: "You're a doggone liar, Fargo. I weren't 'round here no place when the bunch bust out of the corral."

Pete's announcement seemed to have the effect of a bombshell. There was a shocked silence, and then Fargo's worried voice, "If it weren't Pete, who was the feller standin' there? He sure made out he was Pete when I yelled to him."

"It weren't me," heatedly denied the choreman.

"I was back at the house when we heard the bunch stampedin' from the corral. You ask Mercedes."

Kirk found a niche between two haywagons drawn side by side near the barn. He crouched against the wheels, strained eyes and ears. He could see the glimmer of lamplight from the house set back in the trees. Another light came winking up the yard. The man carrying the lantern called out sharply, and Kirk recognized the harsh voice of Clint Sleed.

"What's goin' on here?" bawled the foreman.

Fargo answered him. "We ain't knowin' for sure. Pete claims it weren't him I seen—"

"You bet yore boots it weren't me!" howled the choreman. "You ask Mercedes, ask Clint. He was leavin' the kitchen when I went in with the milk pans."

"Sure I seen you," confirmed Sleed. He came to a standstill, stood there, tall and lean and rigid in the circle of lantern light, head craned forward. "Who in hell turned the cavvy loose?" he stormed.

Fargo gave him the scanty details. "I figgered somethin' was wrong when I heard the bunch stampedin'. Come on the run and seen a feller over by the gate. He let on he was Pete and I told him to fork a bronc and ride hell-for-leather." Fargo hesitated. "Looks like the feller weren't Pete," he finished lamely. "I couldn't see good in the dark."

"You're doggone tootin'!" yelped the choreman.

"Shut up!" rasped Sleed. He glared at Fargo. "Well—what happened when you told this feller to go round up the cavvy?"

There was a dead silence, broken by a malicious guffaw from the choreman. "I reckon the feller done what Fargo told him," Peter chortled. "He sure lit a shuck away from the barn."

An oath exploded from Sleed. "I'm takin' a look," he said, and started on the run toward the barn door. The lantern swung in his hand, made dancing shapes of the men surging at his heels.

Kirk was moving the instant they disappeared inside the stables. Angry shouts told him the loss of the horses had been quickly discovered. He did not linger to hear more and a few moments brought him to the narrow passage between the ranch-office and the patio fence.

Lamplight glowed in a lone window set high in the wall. The window was open. Kirk abandoned his plan to get down into the cellar. He could hear—and with caution, he could see into the room.

He pressed close to the wall and peered inside. Warde Taylor was in his big chair, impatient gaze on the open door. Len Matchett occupied another chair, long legs sprawled, a dejected look on his bandaged face. His head lifted in a resentful look at his glowering companion. "You're not using good sense," he said irritably. "You're letting Kirk Severn stampede you."

"I know what I'm doing," rumbled Taylor.

"Sending Hilda off to Agua Frio is crazy business. She can't do us any harm."

"Listen," Taylor spoke harshly. "Hilda is smart. She'd do some thinking—once she meets that Chase woman."

"How do you know they haven't met already?" queried Matchett.

"They haven't." Taylor's tone was confident. "Hilda doesn't know a thing about the Chase woman. I've talked with her enough to know that Severn hasn't told her."

Matchett's hand went to a bottle on the table. He filled a glass, emptied it with a single gulp. He put the glass down, said sneeringly, "You're too damn scared of Severn. How is he going to get at Hilda with the bad news? She's locked up in her room . . . can't get away—and he can't get her away."

"I know Kirk Severn," retorted Taylor. He fastened cold eyes on the younger man. "He did plenty to you."

"I'll do worse to him." Matchett refilled his glass.

"You'll get yourself drunk," remonstrated Taylor.

Matchett's swollen lips twisted in a mirthless smile. He lifted the glass. "Here's to Kirk Severn," he said. "May the buzzards soon pick his bones." He tossed the liquor down and replaced the glass on the table. "I'm heading for town tonight," he announced. "I'm swearing in a posse." He touched the star pinned to his shirt. "Sheriff Matchett will pay a call at K7 with a warrant for the arrest of Kirk Severn. There will be an accident—the prisoner killed on the way to jail while attempting an escape."

Warde Taylor shook his head. "You're riding tonight, Len," he said, "but you won't be going to Soledad. You're heading for the border, for Agua Frio, you and Hilda."

Matchett scowled, drummed fingers on the table. "I'm all set to get Severn," he objected.

"I've other plans," smiled Taylor. "We won't want the Law with us when we pay our call on Kirk Severn."

"He claims I'm not a sure-enough sheriff—yet," smiled Matchett. "I'd like to show him a thing or two."

"The Association voted you in," reminded Taylor. "What the Association says is law in the Soledad." He paused, added significantly, "I've been talking to Mat Dilley and Rock Sledge. They've got it into their heads that Severn is *El Topo*. They won't want the sheriff with them when they go out to K7."

Matchett swore softly, admiringly. "You've got the brains of the devil," he said.

"Mat plans to have quite a crowd along," continued Taylor. "Those cottonwood trees Kirk's dad planted will have dead men dangling from them when Mat Dilley's crowd is done with the business." The big man leaned back in his chair, fingers playing with his beard. "Kirk Severn's own fault. He's smelling at my heels too close. This Chase woman was all he needed to clinch the thing."

"What about Hilda?" The purr in Matchett's voice put a red mist in the eyes of the man crouched outside the open window.

"I'm not caring any more," Taylor said. "She will never be the same again. I could see the distrust, the growing hate in her when I told her she was to go to Agua Frio."

There was a brief silence, broken by Matchett, the same wicked purr in his voice, "You mean—"

"What happens to her is up to you," Taylor said bluntly. "I'm not taking any more risks. I was a fool not to have got rid of her long ago. The idea seemed good at the time—made a good story." He laughed gratingly. "My little motherless child."

"You're a devil," Matchett said again. His good eye gleamed. "I'll tame her. She'll mind her manners with me. I'll halter-break her." He laughed softly. "I need a new woman out at Walking M."

Taylor frowned. "I won't have her back in the Soledad," he said. "Anywhere else you like, but not on this side of the border."

"That's all right with me," smiled the younger man. "I'll make a Mexican out of her."

Kirk's hand fastened hard on the butt of his gun. He saw the two men through a red mist. It would be easy to kill them as they sat there, so callously deciding Hilda's fate. He resisted the impulse. Gunshots would bring Sleed and his pack on the run. His own death would leave the girl helpless in their hands. Her life—and more, was in his keeping.

He drew back from the window. Immediate action was imperative. Hilda was a prisoner in the house—in her own room. He had to get her away and do it under their noses.

Hurried footsteps, the slam of the office door, drew his eyes back to the window. Sleed stood framed in the doorway. He gave the others a furious look. "There's a feller 'round some place," he said harshly. "He sneaked in and turned the cavvy loose—got the broncs away from the barn."

"You'll probably find our caller wears the name of Kirk Severn," rumbled Taylor. His eyes took on an angry glint. "I warned you. I told you to watch out for him—his tricks."

The foreman snarled an oath, snatched the bottle and tilted it to his lips. "We're left afoot," he grumbled, slamming the bottle down. "The boys is combin' the pasture now, but it's dark as hell's backyard and nothin' save their own laigs to use. No tellin' how long it's goin' to take 'em— roundin' up the cavvy."

"It's going to take not more than half an hour,"

Taylor said coldly. "Len is starting for Agua Frio with the girl. Fargo will go with them. That means three horses, and a pack animal for the girl's clothes. I told her she could take some clothes."

"We can mebbe round up that many inside of half an hour," conceded Sleed grumpily. He scowled. "What about this feller that's prowlin' 'round?"

"No chance for him to get to the girl," reassured Taylor. "I've seen to that, Clint."

"You cain't gamble on what Kirk Severn will do," Sleed pointed out. "Look at what he's done to us inside of a week. Pedro Negro, Rincon, Tate. Three of our best gunslingers sent to hell on a shutter."

Taylor started to speak, lifted a warning hand instead. Kirk, crouched close to the window, heard the quick pad of sandaled feet, caught a glimpse of a buxom Mexican woman hesitating in the doorway.

Warde Taylor looked at her inquiringly. "What is it, Mercedes?"

"Señor— thees paper—" The woman moved swiftly to the desk and placed a scrap of brown wrapping paper in front of the rancher.

Taylor stared down at it. His face showed no expression. He said in a curiously quiet voice, "All right. I'll attend to it."

The woman turned away, gave Sleed an enigmatic look as she passed him. Kirk heard the quick beat of her sandaled feet as she fled back to the house.

The scrap of paper intrigued his interest. A message about Hilda . . . an attempt to escape . . . perhaps a demand to see Taylor.

He continued to watch, saw Taylor hand the piece of paper to Sleed. The foreman glanced at it, gave Taylor a startled look.

"You go attend to it," Taylor said curtly. His eyes held the foreman's, seemed to compel his silence. Sleed was breathing hard. His look strayed to the whiskey bottle, jerked away. "Sure," he said, "sure—you bet." His voice was little more than a strangled whisper, drew a puzzled stare from Matchett.

"You're wasting time," Taylor said irritably.

"Sure—I'll—I'll fix it." Sleed swung on his heel and plunged through the door.

Matchett arched inquisitive brows at the big man behind the desk. "What's the matter with him? He's foaming at the mouth."

Taylor ignored the remark. He slid a drawer open and took out a cigar box. "Have one," he invited, and pushed the box across the desk. His hand drew back and rested casually on the edge of the open drawer, and his fingers slowly tightened over the butt of a Colt forty-five that lay inside.

Kirk was suddenly acutely aware of danger. He could not see the gun in the desk drawer. Nor did Taylor's face betray any emotion. It was the

immobility of the man, his unmistakable tens
ness. Something to do with the Mexican woman's
scrap of brown paper. She had discovered his
presence outside the window—had warned Taylor.

Cold prickles chased up and down Kirk's spine.
He moved past the window and on through the
blackness of the runway. A faint sound drew
him to an abrupt standstill. The crackle of a dry
vine leaf underfoot. He was being stalked, was
already trapped in the narrow runway between
the building and the high patio wall.

He sharpened his eyes against the darkness.
No way over the wall, with its mass of climbing
grape vines. He would be hopelessly entangled,
helpless to put up a fight. It was either go back
the way he had come, or go forward. The warning
rustle of the leaf had come from behind. He had
no alternative. He must go forward, chance what
might come at the far end.

He was within three feet of the corner, moving
with the noiseless stealth of a creeping shadow.
He halted, strained his ears for some betraying
sound, a man's breathing, the stir of hand or foot.

Reassured by the continued stillness he slid
from the passage. Something loomed in the
darkness ahead. A big cottonwood tree. Its
branches reached over the patio wall. Kirk
measured the distance, ran on swift, soundless
feet and came under the widespreading limbs.

The branch that reached over the wall was a

good foot above his grasp. It meant using both hands. He holstered his gun and stooped for the upward spring that would gain him a hand-hold.

Something hard suddenly jabbed his back, held him rigid in that half crouch. A voice said gloatingly in his ear, "Easy, mister, or you won't *never* raise up."

Kirk fought off the nausea that waved over him. He turned his head cautiously in a look at the shape standing close to his shoulder. He said laconically, "Careful with that gun, Sam."

"It's you that's got to be careful," Sam Gaines answered. "Don't you git me narvous, feller. Right now my trigger finger is some jumpy."

Kirk felt a hand slide down his side, the tug of his forty-five as it was jerked from its holster. Sam spoke again, his voice loud. "I've got him, Clint."

Sleed's tall shape materialized from the runway. He came close to Kirk, peered at him. "Keep your gun on him, Sam," he said. His hand closed over Kirk's collar and jerked him upright.

Kirk made no attempt to resist. He could feel the foreman's seething malevolence, a searing, murderous rage. Resistance was worse than useless, would sever the thin lifeline that meant safety for Hilda Taylor. He had to keep his wits, fight these men with all the courage he could rally. Each moment gained was a precious thing, to be cherished, nurtured into the time he must have.

Chapter XIX
LA TOPERA

The Bar T foreman wasted no time with words. He gestured with his gun. Kirk said, "Sure," and moved leisurely toward the glow of lamplight that lay on the ground in front of the ranch-office door.

Warde Taylor watched in grim silence as the three men filed into the room. Len Matchett stirred restlessly in his chair, leaned forward, hand tight on the butt of his gun.

Kirk's eyes took them in with a careless glance, remained fixed on Taylor. He said nonchalantly, "Some little surprise party, Taylor."

The big cattleman studied him curiously, almost admiringly. "You came to see Hilda?" There was a hint of irony in his voice.

"I won't say your guess is wrong." Kirk grinned, fished tobacco sack and papers from his pocket. "Not the first time I've come to see Hilda."

"It's the last time," Taylor said balefully. "I don't approve of my daughter's friendship with you."

"I'm not easily discouraged," Kirk said smilingly. "Have a heart, Taylor."

Matchett half rose from his chair, a murderous

glint in his one good eye. "No sense wasting time with him," he said furiously.

Taylor flapped a hand at him. "Sit down!"

Matchett slumped back in his chair. "I say let's get done with him," he muttered.

"Len's talking good sense," urged Sleed. "This feller is awful tricky. We should fix him pronto."

"I boss this outfit," rumbled Taylor. He fingered his beard thoughtfully. "You boys are too crude. We have got to benefit by Severn's death."

Kirk managed to hang on to his careless smile. "Thanks for the compliment, Taylor." He forced an amused laugh. "You mark me up high."

Taylor looked at him with cold, unwinking eyes. "You are the one man in the Soledad who can do me harm." His smile was unpleasantly significant. "I want to explode this *El Topo* myth even more than you do. In fact, Severn, by eliminating you, I can also eliminate this troublesome *El Topo*. Soledad County will owe me a vote of thanks for unmasking the scoundrel."

Kirk held on to himself with difficulty. He grinned, said lightly, "You'll be sitting pretty, Taylor. The past a closed chapter, yourself the great cattle king, rich and respected."

Taylor nodded assent. "You put it well, Severn." His tone was bland. "It is the goal I have in mind, in fact a goal already achieved until you started smelling around, unfortunately for yourself. You should have minded your own business, young man."

"I suppose you will even acquire my K7 ranch when the *El Topo* myth is destroyed," Kirk said good-naturedly.

"It is possible," coolly admitted Taylor. He combed his beard with hooked fingers and turned an inquiring look on Sam Gaines.

"It was like this," Sam began, "I trailed him clean over to Mesquite Springs. Dunn Harden was thar, and they had a powwow. I couldn't git close enough to hear their palaver. They come out of the old mesquite and Dunn lit away from thar on the jump. You told me to stick to Kirk, which same I done." Sam shook his head. "Wasn't easy. Couldn't take chances on him spottin' me. Soon as I knowed he was headed for Bar T, I struck out on my own. Got here too late to stop him from stampedin' the horse herd."

Taylor nodded, transferred his gaze to Kirk. "Where did you leave your horse?" he asked.

Kirk shrugged. "Does it matter?"

Taylor's eyes interrogated Sleed. The foreman shook his head. "Some place down in the barranca," he guessed. "Come mornin', I'll send Pete down there for a look. Too dark now to spot anythin' in that brush tangle." He gave Kirk an ugly look. "Don't matter a damn where the bronc is hid. We've got the rider and got him good."

"That's right," Taylor agreed. He stared gloomily

at Kirk. "Where was Dunn Harden going when he left you at the Springs?"

"You know Dunn," smiled Kirk. "He doesn't talk much about his plans."

"I'll make *you* talk." Taylor's bearded face was a black, threatening mask.

"You'll have to find Dunn and ask him," Kirk rejoined.

Sleed took a step toward him, fist clenched. A voice said from the doorway, "We got most a dozen broncs back in the corral, Clint." The speaker stepped in from the night, muttered a startled oath when he saw Kirk. "Hell!" he exploded. "So it was *you,* huh?"

Kirk looked him up and down, his eyes hard, unsmiling. "Hello, Fargo." His fingers fumbled in a pocket, drew out a shiny bit of metal. "Found this in the brush where you took that shot at me this morning." He tossed it at the man. "I'm afraid my own shot ruined your Mexican spur."

Fargo scowled, toed at the piece of broken rowel and flung Taylor a nervous glance. The cattleman wagged his head reprovingly at Kirk. "You make a dangerous accusation, young man."

"It's a true one," retorted Kirk.

Taylor regarded him intently, his expression sinister. "No use in our pretending," he said. "You know too much, Severn. I don't know how much you heard just now, listening at the window. The fact that you came here is enough for me. It is your life, or mine." His glance flickered at the intent faces. "The same goes for all the men on Bar T's payroll. Not one of us can afford to let you live."

"Now you're talkin'," muttered Sleed.

Taylor's bearded face moved in an impatient look at the foreman. "That's right," he said heavily. "I'm talking—and that means you keep your mouth shut."

Sleed's face paled. He shuffled his feet, mumbled uneasily, "Sure, boss, but I got a stake in this."

"You bungle things," accused Taylor. "Look how you let the Chase woman slip through your fingers."

"That's why I aim to lift Severn's skelp," sullenly defended the foreman. "I'd have got her if he hadn't butted into the play."

"He won't do any more butting in," promised Taylor. His lowering gaze fixed meditatively on Kirk. "Lock him up," he added, and he got heavily out of his chair. "I'm to see Mat Dilley tonight. I want you along, Clint."

The foreman looked rebellious. "Ain't you goin' to swing him *now?*" He gestured fiercely at Kirk.

"No." Taylor spoke irritably. "I know what I'm doing, Clint." He gave Kirk a mirthless smile. "A lot of good cowmen in the Soledad will want to pull on the rope that swings *El Topo*. We mustn't disappoint them."

Sleed was unconvinced. "I'm scared of him," he frankly admitted. "He's too damn tricky. No tellin' what will happen. I'd ruther we dangle him here and now."

Taylor stood there, massive, dominant, his bearded face darkening with mounting anger. "He can't get away, trussed hand and foot, locked inside adobe walls, armed men watching him." He spoke impatiently. "Get a move on, Clint. You, too, Len. You know my plans—my orders."

"I'm supposed to be the sheriff of this county," sneered Matchett. "Severn is my lawful prisoner, and you send me across the border with the girl."

"My plans for Severn don't include the Law," coldly replied Taylor. "Don't argue, Len." He took his white hat from the desk and pulled it over his thick thatch of grizzled hair. "You're going with Len," he said to Fargo.

Fargo nodded, said tersely, "I'll go throw on the saddles." He disappeared through the door.

Despite his outward nonchalance, Kirk was acutely aware of a sickening despair. Hilda was being hurried away, and he was powerless to save her. Warde Taylor had said he never wanted to see her again. Her fate was in Matchett's hands, a fate too dreadful to contemplate.

His careless smile gone, his face an expressionless mask, he obeyed the gesture of Sleed's gun and stepped outside. The lantern in Sam's hand made grotesque shapes of them as they moved through the darkness.

They came to a small squat building. Sam pulled the door open and went inside with the lantern. Kirk followed, Sleed's gun prodding his back.

The two Bar T men went to work with the swift efficiency of experienced cowmen. In a few moments Kirk was stretched out on the hard mud floor, his hands lashed behind his back, his ankles securely roped.

Sleed looked down at him, a grin of satisfaction on his hard face. "I reckon you'll keep," he said. "I'd ruther dangle you, but the boss figgers to wait some longer." His foot lifted, smashed viciously against the prisoner's ribs. "I'm sendin' Slim over to help you keep the skunk from bustin' loose," he said to Sam. His tall, angular frame slid into the darkness outside the door.

Sam Gaines pulled the door shut and sat on his heels against the adobe wall. The glow from the lantern made an evil gargoyle of his leathery face in the surrounding darkness of the old granary.

"Waal, Kirk—" He spat out a stream of tobacco juice and pulled a whiskey flask from a hip pocket. "I reckon I'm due to be fired from your payroll, huh?" He tittered, tipped the flask to his lips. "I like to have split my sides laughin' at the way I fooled you."

Kirk was not listening. His mind was on other

things. *He had to escape . . . save Hilda. They were hurrying her across the border.*

Sam droned on, gloating, jeering, malicious. Kirk was suddenly listening. He twisted over on his side, gazed hard on the wicked old face framed in the lantern's glow against the darkness.

"I could have talked plenty any time I wanted," boasted the man. He leered at the prisoner. "Wasn't wantin' to dangle on a tree. Sure would have dangled if I'd talked. Wouldn't have dangled by my lonesome nuther. Would have been plenty others keepin' me comp'ny if I'd talked." He tipped the flask to his lips, let the liquor gurgle down his throat. "Most gone," he grumbled. He held the flask to the lantern's light, shook it regretfully.

Kirk spoke softly. "Why would anybody want to hang you, Sam?"

Sam leaned toward him. He was quite drunk, his tongue thick. "You doggone fool! Ain't you got any savvy?"

Something Warde Taylor had said took shape in Kirk's mind. *The same goes for all the men on Bar T's payroll. Not one of us can afford to let you live.*

The answer to the mystery of *La Topera* was in those words. *Bar T was La Topera*—the Mole Hole—long-sought-for secret hideout of the dread bandit who for so many years had scourged the Soledad.

The thought sent a thrill through Kirk. He said quietly, "Sure, I savvy, Sam. You mean this place is *La Topera*."

Sam leered drunkenly, tipped the flask again, held it out to the light. "She's *all* gone," he hiccoughed.

"You can get another," suggested Kirk. "Taylor has plenty of the stuff."

Sam focused drunken eyes on him. "Mercedes won't stand for it," he mumbled. "She's pizen ornery."

Kirk studied him. Sam was the weak link in the chain that held him a helpless prisoner. He spoke again. "I could do with a drink myself, Sam."

"Ain't got no likker." Sam glowered. "Wouldn't waste it on you if I had. You'll be dead awful soon, feller. Jest as soon as the boss gits back here with Mat Dilley's vigilantes." The thought seemed to restore his drunken good humor. "Mat has raised him a vigilantes gang. He's got it figgered you're *El Topo*." Sam broke off, eyed the empty flask. "I should have fetched me a full quart along," he mourned. "I wasn't knowin' that Clint would set me to ridin' herd on you." He hurled the bottle at the wall. It shattered into fragments.

"I can't run away," Kirk pointed out. "You go get another bottle—a couple of bottles."

"Mercedes will tell me to go to hell," grumbled Sam. "She won't listen to nothin'."

"She'll listen to money," Kirk said.

"Sure," jeered Sam. "Where at is money?" He scowled. "I'm broke."

"I'm not broke," Kirk said. "Reach inside my pocket, Sam."

"You got *dinero* on you?" Sam's voice took on new hope. "Doggone me for a fool maverick. I should orter have figgered that one my own self." A wide grin split his face. "How much you got on you, Kirk?" He stood up, an ugly gleam in his eyes.

"Enough to fix Mercedes," replied Kirk. "A couple of ten-dollar gold pieces in the bag you'll find inside my coat."

Sam rocked drunkenly on his heels. "Mister," he said solemnly, "me an' you is due for a wet night. Doggone if I ain't kind of sorry you'll soon be buzzard's meat." He moved closer.

Kirk's long, hard body tensed. As Sam bent over him on unsteady, wide-apart feet, he drew in his legs with lightning speed, swivelled on his back and shot his bound feet under Sam's crotch. His knees arched up with an impact that hurtled the unsuspecting man in a forward plunge that crashed him headlong against the opposite wall. There was a groan, then silence.

Kirk twisted over on his side for a look. Sam lay sprawled against the wall. He was unconscious. Kirk wasted no time. He rolled over, squirmed close to the senseless man. He wanted Sam's gun.

He wriggled into position, fumbled for a moment with his bound hands and eased the gun from its holster.

For a long minute he lay motionless, his back against Sam, the gun pressed hard against Sam's body. He had taken the first trick but was short of an ace for the next play. And the violence of his attack, his initial success, had left him a bit dizzy.

He had to do something, and quickly, before Sam recovered consciousness. His desperately searching eyes saw the fragments of Sam's whiskey bottle. He studied the possibilities they offered. If he could get the jagged piece of bottleneck under his bound wrists he might be able to cut through the tough cord. He abandoned the idea as too dangerous. The fragment of glass would slip, slash his wrists instead of the cord.

A faint groan from Sam sent a chill of apprehension through him. Sam was regaining his senses dangerously fast.

Kirk kept the gun pressed against the man's side. For the moment he was safe. He could keep Sam helpless under the threat of the gun.

The thought brought no cheer to him. Holding Sam a prisoner would not help his own escape. He could not force Sam to cut the rope that bound his wrists behind his back. Once Sam was beyond range of the gun, had moved behind on the pretense of loosing the rope, he could easily snatch the gun from Kirk's grasp.

There was one possible solution, a hundred-to-one chance, a chance he must take. He lifted his bound hands until he felt the gun sink into Sam's big, soft paunch. With an effort he craned his head until he could see the man's face and waited tensely for the first moment of returning consciousness.

A minute passed, two minutes. Sam's eyes fluttered open, stared vacantly at nothing. Kirk spoke softly, "Don't move, Sam. I'll blow your guts out." He emphasized the warning with a hard prod of the gun into the soft belly.

Sam made no attempt to move. His eyes widened in a dazed sidewise look. Kirk spoke again. "I'll kill you, Sam, if you move, or try to yell."

"I ain't movin'," Sam said in a faint whisper. "Don't you squeeze that trigger—"

"It depends on you," Kirk said. "You'll be an awful mess if I empty this gun into you."

"You're holdin' the aces, all four of 'em," Sam groaned. "What do you want me to do, Kirk?"

"Raise up easy," Kirk instructed. "Very slow, Sam, and mind you don't touch the gun, try to grab it. I'll spill your guts the instant I feel your hand on the gun. You savvy?"

"I savvy," grunted Sam.

"All right." Kirk's voice was hard steel,

menacing, deadly. "Raise up, not too high, just enough to let you untie the rope. Keep your fingers away from the gun, or I'll kill you."

"I feel awful sick," Sam muttered. "I ain't in no shape to lock horns with you . . . I ain't touchin' that gun an' have you spill my guts."

He lifted his head with an effort. Kirk saw that he was still groggy, his wits befuddled, submissive to the domination of his prisoner's coolly functioning mind. He felt the touch of fingers on the knotted rope.

"Careful," he warned.

"My fingers is awful shaky," muttered Sam. "Don't go to squeezin' that trigger—" His whisper was hoarse with apprehension.

Kirk felt the rope loosen, drop from his chafed wrists. He rolled over in a lightning move, pulled his legs clear and faced Sam, gun in freed hand. "Now my ankles," he said.

Sam went to work on the knots. He seemed forever about it. Kirk's impatience mounted to fever heat. His eyes were on Sam, his ears intent on things outside; men's voices, hurrying booted feet, the stamp of shod hoofs. He knew what it all meant. Len Matchett and Fargo were making ready for the journey that was to take Hilda Taylor to unthinkable horrors below the border.

Sam slipped the last knot. Kirk was on his feet in an instant. Any moment might bring the man

Sleed was sending to help Sam keep vigil on the prisoner.

"Get down," he said to Sam, "flat on your face." He snatched the tie-ropes from the floor.

"I'm awful sick," complained Sam. "Ain't no sense tyin' me up, Kirk."

Kirk was in no mood for temporizing. Hilda's life was at stake. He could feel no mercy, no pity for Sam. He swung the gun barrel against the man's head. Sam's knees buckled. Kirk grabbed him, eased his fall.

Footsteps approached the door. Kirk dragged the stunned man closer to the near wall where he could not be immediately seen.

The latch lifted, the door swung open, and the newcomer stepped inside. Kirk, crouched close to the door, reached out and jerked him forward. His gun barrel lifted and crashed against the bewildered man's temple.

In another moment, Kirk had the door pulled shut. He hoped fervently the brief episode had not been seen by anybody in the yard. He listened for a moment. The outside night was quiet again. Apparently Matchett and Fargo had left with the girl. And Warde Taylor was leaving immediately for Mat Dilley's ranch and taking Sleed with him. Or perhaps they were already gone.

Reassured, he went to work on the two unconscious men. The newcomer was a lean little man with prominent buck teeth and a broken nose. Kirk had never seen him before.

There were two guns in the belt that Kirk took from him and buckled around his own waist. They were beautifully balanced guns and spoke eloquently of the man's profession. He was a killer, a far more dangerous opponent than old Sam.

Using the two ropes, Kirk quickly tied the man's hands and feet, finishing the job with a gag he fashioned from his bandanna. He became aware of fierce beady eyes staring up at him as he jerked the last knot tight.

Kirk turned from him. The hate in those eyes made him a bit sick. The margin of safety had been scant, a matter of moments.

Sam Gaines was still unconscious. Blood trickled down the side of his face. Kirk could summon no pity. The man was a vicious old scoundrel with a whiskey-sodden body and a soul steeped in infamy.

Kirk found more pieces of rope and tied him up, using Sam's soiled handkerchief for a gag. He was not at all sure that Sam would ever regain consciousness. It was possible he had struck harder than necessary, considering Sam's collision with the adobe wall.

Kirk left him without regrets and paused at the door for a backward look at his two victims. The lantern still burned on the upended box. He would leave it burning. The light would indicate that all continued well if any chance eyes looked that way.

He pushed the door open cautiously and peered into the yard. The coast was clear. He stepped outside and shut the door. A big padlock hung open in the iron hasp. He slid the bar, snapped the padlock and took the key.

Lamplight glowed in the bunkhouse windows, winked from the big house set back in the trees. Kirk stood debating his next move. He dared not leave without first making certain that Hilda was no longer in the house.

The moon was up, made a silver rift in the clouds. He slid into the deeper shadows of the corral and crossed over swiftly to the opposite fence. The threat of a clearing sky, the revealing moonlight, worried him. He was anxious to put distance between himself and the place he now knew was *La Topera.*

He climbed the fence and worked his way cautiously through the tangle of brush that skirted the garden in the rear of the house.

No lights showed from the upstairs windows. Kirk halted under the dense shadow of an umbrella tree and carefully scrutinized the dark windows that opened on a small balcony. Hilda's room, the only one on that side of the house that possessed a balcony.

He was reasonably certain the girl was gone.

The dark windows confirmed his belief—almost. He had to be more than reasonably certain. He must know for a fact that she was no longer a prisoner in her room.

He crept closer to the house, toward the kitchen where lamplight glowed in the windows. Voices reached him, the laugh of a woman.

Kirk slipped across the path and crouched under one of the windows. It was open, and the woman was talking in Spanish. Her words held Kirk rooted.

"She won't be the fine señorita in that place," exulted Mercedes. "You should have seen her face when they took her away, Miguel. She looked like pale death."

"Señor Matchett has all the good luck," grumbled Miguel. "She is pretty enough for any man's fancy—that one."

"She'll be less than trash when Matchett is done with her," sneered the woman.

Kirk waited to hear no more. He sped into the brush, a fast-moving shape in the quickening light of the moon. A wordless prayer was in him as he ran. He prayed that his horse would be waiting for him down in the hidden depths of the barranca.

Chapter XX
A VOICE IN THE CHAPARRAL

They rode single file through a monotony of sagebrush that moved endlessly to meet them from the dark horizon of the night.

Hilda had abandoned all hope of escape. Len Matchett had her mare on a lead-rope, and trailing them with the packhorse was Fargo, watchful of her every movement. Not that he had any need to watch her. They had tied her feet to the stirrups.

She drew a feeble spark of comfort from the chestnut mare under her. Castaña was a link that held her to Kirk Severn, a link worn ominously thin, but still holding her to Kirk. She clung to the thought.

The moon broke through the clouds, threw a filigree of shifting lights and shadows across the landscape. Hilda caught a glimpse of low hills that vanished as clouds again veiled the moon. The clouds lost the conflict, and the hills reappeared, dark and sinister and threatening.

Hilda gazed at them, conscious of a sickening dread. She heard Len Matchett's voice and drew the mare to a standstill. Matchett climbed from his saddle and came to her side. She stared mutely down at his upturned bandaged face.

"That's Mexico over there," he said with a gesture at the hills.

"Yes," Hilda said. She drew a sharp breath that was almost a sob. "Don't—don't make me go—there."

His one good eye took on a sardonic glint. "Your father is bossing this show," he rejoined.

"You can turn me loose," she begged. "He needn't know."

Matchett shook his head. "Won't do you any good," he said. "You won't find Kirk Severn. He'll be dead before sunrise."

She cried frantically, "*Dead?* Oh, *no*—"

"He was fool enough to come to the ranch," Matchett said. "We grabbed him. He's done for, Hilda. He's the one man in the world your father fears. He's got to die." Matchett paused, added softly, "Your father is afraid of you, too. That is why he doesn't want you back in the Soledad—ever."

Hilda was not surprised. She had read the truth in Warde Taylor's eyes. He hated her because she loved Kirk Severn.

"What are you going to do with me?" She kept her voice steady. "Murder me, too?"

"You're too pretty," Matchett said.

"You beast!" Hilda said.

"I've a *rancho* below the border, about fifty miles from here," Matchett went on. "Not a bad place, Hilda. You'll have servants, plenty of

259

pretty clothes—and you'll have me for a master."

She stared down at his upturned face, her eyes scornful. "You mean I'm to be your—slave?"

"My sweetheart," Matchett replied with a short laugh.

"You beast!" Hilda said again.

"I'll tame you," smiled the man.

Fargo drew alongside, the packhorse on a lead-rope. He eased himself in his saddle, grinned at the girl. "I reckon we're close to that spring," he said to Matchett.

"Fine," Matchett said. "We ought to rest a bit before we start into the hills. Can you locate the spring, Fargo?"

"Sure. Stopped there plenty times." Fargo passed them with the packhorse. Hilda's gaze followed them. The first sickening wave of horror had left her. She had to keep her wits, fight these ruthless men with the best she had. She was surprised at her own coolness, her clear, swift-moving thoughts.

She sighed plaintively, put a tremulous smile on her lips as she looked at Matchett. "Won't you untie the ropes? They're cutting my ankles—hurting me."

Matchett hesitated. "It won't be for long," he objected. "You can stand it."

Hilda leaned down to him, her face close to his. "I'm sorry I was mean to you," she said softly.

"I'm not really blaming you, Len, for what father makes you do."

He stared at her, silent, suspicious.

Hilda desperately forced herself to another lie. "I think that being your—your sweetheart will be—nice, Len." Her hand touched his cheek lightly. "Your poor face . . . I'm so sorry—"

Matchett seized her hand, held it tight. She could have screamed. She continued to smile instead. He said thickly, "You should have talked that way sooner—and married me, Hilda. You could have lived the life of a queen at the ranch."

"Is it too late?" Her eyes entreated him.

"Too late," he answered. "Your father doesn't trust you. Too much is at stake."

"I don't understand," Hilda complained. "What is it he fears? What harm can I do him?"

"He thinks Kirk Severn has talked to you."

"Kirk never told me anything," Hilda denied. She thought miserably, *If he only had.* Her voice purposely shrill, she added, "Father should have trusted me. After all, I *am* his daughter."

Matchett studied her with an intentness that made her wonder. "You are either a good actress, or a liar," he said.

She looked at him helplessly. "I don't understand, and I think you're unkind. My ankles are hurting dreadfully."

Fargo's voice reached to them across the

moon-misted sagebrush. "Spring is over here, Len. Plenty of water."

"Be right there," Matchett called. He turned to his horse and eased into his saddle. "I'll take the ropes off at the spring," he said to Hilda.

They moved off the trail, the girl's mare following on the lead-rope. Hilda felt herself go limp. It seemed she was to win the first round. She wondered dully how far she could go. She could only wait, and pray that her courage be equal to whatever came. She *must* escape— make her way back to the ranch before it was too late—before they killed Kirk Severn.

Fargo was building a small brush fire near the spring. He called out without looking up, "I'll fix a pot of cawfee, Len."

Matchett said, "That's fine." He got down from his horse and went to the girl and slipped the ropes from her ankles.

Hilda slid awkwardly from the saddle. "I'm stiff," she complained. She took a few hobbling steps, bent down and began rubbing her ankles.

Matchett watched her. "Stick close," he warned.

"I can't get very far on foot," Hilda pointed out. "I've got to walk around, get the stiffness out of my legs."

"Don't get out of sight," Matchett said. He gestured at an old mesquite some fifty yards beyond the spring. "Keep this side of that mesquite." He led his horse and the mare to the spring.

Fargo had his fire blazing briskly. He went to the packhorse and began rummaging for the coffee pot. "I'm hungry," he announced. "How about throwin' some bacon on the pan, Len?"

"Suits me," agreed Matchett. He waited until the horses had finished drinking, then snagged bridle reins over a scraggly branch of sagebrush and moved leisurely to the fire, fingers fumbling in his shirt pocket for tobacco sack.

Hilda took a few hobbling steps toward the mesquite. Matchett watched her, fingers shaping his cigarette. She halted, glanced back at him and began rubbing at her ankles again.

"I'm so lame from those ropes—" She spoke resentfully. "You mustn't tie me up any more."

Matchett nodded. "We won't need to keep ropes on you," he assented. "You'll stick close enough when we get into the hills." His swollen lips twisted in a grimace. "Lions in those hills, and bears, and some pretty mean outlaws."

Hilda attempted some more painful steps. She wondered if he suspected that her lameness was only pretence. The slight stiffness was already gone. She could have run like a deer. Only there was no place to go. The sky was clearing fast. She would have small chance to hide in that revealing moonlight.

She came to a standstill and looked back at the fire. Fargo was sitting on his heels, busy with coffee pot and frying pan. Matchett was still watching her, cigarette drooping from his lips. He seemed easy enough about her, but annoyingly attentive to her movements.

Hilda bent down to her ankles again, rubbed them slowly, her mind seeking desperately for some way that would offer even the ghost of a chance.

She sent covert glances back at the mare. She knew something about Castaña that would have surprised Matchett. A trick that Kirk had taught his own horse. The mare would come immediately when Hilda whistled a certain note. Even if tied, she would jerk back, snap the rope and gallop to her mistress.

Hilda knew that were she to send that call, Castaña would snap the reins from the sagebrush and race to her side. She could be in the saddle and heading into the chaparral before the men realized what was happening.

She continued to rub an ankle. It was a chance, a desperately long chance. She could not hope to make the escape good. Fargo was a dead shot with a rifle. He would not hesitate to use it. He would tumble her from the saddle like a kicking rabbit.

Growing resolve took the soft fullness from her lips, gave them a thin, hard look. Anything was better than the fate that would be hers in that land below the border. She would rather be dead. Better to be killed trying to escape than to kill herself later.

She stole another glance at the chestnut mare, let her gaze move on to the men at the fire. Fargo's head lifted in a look at her. "Cawfee ready in five minutes," he bawled.

"I'm only going as far as the mesquite," Hilda answered. She hoped her voice sounded natural, stood watching them for a few moments. Matchett was twisting another cigarette. He said nothing, but his eyes never left her.

She took a few more limping steps. She was within twenty feet of the mesquite now. A quick dash would take her from Matchett's watchful gaze, her sharp whistle would bring Castaña to her on the dead run. She could be in the saddle—riding for her life—and Kirk's life.

A faint sound from the mesquite froze her to a standstill. A whispering voice it was, hardly audible, just enough to touch her ears.

Hilda stood transfixed, her heart thumping, her brain refusing to believe, understand.

"Hilda! Don't let them guess. Get behind the mesquite. Don't hurry."

Kirk Severn's voice! It was Kirk, there in the mesquite.

With an effort the girl fought off the impulse to start running toward him. She said in a low whisper, "Yes, Kirk." She took a limping step forward, paused on a pretence of rubbing her ankles. "I can whistle for Castaña."

"Not yet," Kirk whispered. He added worriedly,

265

"Keep moving. I think Matchett is suspicious. He's standing up, starting this way."

Hilda heard Matchett's voice, impatient, harsh. "Not so far, Hilda. Keep back from that tree and stay in sight, or I'll tie you up again."

Kirk said, "Don't run, but keep moving . . . Get behind the tree."

Hilda kept moving, limping, drew alongside the spreading mesquite branches. She heard Matchett's voice again, a loud angry yell. "Come back!" he bawled. The sound of his pounding feet sent her scurrying.

She caught a glimpse of Kirk, crouched low against the branches and hardly visible in the mingling of moonlight and shadows that made him a part of the tree. Had she not known he was there she could easily have missed seeing him.

She heard his sharp whisper and obediently stopped her flight a few paces beyond him, turned her head in a bewildered look. She was not certain she had understood.

Kirk spoke again. "Don't move."

She waited, head turned, frightened eyes fixed on the point where Matchett would hurl himself around the tree. She could hear him cursing as he approached.

He appeared with a rush, and seeing her waiting, he broke his run, came on more slowly, relief apparent in the way he pushed his gun back in its holster.

"You scared me," he said. His voice was soft, purring, and he moved closer, clamped hands on her shoulders. "I need a kiss for that scare." His laugh made her flesh creep. "It's time I started in taming you."

Hilda drew back, fought silently against the pull of his arms. She was vaguely aware of a shape that rose from the branches of the mesquite. It moved swiftly and with no more sound than the slow-crawling shadows that made a black and silver phantasy of the moonlit chaparral. She heard a dull thud, felt Matchett's grasp relax.

Kirk's voice said softly, "The mare, Hilda. Quick!"

She was too dazed for the moment to grasp his meaning. She could only stare with incredulous eyes while he dragged Matchett's limp body close to the spreading branches of the mesquite. A gun was in Kirk's hand and with a rush of realization she knew what had happened. Kirk had knocked Matchett senseless with a single crushing blow.

"Call the mare," he said, "then get back behind the tree." He resumed his crouch, gaze fixed on the winking fire.

Hilda put her fingers to lips, whistled shrilly. A startled snort sounded from the mare, a sharp crackle of breaking branches, and Castaña was off in a circling gallop that turned her head toward the mesquite. She came on the dead run, head high, reins dragging.

Hilda caught a glimpse of Fargo leaping from his crouch over the frying pan he had on the fire. He stood for a moment, obviously puzzled. His hesitation was brief. The next instant he was in his saddle.

Hilda did not wait to see more. She fled around the tree and cowered against the branches. Castaña slid to a standstill. The girl mechanically snatched at the dangling reins.

The hammering hoofbeats drew up fast. A gunshot exploded from the mesquite. Fargo swung into view, his horse on the jump. The man was slumped forward on saddle horn. Another shot crashed out. Fargo pitched sideways and tumbled headlong into a clump of brush. His horse slackened speed, circled around and came to a halt close to the mare.

Hilda's legs bent under her. She wanted to sit down. She leaned against Castaña instead, her gaze on Kirk Severn as he moved swiftly to the limp body sprawled in the sagebrush.

He seemed quickly satisfied, turned away from the dead man and spoke to the girl. "I had to do it," he said. "I had to kill him. It was our only chance."

"Yes," Hilda said faintly. She shivered. "I can't quite believe it—yet. You, here . . . those men— dead. I—I had about given up all hope—and now—" Her voice broke.

He took a step toward her, and the moonlight

showed harsh lines on his face, a deep pity—and tenderness in his eyes. "You've been through hell," he said.

"The thought of you was the only thing that kept me sane." Hilda glanced at the limp body in the brush. "It has been so appallingly sudden—and simple . . . so dreadfully final. You appeared from nowhere—and now they are dead, and I don't have to be afraid any more."

He stood looking at her, then was suddenly moving to the man lying under the shadowed branches of the mesquite. He bent down, stared intently at Matchett's face. "He's not dead," he said in a satisfied voice. He looked back at the wondering girl. "Get some water, Hilda. I want to keep this man alive."

She was mystified. For him to live could only add to the dangers ahead.

She said rebelliously, "Why should we do anything for him? He would have killed you on sight."

"We need him alive," Kirk answered. "*You*— more than you dream."

Impelled by his gravity, the urgency of his gesture, Hilda sped to the spring and snatched up the coffee pot Fargo had left near the fire. It was the only thing handy that would hold water. She emptied the coffee, hastily soused the pot in the spring, filled it with fresh water and hurried back to Kirk.

He had dragged Matchett away from the mesquite, into the moonlight and was examining the gash on the senseless man's head.

"*Gracias*." Kirk grinned up at her. "We'll soon have him out of it." He set to work, bathed Matchett's face and head. Hilda watched in silence, and sensing her disapproval, Kirk said without looking at her, "It's a lucky break for us, Hilda. Matchett can tell us a lot of things. He knows a terrible secret that concerns you. We've got to keep him alive—take him back to K7."

"You know best." Her tone was dubious, touched with fierceness. "He's a beast. I can't feel sorry for him—not if he died this instant."

Matchett's eyes fluttered open, closed again. He groaned, spoke feebly, "Where's Fargo?"

"Dead," Kirk told him.

"What are you going to do with me?"

"Take you to the ranch—my place," Kirk answered.

Matchett sat up with a groan. "I told Taylor you'd pull off some smart trick." He touched his head gingerly. "We should have killed you on the spot. Sleed wanted to kill you."

Kirk helped him to his feet. "You won't need that gun," he said. He eased Matchett's forty-five from the holster and tossed it into the brush. "Hilda," he continued, "my horse is down in that gully."

She nodded, stepped into her saddle and rode

away. Kirk motioned in the direction of the spring. "All right," he said to Matchett. "Let's go."

They moved slowly away from the mesquite. Matchett walked like a man in a daze. Fargo's horse trailed behind, ears twitching nervously.

When Hilda came up, leading Kirk's horse, Matchett was already in his saddle. Kirk tied his hands to the horn and roped his feet to the stirrups.

"You're too valuable to lose," he told Matchett with a thin smile.

Matchett only stared at him vacantly. There was no fight left in him, only despondency, abject resignation. Hilda looked at him curiously. The man was a coward and in the grip of a dreadful fear—completely demoralized.

"Anything you want from that?" Kirk gestured at the packhorse.

Hilda shook her head. "I only want to get away from here," she declared. Anger took shape in her eyes. "I don't want anything my father ever gave me." Her breath quickened. "Kirk—it hurts terribly—to think he is my father. He—he gave me to that beast." She flung an outraged look at Matchett. "He is one himself—and worse. He's a devil."

Kirk gave her a strange look. He said slowly, "Haven't you guessed the truth, Hilda?"

"I know things are awfully wrong at the ranch—" Hilda broke off, stared at him with dilated eyes. "You mean—"

271

Kirk nodded. "Yes, I mean that Warde Taylor is not your father."

She said faintly, "Say that again, Kirk." Her eyes were on him, wide with incredulity.

"It is true." Kirk's eyes narrowed in a hard look at Len Matchett. "He knows it is true. That is why we've got to keep him alive."

A fit of trembling seized her. "Kirk!" She reached blindly for his hand. "I feel so—so queer."

He drew her to him, held her tight. "It's a shock." He was self-reproachful. "I should have—"

Her look hushed him. "A blessed shock," she said. "Thank God, Kirk, oh, thank God! It's been driving me crazy—thinking he was my own father." She was suddenly composed, drew back from his arms. "How long have you known?"

"Not long," he answered. "I first suspected only the other day."

Hilda looked at him searchingly. "Father—" She shook her head impatiently, "I mean that *man* . . . he talked about a woman . . . said you were her lover. Has it something to do with her?"

"She is your sister," Kirk said. He went on quickly, before the girl could find words, "It's a long story, a dark story."

"Tell me I'm not dreaming," she begged. "A—a sister!"

"You're not dreaming," he assured her. "It's ⸱en a long trail—a shadowed trail Mustang called it—but we've come to the end of it and found the truth."

"It's too wonderful," Hilda said. She looked at the packhorse. "I don't want a thing from the pack," she said again. "Only this—" She touched her breast. "I made a pocket for it inside my blouse—my mother's picture. He—that *man*—said it was her picture. I found it years ago—in an old trunk. He let me keep it."

"I'd like to see it," Kirk said.

Hilda turned her back on him for a moment. When she faced around she had the faded daguerreotype in her hand. Kirk took it from her, looked for a long time at the lovely young face. "You are the image of her," he said, "and so is Esther Chase the image of her." He put the daguerreotype back in her hand and smiled at her. "You will think you are looking at yourself in a mirror." He paused, added soberly, "It was seeing Esther Chase that first gave me a hint of the truth."

Hilda drew a long breath. "I don't understand a thing." Her eyes were misty. "Only that it is wonderful—and that *you* are wonderful."

"It's not finished—yet," Kirk said. His look went to the packhorse, to Fargo's horse. "I'll strip off their gear and turn them loose before we go," he added.

It was like him to remember the horses, Hilda thought.

Chapter XXI
THE END OF THE TRAIL

Chuck Rigg was worried. "I'm scared," he said to Doctor Williams. "Kirk ain't showed up since he went to town at sunup yesterday." Anxiety grooved the lanky foreman's face. "I ain't likin' it, Doc."

Doctor Williams climbed stiffly from his buckboard. Chuck's words disturbed him more than he cared to admit. He stood frowning at the foreman. "Kirk was at my office yesterday morning," he said. "I gave him some pills for young Chase."

"He ain't showed up with no pills yet," Chuck said. He fingered his sandy mustache nervously, said again, "I ain't likin' it."

Doctor Williams reached into the seat for his bag. "I promised Kirk I'd drop over for a look at Chase."

"Ain't you knowin' where Kirk has went?" Chuck put the question bluntly. "Dunn Harden ain't showed up, nuther," he added, half to himself.

"Dunn Harden?" The doctor was puzzled. "He's a Bar T man, isn't he?"

Chuck nodded. He made no attempt to conceal

his fast-growing uneasiness. "Kirk and me figgered Dunn was finished with Warde Taylor's outfit. Mebbe we figgered wrong and put too much trust in him."

"Good Lord!" Doctor Williams lost some of his ruddy color. "You mean that Dunn may have laid for him in the chaparral?"

"I ain't knowin' what to think," gloomily rejoined the foreman. His look went to Atilano and Justo, perched on the corral fence, rifles between knees, their eyes attentive on the two men standing near the buckboard. "I'm in a mess, Doc. You see, Kirk told me to stick close to the house until he got back. He's awful scared somethin' will happen to that young Chase couple. If it weren't for him sayin' I was to stick close I'd take the Nueco boys and head for town . . . try and pick up Kirk's trail."

The doctor considered him thoughtfully. "It's a tough problem, Chuck," he said finally. He shook his head. "If I were you, I'd obey Kirk's orders. He has good reasons for wanting you to keep watch here."

"I'll give him until noon," compromised the foreman. "If Kirk don't show up by then I'll sure go on a scout for him." His head lifted in a keen look at a drift of dust in the low hills beyond the corrals. "I sent for the boys to come in from the Burro Mesa camp. Looks like they're on the way."

The doctor shaded his eyes against the glare

of the early morning sun. "Coming fast," he commented.

"I sent word for 'em to make dust gettin' here," Chuck said. "I figger to be ready, if trouble busts loose."

Doctor Williams said soberly, "You're a good man, Chuck. I know what Kirk thinks of you, the confidence he has in you."

"I feel toward him like he was my son," the foreman said. His voice choked. "If anythin' has happened to him I'll kill the man who done it with my bare hands."

"I'm believing you," Doctor Williams said. He looked at Chuck speculatively. "I wouldn't worry too much. Kirk can look out for himself if any man can." He went briskly across the yard and pushed through the garden gate.

Esther Chase must have seen him. She ran down the porch steps. "Doctor!" Apprehension was in her voice, in her fine eyes. "Kirk hasn't returned. He was to have brought some medicine—"

"How is the patient?" Doctor Williams kept on going, went quickly up the steps. "I promised Kirk I'd be out and have a look at that leg."

Esther halted him on the top step, her hand on his arm. "Something is wrong." She spoke sharply. "Is it Kirk?"

"Yes." The doctor studied her intently. The hint of amazement in his eyes seemed to trouble her. "You look at me the way Kirk does, the way Chuck Rigg and the others do." Her tone was exasperated.

"Hasn't Kirk told you?"

"Only that I remind him of some girl he knows," Esther answered. "The resemblance must be quite remarkable."

"It's more than remarkable," asserted the doctor. He started past her, hand reaching for the screen door. Her voice halted him.

"You haven't answered my question. Has anything happened to Kirk?"

"We don't know." Doctor Williams spoke gruffly. "Senseless to worry. Kirk can take care of himself."

She followed him inside and led the way down the hall to the bedroom. Dick Chase grinned at him from his pillow. "Hello, Doctor." His attempted smile faded and he said feverishly, "Can't you get us away from this place? There's death in the air. I can smell it, and I want to get away—get my wife away."

"Must be something wrong with your nose," joked the doctor. He rummaged in his bag. "We'll have to give you something for that curious smell. Can't have you frightening Mrs. Chase with such fancies, young man."

Chase gave his wife a haggard look. "Sorry, dear," he mumbled. "I must be losing my mind."

"Nonsense," scoffed Doctor Williams. "Lying

in bed with a broken leg is enough to get anybody restless." He measured a dose from a
small bottle. "Drink this. You'll feel easier."

"It's the whole crazy business," fretted the sick
man. "Why should anybody want to kill me?
I'm a stranger in this country."

"Somebody's fool mistake," Doctor Williams
said brusquely. "Now for a look at the leg, and
no more talk. You do yourself no good."

Esther suddenly went to the window. "It's
Kirk!" she exclaimed. She faced the doctor, her
eyes wide with excitement. "He has a girl with
him, and a man, roped to his saddle."

Doctor Williams joined her at the window.
Astonishment bulged his eyes. "Hilda Taylor,"
he said in a startled voice, "and Len Matchett!"
An exclamation from the girl by his side drew
his attention. She was very pale.

"Hilda?" Her voice was unsteady. "You say her
name is *Hilda Taylor?*"

"Certainly. Hilda Taylor—Warde Taylor's
daughter." The doctor broke off, a startled look
in his eyes. "Good Lord!" he ejaculated, "I
believe I begin to understand . . . but no—it is
impossible—*impossible*."

Esther spoke again. "Is—is she the girl who
looks like me?"

"Yes," the doctor answered. His keen eyes
bored into her as if searching for the solution to a
baffling conundrum.

"Hilda was my mother's name," Esther said. "Hilda Taylor, but I—I have no sister—" Her voice faded, and she moved with swift, graceful steps to the door, paused and flung a dazed look back at her husband. "I can't bear it!" she exclaimed.

Doctor Williams stood listening to the sound of her running feet, his gaze on the sick man.

Dick Chase said wonderingly, "My wife's father was Worden Taylor. There's a mystery about him and Esther's mother. They disappeared years ago, out here in this country."

"Good Lord," the doctor muttered again. "A mystery indeed—and a damnable one." His voice was unsteady, but his hands were sure as he gently and swiftly examined the injured leg. "Fine," he pronounced, "perfect. Your leg will be as good as new, young man." He hastily rearranged the bedcovers and started for the door.

Hilda was down from her mare when Esther Chase ran into the yard. She gave Kirk a piteous look and reached blindly for his hand. Esther came to a standstill, stood staring at her.

Kirk spoke softly. "Hilda," he said, "this is your sister, Esther Chase."

Chuck Rigg, untying the ropes that bound Len Matchett to the saddle, heard the words. His head jerked around in an amazed look.

Esther Chase broke the silence. She was pale, her eyes very bright. She said quietly, a great

279

dawning gladness in her voice, "Of course you are my sister. I don't understand, but you must be my sister. You are the very image of my—our mother. I have her picture."

The two girls moved slowly closer, their eyes devouring each other. Hilda said faintly, "I have a picture . . . You look just like her." Her fingers went to the secret pocket inside her blouse.

Esther studied it for a brief moment. "It's the same as mine," she said. Her faint smile touched Kirk. "I don't blame you for being puzzled. We are marvelously alike."

Hilda said breathlessly, "I don't understand!"

"Nor do I." Esther's arms went out and they clung to each other.

Doctor Williams hurried up, arched inquiring brows at Kirk. "What does this mean?" he demanded. "It must be true. You only need to look at them to know that. The family resemblance is amazing."

Kirk gestured at Len Matchett. "I think we can get some of the answers from him. That's why I brought him along."

"He's a sick man," declared the doctor after a sharp glance at the prisoner.

"Fix him up," Kirk said curtly. "He's valuable evidence."

They helped Matchett from the saddle. His knees sagged under him, and at a word from Kirk, two cowboys carried him into the house.

Kirk went to the two girls. "You've had a tough night of it," he said to Hilda. "You need rest—sleep."

"I'm all right," she demurred. "I'm too happy to feel tired."

"I'll put her to bed," Esther said firmly.

"I couldn't sleep—not yet," declared Hilda. "I—I'm too confused. My mind is in a whirl."

"Mine, too," admitted Esther Chase. "I don't understand. I only know that I've found a sister." She gave Kirk an imploring look.

He shook his head, said gravely, "We're getting close to the truth. You've got to be brave—both of you."

The two girls stood looking at him, their arms entwined. Seen together the difference in age was apparent, otherwise the resemblance in face and form, their hair, their eyes, was striking.

Esther Chase drew a shuddering breath. She seemed to be fighting off a dreadful fear. Kirk sensed the thought in her mind. He said quickly, in a low voice, "No—not what you think. It was a ghastly mistake—about Pecos Jack."

She gave a little cry, tightened her arms about Hilda's waist. "I—I must tell Dick," she said. "Hilda—come with me—to Dick."

Chuck Rigg spoke softly. "Kirk," he said, "looks like Dunn Harden comin'. Got a feller with him."

Kirk pulled his gaze from the two girls moving across the yard. Relief put a light in his

eyes when he saw Dunn's companion. He heard
Chuck's excited voice. "By grab, it's Tom Holden
with him!" The foreman looked reproachfully
at Kirk. "You could have told me, son. You sent
Dunn to fetch Tom over here."

"The thing broke too fast," Kirk explained.
"I was going to write. I sent Dunn instead, to
Deming."

"I was some worried when you didn't show
up," confessed Chuck. "Got it into my head that
mebbe Dunn had double-crossed you."

Kirk's look took in the group of cowboys
clustered near the barn. He gave the foreman an
affectionate grin. "I'll say you were worried,"
he said dryly. "Pulling the boys in from Burro
Mesa."

"I ain't one to set 'round doin' nothin' when I get
to worryin'," admitted Chuck with an answering
grin. He lifted a hand in greeting. "Hello, Tom,
you old sidewinder."

United States Marshal Holden grinned at them
amiably. He wore a bristling gray mustache and
his darkly tanned face accentuated the blueness
of rapier-keen eyes. His gaze slid to the group of
watching cowboys, came back to Kirk.

"Got here as quick as I could, Kirk," he said.
"How are you making out?"

"You're due for a surprise," Kirk answered.
"I'm mighty glad Dunn found you so soon."

"I was in the telegraph office when Dunn busted

in to get these on the wires." The marshal thumbed the two envelopes from his shirt pocket, smiled bleakly. "I didn't waste time headin' this way." He dropped from his saddle, a compact, wiry little man. "What's this surprise? Couldn't get much out of Dunn."

"The thing's too big for me," Dunn Harden said. He slid from his horse and looked at Kirk with eyes that weariness and anxiety had burned to black holes. "We've wore out five broncs gettin' here. Run into a dust storm crossin' the Sinks." He spat out dust, added sullenly, "I don't savvy enough to do any *real* talkin'."

"You've done fine," Kirk reassured him. He saw the question in the cowboy's eyes, the agony that was making him sick to the soul. "She's in the house, Dunn," he said gently.

Dunn went pale, he put out a hand, caught at the mane of his horse. "Why didn't you say so sooner?" There was no bitterness in his voice. Only a great gladness.

Kirk looked at the somewhat bewildered United States marshal. "Len Matchett is here," he said. "Let's go have a powwow with him, Tom. He's in the house, with Doc Williams."

The marshal looked at him intently, and perhaps what he read in Kirk's eyes was enough. He said simply, "Sure, Kirk."

A sharp exclamation from Chuck Rigg held them rigid. "A feller headin' this way fast," Chuck said. He added laconically, "Plenty dust liftin' a couple of miles back of him."

"I think we're due for callers." Kirk's voice was hard. "Come on, Tom. We've got to finish with Matchett in a hurry."

The two men started quickly across the yard. Chuck called after them, "I'll 'tend to things out here, Kirk." His eyes signaled Justo and Atilano. The two Yaquis slid from their perch on the corral fence and ran toward him, rifles in their hands. A shrill yip came from the group of cowboys lounging near the barn.

"Want for us to git set?" one of them yelled.

"Pronto!" bawled Chuck. "You boys do like I said and do it fast."

Jubilant yells answered him. The men scattered in various directions. It was apparent that they knew what they were doing and where they were going. Dunn Harden gave the foreman a shrewd look. "They sure took cover fast," he commented.

"No harm gettin' set for trouble if she comes," drawled the foreman.

"She's comin'," Dunn told him grimly. "That's Mat Dilley and his crowd, all set to swing Kirk from a tree. Kirk had a tip from Mott Balen yesterday." The cowboy drew his gun, examined it expertly. "You and me, too, Chuck. They won't want to stop with danglin' Kirk."

Chuck Rigg gave him a dry smile. "K7 is awful

tough, feller," he said softly. "That means you, too."

"Sure," agreed Dunn. "I'm a K7 man and I'm throwin' hot lead with the rest of you."

They stood silent, watching the lone rider swing into the avenue. It was Chuck who spoke. "Mustang Jenns!" he ejaculated.

A rifle barrel caught sunlight as it darted like a snake's tongue from the green foliage of an oleander bush. A guttural voice spoke fiercely, "*Alto!*"

Mustang pulled his horse to a sliding standstill and flung an outraged look at the threatening rifle. Chuck Rigg called out, "Mustang's a friend, Justo." The rifle barrel slid from view.

Mustang put his horse into motion. He shook a fist at the oleander bush. "Doggone your ornery hide, Justo," he yelped. "You knowed it was me comin'."

He gave Chuck a dry grin as he rode up and swung from his saddle. "That pesky Yaqui was all set to drop me," he complained.

"Wasn't Justo's fault," explained Chuck. "I told him to stop anybody who come. Wasn't expectin' you'd be along."

Mustang gestured at the trailing banner of dust. "You won't be stoppin' *them* fellers," he said grimly. "There's close to fifty of 'em—" He broke off, glared at the unmoved foreman. "I ain't jokin'," he spluttered. "Where at is Kirk?"

He spun on his heels, ran stiff-leggedly toward the house. They heard the slam of the kitchen door, the indignant protests of the Chinese cook as the excited old desert man clattered through the kitchen, his voice lifted in loud yells for Kirk.

Chuck grinned at his companion. "Mustang's some worked up," he commented. "Salty as they come, that old-timer." He studied the approaching swirl of dust, drew his gaze back thoughtfully to the horses. There were six of them. The three ridden in by Kirk and his companions, the marshal's and Dunn's, and Mustang's weary buckskin.

"Too many broncs here," Chuck said. "Won't look good. Get 'em suspicious." His voice lifted in a low call. A man slid into view from behind the tankhouse, rifle in his hand. Chuck gestured at the horses. "Run 'em into the barn, Jimson," he said. He glanced at the nearing haze of dust. "Move 'em quick. Them fellers will be here inside of ten minutes."

Voices in the garden drew the foreman's attention. He gave Dunn a nod and the two hurried through the gate. Kirk and Mustang Jenns were standing on the steps of the side veranda. The old liveryman grinned at Chuck. "Looks like you wasn't needin' my news," he drawled. His mood hardened. "I ain't sorry I got here in time to line up my sights on the damn coyotes."

Tom Holden came down the steps. The United States marshal wore a satisfied look. He sent a brief glance at the dust now drifting down the avenue and looked inquiringly at Kirk. "Want me to talk to 'em?" he asked.

Kirk shook his head. "Not yet," he replied.

"I'll be ready," the marshal said.

The yard was filling with riders, grim-eyed, silent men. Kirk watched them from the veranda steps. He knew most of them. Mat Dilley was there, and Rock Sledge of the Lazy H, both of them long-time friends. They had known his father, shared many a roundup with him. Kirk's face set in hard, bitter lines.

His eyes roved over them, and he was aware of a shock, a bitterness, a hurt that twisted in his heart like a two-edged knife. These men, his friends, were here to kill him. The poison had been cunningly spread.

He heard Mustang's voice, a rasping, fierce whisper, "Thar's Warde Taylor, and Sleed." The old man's hand fastened on his gun. "I've a mind to drop 'em from their saddles—"

Tom Holden spoke quietly. "Keep your shirt on, Mustang," he said. "Kirk's handlin' this."

A voice called from beyond the gate. "We want to talk to Kirk Severn." The speaker was Mat Dilley, and it was obvious that the cowman was nervous. There was an unnatural thinness to his voice.

The continued silence seemed to worry some of the visitors. The yard was too lifeless. Only the restless stamp of their own horses, the creak of leather as men fidgeted in their saddles.

A man laughed discordantly. "Looks like they got wind of us comin' and hightailed it away from here," he said loudly.

Mat Dilley spoke again, his voice a hard, rasping croak. "Come on out, Severn, or we'll drag you out."

Chuck Rigg nudged Dunn, and the pair moved cautiously across the garden to a small side gate in the patio wall. Mustang Jenns hesitated, followed them stealthily.

Signs of growing uneasiness came from the yard. A man cursed. It was obvious they did not like the business that had brought them to the ranch.

Another voice demanded harshly, "What are we waitin' for? Let's git done with it."

Kirk recognized Clint Sleed as the speaker. He gave the marshal a nod and went swiftly up the steps and along the veranda to the front of the house. He glimpsed the frightened faces of the two girls watching at a window.

Loud shouts greeted his appearance on the front steps, then silence, grim, ominous.

It was Kirk who broke the silence. "What is it you want with me, Mat?"

"We want that cow thief you've got hid in your

house," answered Dilley. "We want you, too, Severn. You've fooled us long enough. You're finished in the Soledad."

"The same goes for your own self, Mat," screeched a voice. "I've got you covered, feller."

Kirk caught a glimpse of Mustang, crouched against the fat trunk of an umbrella tree, his long-barreled forty-five within three feet of Mat Dilley's head.

He heard Chuck Rigg's voice. "The same goes for you, Taylor," warned the K7 foreman. "I'll blow your light out if you make a move."

"I've got my sights lined good on Clint Sleed," announced Dunn Harden from some unseen place. The old reckless gaiety was back in his voice. He was enjoying himself.

Chuck's voice stabbed again through the deep hush. "You're up against K7," he said. "You ain't got a chance. There'll be a lot of dead cowmen layin' 'round in this yard if you start anythin'."

An oath exploded from Sleed. "We've rode slap into a trap," he said disgustedly. "Look around, fellers. There's twenty guns on us."

"All set to blow you to hell," cheerfully announced Dunn Harden.

"You're making a mistake, Severn," warned Dilley. "You can't escape—"

"Escape what?" interrupted Kirk.

"Justice," Dilley answered in a stern voice. "You know most of us, Kirk . . . honest-dealing

289

cowmen and ranchers who believe in law and order—"

"We'll leave the sermon out," Kirk interrupted again. "Get down to facts."

"That's right, Mat," Warde Taylor said in his rumbling voice. "Get down to facts." He sat erect in his saddle, massive, tranquil, hooked fingers meditatively combing his great beard.

Dilley glanced uneasily at Mustang's menacing gun. Kirk said quietly, "Go on, Mat. Say your piece," and then, when Dilley still hesitated, "You're looking for *El Topo*. Is my guess right, Mat?"

Dilley found his voice. "Your guess is right." His tone was acid. He went on, gathering courage. "We're here to destroy this evil thing that has scourged the Soledad too long."

"You accuse me of being *El Topo*?"

Dilley flung a defiant look at Mustang's gun. He was not lacking in courage. "I do accuse you," he said. "For the moment, you have the whip hand, but you can't escape justice."

"You should orter be in a pulpit," admired Mustang from behind his umbrella tree. "Or mebbe run for Congress, or somethin'."

Kirk kept his face straight. "I'm not saying I am *El Topo*, Mat, but I've got a confession for you—" A stir passed through the clustered riders, a brief shiver of sound, like wind in the trees. Kirk waited, his face a hard mask.

Warde Taylor cleared his throat. "You mean you want to confess?" His voice was sharp, brittle with suspicion.

Kirk looked at him with narrowed eyes. "I mean I've got the man who signed the confession." His hand lifted. "Bring him out, marshal."

Holden pushed Matchett through the door, stood by his prisoner's side, gun in hand. Kirk said bleakly, "You know Len Matchett, Dilley. Ask him about Pecos Jack."

Warde Taylor's restless fingers slid stealthily under the beard that covered his shirt-front, and when the hand reappeared, it gripped a gun.

Kirk sensed the purpose of that moving hand too late. A shot crashed out even as he reached for his own gun. Matchett crumpled to the floor.

A man shouted. Kirk took a flying leap down the steps and halted. Taylor was spurring his horse into a mad run through the clustered riders. It was impossible to get a shot at him.

"Stop him!" Kirk yelled. "He's your man, Dilley. He's *El Topo*."

Dilley looked at him stupidly. Surprise held him in a paralyzing grip. Kirk pushed past him, caught a glimpse of Sleed and several riders surging alongside Taylor.

Justo rose from behind his oleander bush, rifle leveled. Sleed's gun whipped up, Kirk saw Dunn Harden spring into view from another bush, smoke and flame pouring from his gun. Sleed slumped forward and pitched from his running horse, his gun exploding harmlessly. Another shot crashed out, a loud reverberating report from the Yaqui's rifle. Warde Taylor fell heavily from his saddle, lay motionless in the dust several yards beyond the dead Bar T foreman.

United States Marshal Holden elbowed his way through the dazed vigilantes. He gazed with grim eyes at the big bearded man sprawled on the ground. Dilley and several other cowmen joined him. Bewilderment held them wordless. They could only stare unbelievingly at the lifeless body of the man they had so long trusted and respected.

Holden narrowed his eyes at them in a look that held both contempt and anger. "They don't believe it," he said to Kirk.

"It just ain't possible," muttered Dilley. "Warde Taylor was a friend of mine . . . owned the biggest ranch in the Soledad. Why—he was president of our Stockmen's Association— president of the bank."

The marshal shrugged a dusty shoulder. "You tell 'em, Kirk," he said.

Kirk met their questioning eyes with a bitter smile. "You were ready enough to believe it of me." His voice was the lash of a whip in their faces. "You found it easy to swallow the poison Taylor spread around."

"We've been damn fools," Mat Dilley admitted

gruffly. He looked at Kirk curiously. "I reckon it explains why you wouldn't be sheriff on Warde's say-so. You were already readin' sign on him."

"That's right." Kirk's smile was grim. "Taylor guessed I was on his trail. Jim Shane got suspicious of him. That is why Taylor killed Jim."

Rock Sledge pulled his scowling gaze from the dead man. "What for did Warde go for his gun and kill Matchett when you spoke of Pecos Jack?" The Lazy H man hesitated, his expression embarrassed. "Pecos was hung years ago. I was there when they swung him."

"The man you helped lynch twenty years ago was not Pecos Jack." Kirk stared with cold eyes at the cowman. "You helped murder an innocent man, Sledge."

"By God!" exclaimed Rock Sledge, "what are you trying to tell us?" His aghast look went to the lifeless body.

"Yes," Kirk said. "He's Pecos Jack, alias *El Topo*."

United States Marshal Holden nodded. "That's right," he confirmed. He spoke solemnly. "I have Matchett's confession."

"The thing goes back a lot of years," Kirk continued. "A man named Worden Taylor came West with his wife. He'd bought a big cattle ranch through an agent whose name happened to be Warde Taylor, who was also Pecos Jack, border desperado and stage robber. He framed the innocent tenderfoot for a stage hold-up he had himself pulled off. Worden Taylor was lynched."

"What became of the wife?" queried Dilley. "This Worden Taylor had a wife, you said."

"Worden Taylor and his wife were staying at a hotel in Socorro," Kirk explained. "Len Matchett was the clerk there. His confession states that Mrs. Taylor died in childbirth brought on by the shock of her husband's death. Nobody knew the Taylors. Warde Taylor, alias Pecos Jack, stepped in as the dead woman's husband, and father of the baby." Kirk paused, added grimly, "He also stepped in as owner of Worden Taylor's Bar T ranch."

"That's right," Holden said again. "Warde took Matchett into the plot. Matchett was his outside man in the *El Topo* business. Handled the stolen cattle and other loot the gang got from robbing stages."

Mat Dilley frowned thoughtfully. "So Hilda ain't Warde's daughter," he said. "She's no kin to him."

Kirk shook his head. "She's the other Taylor's daughter."

Dilley nodded. "The other Taylor was the *real* owner of Bar T, and that makes Hilda the owner." He grinned triumphantly at his listeners.

Kirk stared at him blankly. It had not occurred to him. The thought was something of a shock.

Hilda—and Esther, so long kept apart by the tragic years, were now the rightful owners of the ranch their unfortunate father had never seen.

He turned abruptly and went with swift, long strides toward the house. Chuck Rigg broke away from a group of excited cowmen. The foreman wore a contented grin.

"I reckon the lynchin' party is busted for keeps," he said. "Kirk—you're the big man in Soledad. There's already talk they're goin' to make you president of the Association."

"That means a job for *you*," Kirk told him. "How would you like to wear a sheriff's star, Chuck?"

"I'll get me a fancy new shirt," grinned the foreman. "The best shirt Mott Balen has in his store." His face sobered. "I don't know, Kirk. How about Dunn Harden? He'd make a sure good sheriff."

Kirk shook his head. "I've got another job picked for Dunn," he said. "If my word means a thing to a couple of girls we know, Dunn is going back to Bar T as foreman."

He left Chuck open-mouthed with astonishment, and pushed through the patio gate. Hilda was standing there, on the veranda steps. She seemed to be waiting for him.

Kirk's eyes took on a warm, eager light. He went quickly toward her.

Center Point Large Print
600 Brooks Road / PO Box 1
Thorndike, ME 04986-0001 USA

(207) 568-3717

US & Canada:
1 800 929-9108
www.centerpointlargeprint.com

D.L.

AB